P9-DCD-657

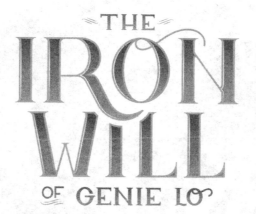

THE IRON WILL OF GENIE LO

AMULET BOOKS
NEW YORK

THE IRON WILL

OF GENIE LO

F. C. YEE

PUBLISHER'S NOTE: This is a work of fiction. Names, characters, places, and incidents are either the product of the author's imagination or used fictitiously, and any resemblance to actual persons, living or dead, business establishments, events, or locales is entirely coincidental.

Cataloging-in-Publication Data has been applied for and may be obtained from the Library of Congress.

ISBN 978-1-4197-3145-7

Text copyright © 2020 Christian Yee
Jacket illustrations copyright © 2020 Studio Muti
Book design by Hana Anouk Nakamura

Printed and bound in the U.S.A.
10 9 8 7 6 5 4 3 2 1

Amulet Books are available at special discounts when purchased in quantity for premiums and promotions as well as fundraising or educational use. Special editions can also be created to specification. For details, contact specialsales@abramsbooks.com or the address below.

Amulet Books® is a registered trademark of Harry N. Abrams, Inc.

ABRAMS The Art of Books
195 Broadway, New York, NY 10007
abramsbooks.com

for
IAN

1

SEVERAL MONTHS AGO

"I believe you," Yunie said.

I ground my knuckles into my eyes. This wasn't going how I'd imagined.

"I—I don't think you're listening," I said. "I'm trying to tell you that I'm the reincarnation of a legendary weapon once owned by Sun Wukong, the Monkey King."

"I've heard of him, Genie. You don't have to recap *Journey to the West* for the umpteenth time. Not all of us suck at being Asian as much as you."

Yunie and I were having a heart-to-heart in the most secure location I could think of when it came to our friendship: the basement rec room of her house. As kids, we'd ousted her father from his mahogany-walled man cave to hold countless sleepovers here, next to piles of outdated golf clubs and liquor cabinets we had no thought of pilfering. As we got older, we stopped hanging out here, preferring to meet aboveground in the light of day. But I thought I needed the emotional backdrop for a confession as weighty as this one. I wasn't prepared for her treating it like she'd gotten my favorite color wrong for seven years.

1

"*Quentin* is Sun Wukong!" I cried. "The guy in our class! He's *him*!"

"I believe you said that multiple times."

I nearly pulled my hair out with one yank. "Demons, Chinese demons called *yaoguai*—they're real! They're wandering the Bay Area as we speak! You know the Boddhisatva Guanyin? I've *met* her. We saved the lives of everyone in the city!"

Yunie looked up at me with her calm doe eyes, as placid as could be. "That sounds like something you would do."

I'd reached my breaking point. I didn't want to have to do this.

Before I cut loose, I looked around for anything fragile nearby. Her basement was spacious and floored in fluffy, sound-muting carpet. As long as I kept away from the giant TV mounted on the wall I'd be okay.

I took a deep breath, feeling oddly naked in front of my best friend. "*Grow*," I said to myself.

I had been practicing this with Quentin and had gained some semblance of control over how big I got. So instead of shooting through every single story of Yunie's house and bursting through the roof like a xenomorph, I "merely" changed to about ten feet in height. Enough to make me hunch forward under the basement ceiling.

Yunie shrieked and scrambled backward until the sofa took her legs out from under her. She clambered over the cushions and fell to the floor behind the back with a bruising thud. For a moment I was scared she'd knocked herself out, but then she peeked over the edge, taking cover from my massiveness.

Her eyes were so wide they were mostly whites. "GENIE, WHAT THE FU—"

"Ha!" I pointed a finger the length of a pencil at her, my voice booming an octave lower. "You *didn't* really believe me before! You were lying!"

"I believed that what you were describing was real to YOU!" Yunie screamed. "If you told me you saw gods and demons, then of course I would believe that's what you were genuinely seeing! Genie, what the hell is this!?"

I could tell that forcing her to look upon my perspective-breaking size for too long would make her panic. I was putting her through an experience like the first time I saw magical shenanigans, when I was attacked by the yaoguai named Hunshimowang.

I shrank down to normal size but did it too quickly. Dizziness like a bout of low blood pressure forced me to sit down on the floor. As soon as she saw me collapse with my head between my knees, Yunie's switch flipped into protective mode.

She leaped over the couch to my side, grabbed a nearby blanket, and wrapped my shoulders with it like she'd been waiting for me at the finish line of a marathon. I breathed in and out, regaining my senses.

"Don't push yourself too hard," she said, sensing how much the effort had taken out of me. She stroked my back, trying to generate as much comforting friction as possible. "I believe you. I'll always believe you."

I knew she was telling the truth. Yunie would accept a new reality simply because I was the one laying down how it was. I didn't deserve a person who trusted me so thoroughly, who was so completely on my side.

It should have been *me* trying to steady *her*. I started to tear up.

"I'm sorry," I said. "I should have told you from the beginning instead of blowing you off and being distant. I was trying to protect you. I wanted to keep you as far away from this nonsense as possible."

Yunie sniffled a bit, the closest I had ever heard her come to crying. I knew if I looked her in the eyes right now I'd start to bawl uncontrollably. I kept my face pointed downward to maintain a controlled drip on the floor.

"It's not your fault," she said. "*I'm* sorry."

"For *what*?"

"I don't know. Thinking that you were sick of me, maybe? Making you feel so beholden? Of course you're going to have your own important stuff going on. Your own secrets, too. I can't be part of every single aspect of your life."

I wasn't sure whether I felt absolved or heartbroken to hear her say that. But once again, Yunie was speaking the truth. In the long run, clinging too hard to each other would only end in sadness.

Right now, though, we could hug it out as much as we wanted. I squeezed her to my side, my friend's slight stature making her easy to embrace with a single, normal arm. "You're okay with all the . . . you know . . . demons?"

"Oh hell, no. I am completely weirded out by the demons. And the gods, too; I don't even want to think about that. I mean, *ew*. Are they *watching* us? Can a god see straight down into my room? Or my brain? Are they reading my thoughts right now?"

I laughed and a tear went up my nose, the salt burning. I'd never grilled Guanyin over the particulars, mostly because I still needed my rational side to function. Yunie was taking the same approach—only faster and better, as I should have expected from her.

She tapped the side of her head. "Your mumbo-jumbo is going straight into the vault of horrible things that don't exist, right between my stage fright and Australian spiders. Don't feel obligated to bring me into Chinese Narnia or whatever."

That was absolutely fine by me. Perfect even. My original plan of keeping Yunie safe through distance was still a go, only I didn't have to lie to her anymore.

There was one remaining problem, though, a magical, rock-hard lump that would be impossible to dislodge from our normal lives.

"Quentin is going to be around for a while," I said.

"Eh, he's allowed to stay." Yunie leaned against me and sighed, trying to digest what his existence meant. "Sun Wukong, the Monkey King, huh?" she said. "You know what's funny? I originally thought the reason you didn't have time to hang out anymore was because you and he were hooking up after school. Guess I was wrong. You didn't fall for each other."

Ah, hell.

I didn't say anything fast enough. Yunie must have detected a subtle temperature change in my body, because she pushed me away so she could stare at my face.

"No!" she said, her grin swelling like the crest of an oncoming wave. "Yes?"

Each additional moment I kept silent was another rev of her engine. She brightened and brightened until finally I nodded ever so slightly.

"YES!" she crowed in triumph. "I *knew* the two of you were going to become a thing! Called that from day one!"

I couldn't do anything but turn into a beet.

"Okay, spill. How long has it been official?"

"Not long," I mumbled.

"I take back everything I said. I hate you, and the only way you can ever earn my forgiveness is by spilling some juicy details."

I couldn't believe that this—of all things—was what Yunie wanted to hear about. Not the magic or the size-changing or any of that. I tried to come up with a small slice of information that might appease her, but I couldn't get any words past the gate of sheer embarrassment.

"Come on, out with it," she said. "How far have the two of you gone?"

I scratched my head. "Uh, us or our clones?" There was a pretty meaningful difference.

Yunie blinked slowly at the word *clones* and sat back down, disappointed.

"Okay, now you've made it weird," she huffed.

2

TODAY

"No!" I screamed. "No! No! No! I hate you!"

"Genie, stop being dramatic," Jenny Rolston said from where she was sitting on my chest. Weekend morning practice had just ended, and I'd been taken by surprise in the locker room. "You're team captain next year, and that's final. Now quit struggling and hold still."

Despite my best efforts to thrash around on the cold, dirty floor, my volleyball team's former leader managed to pin me down long enough to clip the enamel badge in our school colors to my shirt. Jenny got off me and blew strands of surfer-blond hair out of her face. The freshmen and sophomores watching us giggled and whispered to themselves about the most undignified transfer of authority they'd ever witnessed.

"It's official now," she said, leaving me on the ground instead of helping me get up. "If you take that off, I'm going to iron the C-patch to your jersey while you're still wearing it. What the hell's wrong with you anyway? I thought you wanted to be captain. Colleges love that kind of thing."

"Leadership is not my personal brand! I have to rewrite my essays if I want to make use of this!"

Jenny scrunched her face like I was giving her a nosebleed. Maybe she'd thought she could exploit my need for as much application fodder as possible, but she had no idea how deep that swamp went.

"Look," I said in an attempt to explain. "It would have been okay if I didn't have to do anything but the coin toss. But you had to go ruin it by setting standards and being an actual team leader. You've made us rely on you, and I can't handle that level of responsibility. You've doomed us all!"

"Genie, you'll learn. And lesson one on being captain is not screaming about how your team is doomed."

"See? You haven't left the room and already you regret your decision."

■ ■ ■

"I mean, seriously," I said to Quentin as I ducked under a tree branch. "What does she think is going to happen? If I'm captain I have to do things like watch game film, plan team outings, and tell Jiayi she's doing great even though she sucks and should quit the sport forever."

"That's the point," Quentin said. His hand flashed out, plucking a bug from its flight path. He examined it with mild curiosity before letting it fly away unharmed, his gentleness and control matching his speed. "Jenny knows you'll be fantastic at all of those things. She wants the job done right, so she gave it to you. You're the best choice and everyone knows it."

Even though that statement was patently false, it made me smile. Quentin knew exactly what to say at times.

"All hail Empress Lo Pei-Yi," he went on. "May her reign be as long and cruel as she is."

I flicked my boyfriend in the back of the head.

We trudged through the woods in silence. In between the trees, bright green ferns littered the floor, bobbing and weaving as I tried not to trample them. We were technically on public park grounds, in a mountain popular with Bay Area hikers, but far enough off the beaten path that no one would ever find us. There was no obvious reason for anyone to be in this part of the forest as opposed to the other thousands of acres.

I was the only one making any noise with my footsteps. Quentin pulled a Legolas, stepping lightly over the terrain like he didn't weigh anything. He could probably springboard off a leaf if he wanted to.

"We're here," Quentin said, stopping at a clearing in the forest that looked no different from any of the other dewy green patches we'd passed. He took a few steps forward and rapped the air in front of him with his knuckles.

It made a dense, hollow noise. The length of the echo implied that he'd hit something very, very big.

When nothing else happened, Quentin made an annoyed sound with his teeth and knocked again, this time to the tune of "Shave and a Haircut."

"You're late," said a female voice, completing the beat.

A rippling vertical surface appeared, as if we'd been leaning over the edge of a pond this whole time. Out of it stepped a tall, elegant woman who was completely unaffected by the grossness of the heat and insects around her. Guanyin, the Goddess of Mercy, had her arms crossed in a way that demanded answers from the lowly mortal in front of her.

"I'm sorry," I said. "I was ambushed at school."

Her annoyance at me vanished, replaced with concern. "By whom?"

"My volleyball captain. She's making me take over for her once she graduates."

"Genie, that's wonderful!" said Guanyin. She rushed forward and gave me a bone-crushing hug. Despite not being known for her physical strength like Quentin, she lifted me into the air with her embrace as easily as a Goddess of the Clean and Jerk.

"I'm so happy for you," she said after putting me back down. "I know how much you wanted more control over your team."

"I never said that!"

Guanyin shared a knowing look with Quentin. "Sure, you didn't say it."

Before I could protest any further, she dropped her fun-time demeanor. "All right, now get inside, you two. We're behind enough as it is."

The three of us stepped through the invisible barrier. I always expected to feel the sensation of crossing over the threshold on my skin, but that never happened. Instead I felt the tug and resistance of the magic deep inside my organs, where my different types of qi supposedly collected and flowed from.

Inside, the landscape of the park grounds was perfectly normal. Except for the fact that it was covered in demons.

Sweating, snarling yaoguai. Fallen Chinese spirits. Animals who'd learned the Way to take partial human forms. Sinners from Diyu, the Chinese Hell with either eighteen or one hundred and eight layers, depending on whom you talked to.

Hackles raised, they all attacked at once.

3

QUENTIN DID A BACKFLIP, AND WHEN HE CAME DOWN, THERE were six of him.

"Stay put!" he roared in unison, forming a chain in front of me and Guanyin. "Stay put! You'll all get your turn!"

The tide of yaoguai surged against his multiple bodies. Quentin's line held, but the demons were still close enough for it to feel like they were shouting their problems in my face.

"Shouhushen!" they screamed, half teenagers at a pop concert and half an orcish horde storming Helm's Deep. "Shouhushen!"

Back when demons first came to Earth it had been an invasion wave, convicts plucked from Hell by the traitorous god Erlang Shen and let loose in the Bay Area to wreak havoc. Quentin and I had defeated the worst of them and foiled Erlang Shen's schemes to the point where it would have been an exercise in cruelty to forcefully send the rest back to Diyu.

But the Jade Emperor, the ruler of Heaven, had tasked us with managing the yaoguai we'd shown mercy to, rather than dealing with them himself. I was now responsible for the well-being of the slavering demons, by virtue of being the only one who gave a rat's ass about the consequences. If I didn't want ogres and goblins

12

wandering around populated areas into the nearest juice bar, I had to keep them away from civilization and hope for the best.

The best, as it turned out, was some kind of quasi-medieval system where each yaoguai theoretically kept to itself on its own plot of land in a centralized area of wilderness. About once a week, I had to visit them to hear grievances, settle disputes, and make sure they weren't inching closer to the boundaries of humanity.

I didn't know how we'd settled into this pattern. Maybe it was what the yaoguai gravitated toward, or maybe I'd watched too many fantasy miniseries and they'd imprinted onto my subconscious. I would have been open to alternate solutions because I really, really did not like holding court.

The yaoguai were impossible to get a read on. They seemed to hate every word that came out of my mouth during these sessions, and yet each week, more and more showed up in this designated meeting place to demand my judgment on this matter or that.

"Ugh, what is this, double the number of demons since last time?" I said.

"It *was* double," Guanyin said dryly. "Until I took care of most of them. What you see right now are the ones that refused to deal with me and insisted on addressing the *Great Divine Guardian* in person."

The slightly irked way she spoke my official, Heaven-appointed title highlighted the other issue here. Really, it should have been Guanyin in charge of all things supernatural on Earth. She knew it, I knew it, and the Jade Emperor knew it, which made appointing me the Shouhushen his way of spiting us both.

By mutual agreement, we'd shifted as much as we could to her plate while I tried to gain my footing as the Divine Guardian.

It was . . . an ongoing process. Without her help, the entire Bay Area would have probably been awash in human and demon blood combined.

I was determined to make my own contribution, no matter how meager, even if it was mostly for the sake of not looking worthless in front of Guanyin. Deciding to go in reverse size order, from smallest to largest, I pointed at a yaoguai who'd squirmed his way to the front.

"State your name and your business," I said.

A chorus of disappointed howls filled the air. The Quentins bellowed for everyone to shut up but didn't get compliance until they started showing their fangs.

The imp who shuffled forward grinned obsequiously. He was only about three feet tall and barely human-shaped. He rubbed his clawed hands over each other as he spoke with an accent I'd never heard before.

"Oh most Great Divine Guardian, I beg a thousand pardons for disgracing your presence with my filthy visage," he said, never dropping his over-toothed smile. "I am but a poor spirit known as Benboerba, an unworthy minnow looking only to survive in a shark-filled ocean by the grace of your hand."

Ugh. *This* guy.

"That's . . . great," I said. "What is it you want?"

My question caused the already tiny demon to wither before my eyes. "Oh Shouhushen, you have already provided so much for such a despicable character such as myself," he groveled. "A lair in this blessed Kingdom of California to call my very own, where I neither have to fear the wrathful eye of Heaven upon my

14

brow, nor the grasping claws of Hell around my ankles. It would be a crime against the justice of the Universe to ask you for anything further."

Pfft. If that were true, he wouldn't be wasting my time right now. I made a rolling motion with my hand. "But?"

"I should be flayed for my impudence in even mentioning this," he said. "In the past, I was accustomed to gardening as part of my meditative rituals, raising *gouqi* as a technique to cultivate the Way. I do so miss that practice . . ." Benboerba trailed off to let me put two and two together.

The Way, huh? He was definitely using a scripted catchphrase that was becoming common among the yaoguai petitioners. A demon could make a request on the grounds of personal development by mentioning the Way, but the Way was vague enough it could encompass nearly any activity. I was waiting for the day when one of the yaoguai grew bold or dumb enough to claim eating babies was crucial to understanding the Way.

This, however, was harmless. "Sure," I said. "Gardening is fine. Keep it to a ten foot by ten foot patch, and only what you can raise by hand. If I see a plague of magic wolfberries taking over the country, there'll be hell to pay. Got it?"

"Oh, supremely understood, Shouhushen," said Benboerba. "Your clarity befits your skills as a leader, as does your illuminating beauty."

Oh my god. I might have thrown up on my shoes right there on the spot, had Guanyin not given me a look that told me to maintain composure. I shooed the demon away before his "thousand thanks" became more than a metaphor.

I thought that one went pretty smoothly, all things considered. But as soon as Benboerba turned his back, his obsequious grin re-formed itself into a cold smirk. He walked away not with the hunched, submissive posture he'd used to approach, but with an upright swagger, hands clasped behind his back.

I pulled one of the Quentins closer to me.

"Why's that guy trying to make an exit like he's a stone-cold badass?" I whispered. If Benboerba was hiding something, he'd forgotten that I could see straight through his skull to his face on the other side if I wanted to. The only reasons why I hadn't had true sight on was because it had been hurting a lot more lately, and Guanyin said that not using it would establish trust.

"He thinks he's gotten one over on you," Quentin said.

"What? How? He asked for a favor that wasn't a big deal and acted like a turd while doing it."

"That's not how he sees it. The gouqi were his way of proving his mental superiority. When he tells his yaoguai friends about them, he'll claim he tricked you into disgracing your authority by using your weakness for flattery. It'll be a big boost to his status around these parts."

I was running out of ways to be exasperated with this job. It would have been easier if everyone weren't so concerned with maintaining face and playing games and climbing a demonic social ladder that I didn't know existed until recently.

I mean, they couldn't even help me out by lining up. Chinese yaoguai didn't queue at all. At least Dante's demons kept themselves in ordered levels of the Inferno.

An unfamiliar noise caught my ear. A cluster of yaoguai was cheering. And it wasn't for me.

A very large demon stepped forward from the group. His smaller friends pushed him forward, slapping the parts of his back that they could reach, hollering encouragement at him. The champ was here, making his way through the crowd.

I noticed that the giant yaoguai's fans might have hailed him enthusiastically as he walked by, but as soon as they were safely behind him, they adopted the same cynical, probing look as Benboerba, doing mental math while pumping their fists, flexing their claws. Waiting to observe what came next. Quentin's little refresher on demon politics had made it so I couldn't unsee the layers of scheming.

The big guy took his place at the head of the crowd. There was still a fair amount of distance between us, but his stance was all challenge and aggression.

"Hear me!" the demon shouted. "I am Yellow-Toothed Elephant, and I declare you, the so-called Shouhushen, to be unworthy of deciding our fates on Earth!"

I crossed my arms over my chest. "No cutting."

"You operate under a false mandate!" Yellow-Toothed Elephant went on. "It is perverse that a human should govern yaoguai. I will end your reign of terror, harlot!"

Well of course. It wouldn't be a proper reign-of-terror ending without a dash of misogyny.

I sized up Yellow-Toothed Elephant. He was even bigger than the giant Demon King of Confusion, the first yaoguai I had ever laid eyes on. Yellow-Toothed Elephant's wrinkly gray hands and feet ended in blunt cylinders as thick as telephone poles, and the long trunk on his face pointed at me in contempt.

Great. I was about to get attacked by Babar.

The Quentins sidled away from me like I was in the middle of an embarrassing argument. *What? No, I don't know her. What gave you that idea?*

I let the demon have one more chance. "I'm going to have to ask you to step back," I said.

Yellow-Toothed Elephant stamped his feet and trumpeted. His body went tense and began to expand, his muscles ballooning around the limits of his joints. It was as if he was undergoing a yearlong 'roid bender over the course of ten seconds. Webs of veins rose to the surface of his skin. His temples started to leak a sticky orange tar. The liquid spilled down his head like tears of rage.

I recognized that last symptom from a nature documentary I watched once. It was a sign that he was going berserk. His testosterone levels were spiking uncontrollably. He needed to kill the object of his aggression. Namely, me.

"Genie," Guanyin said with an edge of concern in her voice. "This is going a little too—"

Yellow-Toothed Elephant lowered his head and charged.

■ ■ ■

The demon's flat feet thundered over the clearing, knocking down a few of the nearby yaoguai from stampeding force alone. His eyes were inflamed with bloodlust, and they seemed to grow bigger and bigger as he approached.

In the instant before he made impact I raised my arm, palm outward, in the *stop* gesture, like a crossing guard. Yellow-Toothed Elephant smashed into my hand with what must have been a half a ton of weight moving at twenty miles per hour.

I didn't budge an inch.

It was a lot of mass coming to a dead stop. The demon compressed like a slow-motion video of a tennis ball hitting the strings of a racquet before bouncing backward into his normal elephantine shape.

The only effect his charge had on me was that my hand turned glittering black, the original color of the Ruyi Jingu Bang. It spread from my wrist down to my fingers and up to my elbow. Quentin's illusion that kept my arm looking like normal flesh often faded away when I used my full strength. He would have to recast it once this was done.

I heard a groaning noise at the painful-looking collision. It could have been Yellow-Toothed Elephant, the collected crowd of witnesses, or both. The demon staggered in front of me, waiting for the KO.

I looked over my shoulder to see if Quentin and Guanyin were clear. Then I grabbed Yellow-Toothed Elephant by the tip of his trunk.

I whirled my arm around my head, taking the massive yaoguai into the air with it. I spun his entire body off the ground using his trunk as a tether, making two full rotations, and slammed him onto the earth. Demons who had just gotten to their feet fell back down again from the tremors.

The dust finally settled over Yellow-Toothed Elephant's unconscious, laid-out form. I looked around defiantly. "Anyone else want to call me names?"

No answer. If there had been a pebble in front of each yaoguai, every single one of them would have kicked at it morosely instead of meeting my gaze.

It was Quentin, surprisingly, who remembered why we were here to begin with. The real one stepped onto Yellow-Toothed Elephant's heaving belly to use as a podium.

"And let that be a warning to the rest of you!" he shouted. "Exhaust the Shouhushen's patience, and pain will be your lot! Now line up for your audience in the order you arrived, or else!"

There was a moment of silence before panicked shuffling broke out. The yaoguai mushed themselves into a reasonable column like frightened penguins.

But I could tell the cynical ones only considered this a minor setback. If they couldn't test me through physical force, they'd find another way. They were never going to leave well enough alone.

Quentin hopped down from his stirring platform and rejoined me and Guanyin. The goddess glanced at what was left of Yellow-Toothed Elephant.

"Was that whole show really necessary?" she said to the two of us. True to her nature, she would never look at violence with anything but distaste, no matter how much she was personally involved.

"Of course it was," Quentin said. "We should thank him once he wakes up. This little circus bought us at least two weeks of good behavior from the rest of them."

I made a noise with my teeth. The going rate on demon obedience was getting worse all the time.

4

BY THE TIME I'D HEARD MOST OF THE YAOGUAI OUT, YOU COULD have watered the grass with my brain. The simple act of listening for hours had drained more energy from me than any fight in recent memory. If the demons couldn't take me down with a direct challenge, they were going to whine me to death.

The field was nearly empty. No demon cared to stick around once they got what they needed. At the end of these sessions they vanished back into the woods without a trace. Today was an exception, as a large trail of broken shrubs marked where Yellow-Toothed Elephant's friends dragged his slumbering carcass away.

I plastered my hands to my eyes as I called for the last one to step up. One away from going home. Depending on how low on patience I was, this last yaoguai might either get nothing or way more than it asked for.

Only it wasn't a yaoguai who appeared when I took my hands off my face. It was an old man.

He was dressed in an embroidered robe that might have once been bleached and elegant but was now frayed down to dingy gray patchwork. The ends of his bushy white mustache swept back

21

around his head in a perfect horizontal arc. He carried a wooden staff riddled with knots and knobs that widened to the size of a fist on top.

Before I could say anything, Quentin whooped out loud and leaped onto the old man's back like a panther on a gazelle.

My first instinct was to scream at him to stop, but then again, maybe he detected a threat. It wasn't out of the question for a yaoguai to have a really good human disguise. If anything, the better camouflaged ones were more dangerous.

The old man took the attack in stride, flipping Quentin over his shoulder. In the same smooth motion he twirled his staff with both hands and locked it around Quentin's neck in a chokehold. I would have stopped him from strangling my boyfriend right there, except the two of them were laughing and having a grand time of it. Quentin was obviously not using his full strength.

"I take it you two know each other?" I called out.

Quentin relented first and snaked out of the old man's grasp. "Genie," he said, proud to make the introduction. "This is the Great White Planet. Herald of the gods, and maybe the only one who's not an ass."

If I remembered the story of Sun Wukong correctly, the Great White Planet was the embodiment of Venus. And he was the first being to recognize that the Monkey King was not a mere beast but a special, uncategorizable being. He'd recommended that Sun Wukong be given a role in the celestial pantheon, like a real god.

That explained the friendly terms he and Quentin were on. While Sun Wukong's entry-level foray in Heavenly duties had been a disaster, at least the Great White Planet had tried. It didn't matter what culture or plane of existence you were talking about. Anyone who got you a job, who tried to get you your money, was as good as gold.

Dude's name still sounds like an online forum that needs to be monitored by the FBI, I thought to myself.

Guanyin, who Quentin had forgotten was also not an ass, stepped forward and smiled. "It's good to see you again, Grandfather."

She was calling him by an honorific. True family relations between gods, like the one between the Jade Emperor and his nephew Erlang Shen, were somewhat rare. The Great White Planet took her hand and bowed. "My lady, you are as radiant as ever," he said in a warm, raspy voice. Then he turned to me.

"The Shouhushen." He made the title sound grander and a lot less sarcastic than the Jade Emperor or anyone else had. He gave me the kindest, crinkliest smile, his gentle eyes positively dancing with wisdom and understanding.

Then he bashed me in the face with his staff.

His attack moved me as much as Yellow-Toothed Elephant's did, which is to say not at all. The head of the shillelagh shattered along the grain, splitting the body down to where he gripped it. The sudden cracks in the wood must have pinched the Great White Planet's skin, because he yipped and put the web of his thumb into his mouth.

"You were supposed to dodge that," he said, looking disappointed. "I suppose reflexes aren't your strong suit." He planted his ruined staff into the ground, pulled out a faded yellow booklet from his sleeve, and began scratching in it with a surprisingly modern ballpoint.

A lot had happened in the past three seconds, and my senses, dulled from yaoguai complaints and introversion fatigue, were only now beginning to catch up. The first thought that went through my head was that I, unlike Quentin, didn't owe this guy a damn thing, and second, I was perfectly willing to commit eldercide right here and now.

I cracked my knuckles loud enough to make the Great White Planet look up.

Quentin put his hand on my elbow. "He was testing you. That's part of his job. Besides carrying messages, he's also like the inspector of Heaven."

"That is correct," the Great White Planet said in a distracted cadence, scribbling all the while. "I'm here to evaluate the performance of the Shouhushen in her Earthly duties on behalf of the Jade Emperor, whose mandate she is blessed by."

Quentin and Guanyin seemed to be blind to how infuriating that was. "I'm being judged on a job that I was forced into and don't even want?" I said incredulously.

The Great White Planet glanced at me over the top of his notes. "I see motivation could be improved as well." He went back to his scrawling, this time at double speed.

I knew what points being deducted sounded like. The Great White Planet was making blatant use of negative reinforcement. And it was working. The instinct to simultaneously grovel for a better grade and try harder at whatever I was lacking rose to the forefront. *Motivation? I'll show you motivation, you wrinkly old windbag. Also, please kind sir, don't fail me, I beg you.*

I cleared my throat. I wasn't Little Miss Perfectionist anymore. I'd grown. I could call his bluff.

"I don't have to put up with this nonsense," I said as casually as I could. "This is horse crap."

The Great White Planet gave me a mournful look before shaking his head and *tsk*ing with his teeth. He put his pen away and brought out a bigger, redder one. The tip of it glistened with ink like a snake's fang, wet with crimson venom.

Quentin and Guanyin had to restrain me from grabbing the pen and shoving it up his nose.

"Tea!" Guanyin shouted as she twisted one of my arms into a hammerlock. "We should have some tea and catch up. It would be nice to sit down with a drink instead of being under the hot sun, no?"

The Great White Planet's eyes lit up, and he put away the Red Pen of Doom. "That sounds like a wonderful idea," he said. "There is a particular Earthly confection I'm interested in trying."

■ ■ ■

I stared at the Great White Planet from across the table in the bubble tea shop, plotting out how I could grab his booklet and force-feed it to him. My best option seemed to be waiting for him to slip on the greasy, canola-oiled floors.

The cafe was right around the corner from a more popular one that served the same menu, so we didn't bother with disguises or illusions or the like. The clerk was sitting in the back unhygienically on the prep counter, more interested in his phone than the Great White Planet's odd robes. If anyone cared, we could have passed him off as a cosplayer.

In our booth the old man sipped his boba'ed, jellied, foamed abomination through an extra-wide straw with satisfaction.

25

"I think there's been an issue with communication," the Great White Planet said as he wiped milk froth off his mustache. "No one ever gave you the inside track on what having the mandate of the Jade Emperor means."

Guanyin got a little defensive upon hearing him suggest she'd failed at bringing me up to speed, though she hid it much better than me. "We explained to Genie that the source of her authority on Earth comes from the fact that the Jade Emperor granted her his official approval. The exact same way that early human kings were dependent on Heaven's favor to rule their lands."

Quentin and Guanyin had indeed explained it to me. And I'd expressed my distaste for the lesson vehemently. In my opinion, the reason the demons did what I told them was because they didn't want me punching them straight into the bowels of Hell.

Plus I hated what the whole concept of a mandate implied. The idea that you could only hold power because a higher-up gave you permission was utterly terrible. That meant your personal merit counted for nothing. The well-being and opinions of the people you were supposed to be leading counted for nothing.

"Yes, but what can be given can be taken away," the Great White Planet said. "When a king of old lost favor with Heaven by making one too many mistakes, the gods withdrew their mandate and visited disaster upon him until he was overthrown. The mandate passed on to the new leader, who was able to overcome said disaster and right the course of governance."

"I know my actual Chinese history, thanks," I said. I was better versed in Things That Had Really Happened than legend and folklore. "The Zhou Dynasty supplanted the Shang Dynasty, the Qin took over from the Zhou, and so on and so on. The conquerors always used the idea of a mandate to justify and legitimize their conquests. Which to me smacks of post-hoc rationalization, survivorship bias, and a whole bunch of other logical fallacies. Someone takes advantage of a flood or a famine to create a violent rebellion, beheads the ruler, and then screams 'Look at me, I have the mandate now.'"

The Great White Planet poked at the slush gathered at the bottom of his drink. "You have a point. To an ordinary human being, the concept of a mandate can be opaque. But it's a little harder to argue when the god who personally judged those rulers over several millennia is sitting right in front of you." He stared at me while making a slurp of great import.

Even though he seemed to be more concerned with getting his pearl-to-liquid ratio right, the Great White Planet's words carried a load of warning. That big red pen of his had caused the fall of empires. I had been right to fear it.

"The big lesson here is that everyone can be replaced if they're not doing their job well enough," he said. "You can be replaced. *I* can be replaced. Hell, the Jade Emperor can be replaced."

The atmosphere went rigid. I certainly had my opinions about the King of Heaven, given how many problems he'd dropped in my lap. But the one time I'd brought up the scenario of him not being in charge, Guanyin had nearly drawn and quartered me. The hierarchy was to be respected. Insubordination was not tolerated.

Maybe that rule didn't apply to the person doing the judging. I tried dipping a toe in the water, carefully. "I'm a little confused. I thought the Jade Emperor passed out mandates, not held them. Are you saying he's subject to the same laws as the rest of us?"

"King of Heaven is an office," the Great White Planet said. "And the Jade Emperor didn't always hold it. So while deference is certainly due, the answer is yes. He *is* playing the same game. And right now he's not scoring as high as he used to."

Oh my god. God gossip. About one of my least favorite gods. I fought to prevent a massive grin from spreading over my face.

"Oh nooo," I said in a register of polite concern. "How so?"

"Well, to begin with, there was the whole embarrassment with his nephew."

"Embarrassment" was a funny way of boiling down my efforts to stop the rogue god Erlang Shen from destroying the Bay Area and usurping the throne of Heaven to a family squabble. A tiff really. I was barely even there when it happened.

Still, I was glad that the King of Heaven hadn't gotten away unscathed. It was immensely gratifying to know his negligence had caused him to lose face. "To begin with?" I said as demurely as I could, ravenous for the next course. "You mean there's more?"

"Yes. So far he's done nothing about the massive demonic energy that's been gathering in the cosmos." My nascent smile vanished. That wasn't funny at all. I wanted tea spilled, not blood.

"Back that up a bit," I said. "*What* exactly is gathering *where?*"

The Great White Planet brushed a bit of candied debris off his mustache. "Not long ago, a very, *very* hefty source of demon qi was detected in the Blissful Planes."

Guanyin preempted my next question. "A Blissful Plane is like another layer of existence in the Universe," she explained in a hurry. She looked as concerned as I felt and didn't want to waste time. "Imagine reality as a book. You know, a real one with paper. Heaven, Hell, and Earth would only be three of the pages. There are many other realms, each one physically separate from the other, full of lesser spirits and yaoguai who aren't evil enough to be consigned to Diyu."

"I used to live in one," Quentin said. "The Mountain of Flowers and Fruit."

"Okay, so alternate dimensions," I said. The concept was easy enough to grasp after the mystical wackiness I'd been through last year. "I want to hear about this demon energy. What's causing it?"

"We don't know yet," the Great White Planet said. "Only that it's growing stronger by the hour."

Fantastic. "Is Earth in danger?"

"Earth is many layers of reality removed from this menace," he answered. "And the boundaries between realms are nigh inviolable to any but the most powerful gods."

I noticed he didn't explicitly say *no*. "Red Boy and Erlang Shen managed to break through them. If I should be worried, I'd like to know now."

"You need not," the Great White Planet said. "The mighty dragon Ao Guang has been dispatched by Heaven to contain the demonic threat. He commands a vast army of warrior spirits who will be more than enough to combat any enemy he encounters."

Ao Guang. I dredged up the familiar name from the stories of the Monkey King. Ao Guang was the Guardian of the Eastern Sea, and if the stories were to be believed, he and I went way back. Sun Wukong first encountered the Ruyi Jingu Bang, i.e. me, in the treasure hoard of the great underwater dragon while a guest in his palace. If not for that chance encounter, the legendary staff would have sat collecting dust in a sunken gallery for who knew how many millennia.

The Great White Planet took my silence for skepticism. "Might I remind you, Shouhushen, these problems aren't taking place on Earth. They're not your jurisdiction. They're the Jade Emperor's."

Odd. For once someone was telling me I didn't have to take responsibility for a brewing crisis. And that the guy who *was* in charge would have to step up in accordance with his title. I didn't know what to do with my hands.

"Okay," I said cautiously. "And what happens if the King of Heaven flubs this? Whose mandate is he losing? By the rules you've laid out, there has to be a greater authority above him."

The Great White Planet lifted his plastic cup and peered at the chaotic melted slurry inside. "Things start getting a little . . . primordial once you follow the chain too high," he said. "It is my sincere hope that you never behold any of the entities, ideas, or conceptual forces that comprise the level above Heaven. Take it from me; it's unhealthy even for a god."

My curiosity got the best of me. "You've seen what's beyond Heaven?"

"I did, once, and let me put it this way." He gave me a thousand-yard frown. "My hair used to be black."

The Great White Planet shook his head clear of the unpleasant memory and slapped his notebook on the table. He pulled out the normal pen and twirled it like a mathlete before going to town. I heard the distinct down-up swishes of check marks, instead of the down-down separate strokes of *X*s. He went through the rows of his ledger with the swiftness that only a teacher dedicated to handing out nothing but B grades could do.

"I advise you to keep your eyes on your own paper, Ms. Lo," he said, startling me with the use of my actual name. "So far you're doing . . ." He tilted his head side to side. ". . . well, it could go either way in the end."

Before I could protest his choice of words, he clamped his notebook shut around his pen and tucked it back into his robe. "My job here is done for the day." He cleared his throat of the sugar buildup. "I'll pop in from time to time. You might see me or you might not. Which is more warning than I gave the King of Shang before the Battle of Muye. Ha!"

With that he vanished. Disappeared into the ether like a popped soap bubble in the moment the few other patrons were distracted by an order being called. I'd never seen a god make an exit like that, and I waved my hand around the space he'd been in to make sure he was truly gone. Quentin and Guanyin took a similar approach. There was a solid minute of silence among us until they broke it at the exact same time.

"That wasn't so bad," Quentin said.

"This is *not* good," Guanyin said.

They glanced at each other. Quentin made a shrug of deferral for Guanyin to go first.

"I think the Great White Planet is understating the problem," the goddess said. "For the Dragon King of the Eastern Sea to get involved means this potential foe is incredibly powerful."

I took it that since deep-sea sonar hadn't revealed any draconic armies in the Pacific Ocean off the coast of China, the "Eastern Sea" had to be a Blissful Plane outside of my own reality, like the Mountain of Flowers and Fruit. "But that means he's handling it, right?" I said.

"It's his job as a spirit general of Heaven," Quentin said to me. "That's why there's nothing to worry about. Ao Guang is a tough

31

old bastard who absolutely *lives* for battling the forces of evil. I mean, during the whole deal with Red Boy and Erlang Shen, you and I wanted nothing more than for someone else to step in and help with demon troubles."

"Yes, and that 'someone else' ended up being me," Guanyin said curtly. "I'm not comfortable with happily distancing ourselves from a potential catastrophe."

"You heard the Great White Planet," I said. "What are we supposed to do? What are we allowed to do?"

"Gather information?" Guanyin said. "Train, rest, prepare? Be vigilant and available?"

Uh-oh. I had a sense where this conversation was leading. My fingers tightened around the spoon I'd been toying nervously with after the Great White Planet left.

"Genie, I know you have your big trip with Yunie coming up soon, but I don't think it's a good idea to step away from Shouhushen duties for so long," Guanyin said. "You should reconsider going."

I snapped the cheap disposable utensil, and the head went skittering across the table. I knew it would come to this. I had told Guanyin and Quentin months ago that I had this excursion planned. Guanyin hadn't said anything back then, only smiled and nodded in a way that said she didn't approve of it at all.

"I can't bail on that," I said. "It's important to the two of us."

"And so is maintaining planar harmony," Guanyin said. "Or so I assume."

The Goddess of Mercy was correct, technically. But she was conflating my wants with her wants. I had no overwhelming desire to be a champion of the cosmological order, only to see Earth and the people I cared about safe. I'd kept at the role of the Shouhushen because it seemed like the best way to ensure that.

"I'm with Genie on this one," Quentin said. "She'll be off-duty for four days. A long weekend. The multiverse isn't going to collapse the moment we take our eyes off it."

Guanyin had too much experience cleaning up the messes of gods and humanity alike to look convinced by that claim. She wrinkled her nose.

"Look, these still work, right?" Quentin tugged on his earlobes, where the demon-detecting earrings permanently sat. They were mine but infused with Guanyin's magic. If a yaoguai ever got too close to a normal human, they'd start buzzing like angry flies. "If there's trouble on Earth, Genie and I drop what we're doing and take care of it. Like we always do."

I wasn't one hundred percent certain that I was making the right decision. It was usually easiest to do whatever Guanyin said. But in this case, I had to navigate the big gray area of whether she was my boss or my adviser.

"I'm going on my trip," I said. "And that's that. If we want to help Heaven with this problem, then we'll figure out how after I get back."

And hope it doesn't bite us in the ass before then.

5

"THANKS FOR BACKING ME UP," I YELLED INTO QUENTIN'S EAR.

We were in our standard mode of transportation, him using his Cloud-Leaping Somersault to cross mighty distances in a single bound with me perched on his back for the ride. It was cheaper than paying for train fare.

"Hey, I know what it's like arguing with Guanyin," he said. "It's impossible to have the moral high ground. Plus we're talking about what could be your last high school trip with your best friend. Some things are sacrosanct."

That he understood the situation and supported me made me want to wrap my arms around him tighter and bury my nose in his hair. A conscientious Quentin was like Superman without the kryptonite. Sun Wukong could shapeshift into nearly any form, and so far a decent boyfriend was among them.

He and I sailed toward an empty patch of highway. I hung on as his feet slammed into the gravel shoulder. I could hear the muscles of his quads and calves threatening to burst through the seams of his clothes from the effort of absorbing the shock while shooting us skyward again in a single touch. I blinked away the dryness from my eyes. Maybe we needed to invest in old-timey pilot goggles. There were a few kids at school into steampunk I could ask.

My town came into view. From up here, lit by a purple and pink sunset, Santa Firenza didn't look quite as claustrophobic as it felt at ground level. Sure, it was mostly patchy lawns and vacant office parks, but there were no borders to be seen from this altitude. Santa Firenza dissolved into its surroundings, setting the precedent that one day I could drift far away myself.

There was something wrong with our descent, though.

"Quentin," I said. "We seem to be heading straight at my house instead of a clear landing zone."

"I'm going to touch down inside your room. I left the windows open."

I nearly choked in outrage. "You moron!" I shouted. "Even if you can land without making noise, we're never going to fit through the window!"

Quentin pondered the situation with a handful of our precious remaining seconds before impact. "Ummm . . . you're beautiful?"

"Goddammit, Quentin!"

With a skydiving instructor's precision, he flipped his orientation to me in midair and embraced me with my head cradled over his shoulder.

"Shrink," he whispered into my ear.

The front-row view of our impending crash into my house loomed large. And then larger. And larger. Instead of flying through the air, which strangely enough I'd become accustomed to, it suddenly felt like were falling down a hole. A gaping abyss where the bottom layer was the interior of my bedroom, stretched to infinity.

We landed on carpet strands the size of Saguaro cactuses. Quentin chose not to roll with the impact and took the brunt of it all by himself, acting as a sledge underneath me. The friction tore his shirt from his shoulders; had he not been Sun Wukong, he would have lost the flesh from his bones as well.

The chivalrous gesture only pissed me off more. As the reincarnated Ruyi Jingu Bang, I was at least as invulnerable as him. If not more so.

The world shrank quickly as we ground to a stop. What looked like a burnout skid the length of a drag strip turned into mere inches in my bedroom. Quentin and I were full-size before I could even get nauseous at the perspective change.

Underneath me, his glorious torso was laid bare, the cover of a romance novel brought to life. He glanced at my hands braced against his chest and looked up at me hopefully, like this might lead to something.

I slapped his body as hard as I could, leaving two bright red handprints on his skin.

"You asshole!" I shouted. "I can't believe how stupid that was!"

"Ow! I'm sorry! I only wanted to see if you could learn to shrink under pressure!"

That got me even angrier. "You can't *trick* me into learning new powers anymore!"

"But that's the way we used to do it!"

His words gave me pause. Yes, back when Quentin and I were still feeling each other out, a lot of my former Ruyi Jingu Bang powers required an unpleasant jolt to kickstart them back into action.

But that was then and this was now. I felt like I had the right to demand more honesty from Quentin these days, and that included how we trained together.

I tried to smack him across the chest again, but he caught my wrists and sat up, knocking me off balance. To keep me from tumbling backward he threw my arms over his shoulders like he knew I wanted them there and gripped me tightly by the waist.

He looked up at me, his apologetic puppy-dog eyes driving me nuts half in a bad way and half in the *really* bad way.

My heart was pounding. From the mishap, of course. "Don't do it again," I muttered.

He craned his neck up, filling my vision, and brushed his lips against mine. "I won't," he said, the vibrations of his voice tickling me where my skin was most sensitive. "We'll train the right way. Maybe on the top of a mountain. We haven't done that in a long time, have we?"

Somewhere along the line he'd picked up the habit of talking about routine things *while* gently kissing me, and it drove me wild like nothing else. Despite my frustration with him, I gave in to temptation and ran my hands down his back, using both of them to seize his perfect, wondrous—

"Ahem."

We looked over to the corner of my room.

Where Yunie had been sitting in my desk chair the whole time.

Quentin and I scrambled in front of her gaze. He found one of my hoodies on the floor and pulled it over his head. It was too big for him and he'd put it on backward, but at least he was covered up.

Even though he was the more naked one, I patted myself down to make sure I wasn't exposed. I looked like I was searching for missing keys. My friend was enjoying our tango of embarrassment immensely.

"Your mom let me in," she said. "Plus I texted you a bunch."

She didn't need an excuse to be here alone. Yunie and I had an open-door policy between our houses and parents. She'd waited in my room for me tons of times before.

A casual observer might have thought I was mortified that my best friend nearly saw me make out with my boyfriend like a couple of lake boaters during Spring Break. They would have been right, but it was more about the fact that I'd test-driven a power right in front of her. One was awkward, the other was dangerous.

Ever since I'd confessed to Yunie about my . . . situation, I'd kept the supernatural as far away from her as possible. Zero tolerance quarantine. No contamination.

I had a reason for my paranoia. Back when the original jailbreak from Diyu occurred, a particularly dangerous yaoguai named the Six-Eared Macaque had kidnapped her to use against me. Yunie didn't remember it, but for me it was the worst moment of my life. The mere thought of the yaoguai laying its hands on her was enough to make my teeth crack.

Afterward, I'd made Quentin and Guanyin swear to keep a mundane dead zone around her. No magic, no demons, and no powers near Yunie. The possibility of our dealings causing her harm made me sick. So I was extra-peeved at Quentin now, for the way we'd made our entrance. We could have taken out her eye or something in our tiny state—two superpowered pellets from a BB gun.

Yunie tilted her head. "You can shrink?" she said. "It doesn't look anything like it does in the movies. It's got like a . . . *you're receding into the distance very fast* quality, only you're not going farther away."

"That was the first time," I said. I gave Quentin a glower. "It's not happening that way again."

"You know, if you'd just stayed small, you two could have finished your business without me even knowing," she said with a giggle. "How's Guanyin?"

The two of them had never met. But once Yunie realized how much I flipped out over her proximity to the supernatural, she started using it to intentionally push my buttons. She was too smart and too good of a friend to insist on getting personally involved with the supernatural; she'd told me as much that day in her basement. But she was also too good of a friend to pass on riling me up by making statements of sly curiosity, probing closer and closer to the worlds beyond Earth. Which I should have expected from her, the little troll.

"Guanyin's fine," I said.

Yunie chuckled. She'd successfully poked the bear; no need to be cruel about it. "I came over to talk plans for the weekend trip, but it's getting kind of late. I don't think we really need a plan. We'll just follow my cousin around and figure things out on our own if she's busy."

This older cousin of hers was the reason why we were allowed to go on this campus visit over the long weekend without adult supervision in the first place. To hear it, Ji-Hyun Park was a superwoman, currently slicing her way through pre-med at the most prestigious college in our state like a hot knife through butter.

Yunie had spotted an opportunity in her aunt's relentless bragging about the next soon-to-be doctor in the family.

Some weeks ago, my friend had floated the idea to our parents that combining a girls-only campus tour with a stay in Ji-Hyun's apartment over a four-day weekend would help us learn about the school. The experience would improve our characters as we got to witness an upstanding older woman in the real world ignoring the temptations of college life while adhering strictly to a high-status academic path.

That was the surface story. My parents had bought into it hook, line, and sinker. But my alarm bells went off based on the rack of new going-out tops I'd spotted in Yunie's closet afterward.

"A college party's not going to kill you," she'd said when I'd confronted her about our true plans. "If anything, this is a good opportunity to blow off steam. No demons or magic or any of that. I told you a while ago that I hated seeing you so stressed out, and instead of relaxing you got wound up even tighter. And we *are* going for an important campus tour. During the day. That's not a lie."

I knew why Yunie was leaning so hard on this. It was our chance for one last adventure, the two of us. She knew I couldn't afford to go traveling any great distance with her. Grand tours of Europe or South America like the ones some of our classmates took were out of my reach. And the resource disparity between our families always made Yunie more uncomfortable than it did me. So in her mind, she saw this as the perfect way we could both explore new territory, hand in hand.

That was how she'd sold me on a vacation, albeit one that was still focused on college. You could take the girl out of the high school, but you couldn't take the dork out of the girl.

I was still both wary and guilty about the trip, though, to the extent that I'd told Quentin and Guanyin the same version that my parents got. We were going for academics only. No one else but Yunie knew about the partying we'd likely do at night.

"How long did we keep you waiting?" I said.

"I don't know." Yunie held up her phone. "I've been too busy playing this game you made to notice the time. How many levels does it have?"

"They're procedurally generated on the client, so . . . infinity?"

She shook her head. "That's evil. People are going to waste their lives trying to beat this thing."

The game that I'd made as coding practice wasn't very complicated. You played as a little monkey trying to hop between clouds. If you fell, you had a limited number of special items you could use to save yourself, the most common being an iron pole that extended all the way to the pits of death below and propped you back up to safety.

Rutsuo Huang, our school's resident CompSci wiz, had to look over my shoulder a lot while I developed it. Over the course of our hangouts in the computer labs, I got to see a new side of my quiet, unassuming classmate, the one that had utter contempt for a half-assed job. I could have made the game in much less time if he hadn't scowled most of my early code into oblivion.

"I never fixed the randomization," I said. "It's too hard, and you end up dying every other round. I don't think anyone's actually going to play it for real."

"Uhh, I don't know about that," said Yunie. "This says you're number ninety-six out of one hundred on the app store."

The three of us gathered around her phone. Sure enough,

41

Monkey King Jumps to Heaven was right there on the bottom of the chart.

"You have to have a ton of users to get any rank at all," Yunie said. "This is a pretty big deal."

"Woo!" Quentin shouted, raising his fists into the air. "I'm going to be famous!"

"You're already famous, you dip," I said. "I learned who you were through one of the oldest stories still being told. You are *literally* legendary."

Quentin grinned. "Yeah, but now I'm going to be New Economy famous. I've gone multi-platform."

I flipped up the hood over his face.

6

YUNIE COULDN'T STAY FOR DINNER DESPITE MY MOTHER'S impassioned pleas. She had a prior commitment at her aunt's, and blood marginally won out in that scenario. But Quentin knew he had to stick around. There was no way in hell that my mother was going zero-for-two on feeding her favorite people in the world.

He sat next to me at our kitchen table while Mom cooked and I brought her up to speed on what happened at school. Today had been so hectic that my promotion on the volleyball team felt like ancient history. It had already petrified. I had to dig the story out from the surrounding layers carefully for my mother, without getting any residue of gods or demons on it.

"Captain?" she said, tossing a pan of string beans into the air and catching them over the burner without looking. "What's so good about that?"

Yes, she was doing the *denigrate my child's accomplishments compared to other people's kids* thing. But in her defense, the last time she'd heard the term used in relation to one of my sports teams was in grade school gym class, where each kid took turns being the "captain" so everyone would get a chance to feel in charge. It made very little sense on the days we did Parachute.

43

"It's a big deal," Quentin reassured her. "Varsity captain is a position with a huge amount of prestige. It looks great on college applications." He sat next to me at the table and placed a hand on mine like we were announcing a newborn.

Such a public gesture of affection and commitment made me flinch. "Why are you talking like you're the expert?" I said, snatching my hand away. "What were you ever captain of?"

"Nothing." He grinned. "That's why I was such a horrible person when I was younger."

I thought back to the story of Sun Wukong. You could have argued that he was technically the head of Team Xuanzang on their quests to find the holy sutras, with Sandy and Pigsy as the subordinates he regularly trod underfoot. But beating the freshmen into submission wasn't a leadership style I wanted to emulate. Despite what had happened today with the yaoguai.

"It's going to help a lot when you're searching for a job, too," Quentin said. "Companies want to recruit leaders out of college. It's the number one thing they look for."

He'd oversold the concept a little, jumping a couple of steps. I didn't know how he came upon that factoid. "Jobs are like . . . ugh. That's thinking too far ahead right now."

"You don't need to worry about what happens after school," Mom said over her shoulder. "If you can't find a job, Quentin will take care of you."

Quentin's eyes went wide, like a boxing referee who noticed both fighters were suddenly holding knives. He waved his hands at me behind my mother's back to show he didn't share her opinion on the matter.

I took a breath through my nostrils so deep I could have made a wish on a birthday cake. By the time I counted to three and exhaled, the dangerous moment had passed. It was okay. Another one of my mother's stupid, old-fashioned statements. Not worth picking a whole fight from scratch about.

I felt proud of myself. I was the embodiment of serenity and forgiveness.

"No one has considered whether or not I have time to be captain," I said. "You know. Given my other *extracurriculars*?" I made a hint-hint face at Quentin.

"If it's valuable, then make the time," Mom said. A mouthwa tering bloom of garlic and ginger filled the air as she added the aromatics to the pan. The smell would last in our cramped, unventilated kitchen until tomorrow. "You always have more time than you think, lying around in little bits. Back when your father and I were opening the furniture store, we were so busy that we used to make schedules of what we were doing in fifteen-minute . . ."

She paused. I looked away. I'd seen this before; the sentence wasn't going to be finished.

The experience of those days, of the unmitigated disaster that was my father, and really my mother, too, going into business for themselves, had surfaced in the disguise of a wistful memory. The clash of feelings caused my mother to short-circuit.

I might have had an American set of values to help relieve the pressure caused by the tragedy. *Stuff happens. People change. TV's too good right now to care.*

But to her, what had happened to our family was a fermenting cauldron of bitterness that would only grow thicker and fouler over time. It would be there forever. Asian parents did not have the widest psychological toolset.

Quentin tried to break the silence. "You know, you could make things easier for yourself by delegating. Create an assistant captain position."

Yeah right. He'd seen how well that worked with Guanyin. Trying to command someone who'd been passed over for your job was only a good idea on paper. The other seniors who'd been playing the sport way longer than me would *looove* taking my orders. And forget the young'uns. This incoming crop of sophomores and freshmen barely knew which side of the net was theirs.

And secondly, I didn't want to talk about it anymore. Mom's mood had infected me, ruining my short-lived moment of tranquility, and the two of us had regressed into the emotional state we'd spent most of the last five years in. Mother and daughter were both sullen cocoons now. Who knew when we'd emerge. It certainly wouldn't be this evening.

Quentin made a little inward sigh when he saw my face and moved on to safe questions he already knew the answer to. "Can I help with anything?" he called out to Mom.

"Don't be silly," she said. She tipped the beans onto a plate and set them down in front of us, the steam wafting in front of Quentin's face like a veil. Then she paused in front of the rice cooker.

"Forgot something?" I said.

"No, I . . ." She shook her head. I could hear her jab the paddle roughly against the insides of the chamber as she filled a large bowl.

Ugh. Now we were in angry chore mode. The sound of dishes being passive-aggressively put away, the roar of an unnecessary vacuuming, was pretty much the soundtrack of my childhood.

Mom turned around and, sure enough, her face was slightly red. She stopped again halfway to the table.

But then her hands trembled. I'd never seen that before. Something was very wrong.

"I'm fine," she said in response to a question no one had asked out loud. She tried to put the food on the nearest flat surface. The bowl tipped off the edge of the counter and crashed to the floor.

"Mom!" I knocked over my chair in my attempt to reach her before she collapsed.

"I'm *fine*," she declared, this time in a loud, strong voice. But she thumped hard down on the floor, like a child refusing to walk anymore. She took the landing so hard on her wrist that I was certain she'd broken it.

Quentin was gone. I knew without needing to look that he'd vaulted over the table to get help.

I wouldn't have seen him go anyway. My vision had tunneled. My whole world had shrunk down to the size of my mother in my arms, and it was fragile and small and shaking, and I was going to sit here and cradle it in my arms and pray to every god in existence that it would be okay.

7

"GENIE, I'M FINE," MOM SAID.

She would have looked pretty stupid saying that, had we been inside a hospital room, with her lying on an incline bed, an IV stuck in her pale, thin arm. But we weren't. Instead, the two of us were sitting on dull tartan chairs in front of a pile of *Runner's World* magazines in the lobby. We hadn't even made it into the ER proper.

The scattered handful of other people in the waiting area held ice packs to their faces or cradled swollen ankles. Their presence made me indignant. *Get up on out of here with your superficial injuries distracting the staff from my mother. You assholes aren't related to me.*

"You are not fine," I said. "You had a hypertensive episode."

"A *likely* hypertensive episode," she said, as if that word bolstered her argument instead of mine. "You heard the EMT people."

"That means you're not fine! You could have had a stroke!"

"Keep your voice down." She looked around at the other patients apologetically.

I hated that so much. The little gestures of hers that showed how warped her priorities were. How low her own well-being fell on that list. I was so pissed off at her. I couldn't remember the last time she'd had a checkup.

Whenever I'd pestered her about her health, the answer was always the same. *I can't afford to see a doctor.* She'd let years of aches and pains build up in her body, untreated, and now an actual life-threatening issue had settled in there, claiming squatters' rights.

Like we can afford THIS! I wanted to shout at her. She was so worried about money? How much did she think it cost to ride an ambulance to the hospital at night for an emergency? Like any amount of nickel and diming would make up for the incoming bill. My mother might have been willing to gamble with her health, but she didn't understand the basic rules of the game.

"See?" she said, holding up her arm and flexing it. "I thought I hurt my wrist, but it's completely fine now. And they wouldn't put me in my own room because I had no bad signs once we arrived. This is a big fuss over nothing."

Before I could launch into a fresh tirade, Quentin burst in through the doors, clearing a path for my father behind him. Dad was breathing heavily, and I had a brief panic that I would see both of my parents collapse this day. But he was a normal color and his posture was as upright as any of the models on the outdoor magazines laid out on the table. I reminded myself that he worked at a gym, and if anything was now fitter than most people his age.

"What happened?" he said. "Somebody tell me what happened."

Before Quentin or I could respond, my mother cut us off. "Could you give me a moment alone with him?" she said to us.

Him. There was no emphasis on the word, and no insult behind it. My mother had the habit of continuing conversations with my father as if zero time had passed since they last spoke, whether it was hours or months. For an outsider, it would have been impossible to tell that anything had transpired between them. Which was probably the way they liked it.

"You'd better let us catch up," Dad said.

It was good that he was here to sub in for me. A few more minutes and I would have blown up at her and caused the scene she was so afraid of. But I let Quentin pull me away by the elbow so that Mom could see that it was taking their combined efforts to keep me from arguing with her.

Quentin and I went into the hallway. It needed maintenance. The glow of a Coke machine provided the majority of the light, and the water fountain push bar was pushed in and stuck, causing a wasteful, continuous drip. I had the feeling if I walked down the hall, the surroundings would scroll by me infinitely like an old cartoon with no budget.

"Your dad's going to think I'm bad luck," Quentin muttered, semi-seriously. "I don't see him that much, and then all of a sudden I'm telling him your mom's in the hospital."

Unlikely. On the day I introduced them, at a nice cafe in the city, Quentin had charmed my dad as much as he had my mom. Over shots of espresso and six-dollar slices of hazelnut toast, the two had a raucous conversation in Chinese that was so loud you would have thought they were old army comrades. I had to remind them repeatedly to keep it down, and by the end of the afternoon, Dad was already dreaming about playing catch with his grandkids.

"You did fine," I said. "You passed."

Quentin blinked. "Passed what?"

The Test. Being There. Seeing the worst, weakest part of me and not flinching. Wasn't that supposed to be the ultimate boyfriend move? Being a rock-solid presence in an emergency? I didn't know, really. I had very little to go on.

His puzzled face was as cute as a dog tilting its head. Despite how inappropriate the timing was, or maybe because of it, I wanted nothing more than to shove him into the dusty recess next to the hand sanitizer dispenser and finish what we started in my room before Yunie caught us. If there wasn't enough space, maybe we could shrink, him and me together again. I wouldn't have to think about the bigger world.

Luckily for my dignity, we were interrupted by another presence, warm and comforting, that pushed away the medicinal sterility of the hospital.

Guanyin was here. All would be well.

The washed-out lighting only made her look more angelic. She reached out and put her hand on my shoulder.

"You acted pretty quick," I said, smiling.

"I keep an extra eye out for the people close to you," the goddess said. "I know your priorities."

"So she's going to be okay." I slumped against the wall in relief. "Thank you for fixing her."

The silence that came from Guanyin didn't feel like an acknowledgment. It wasn't a good enough silence. I straightened back up.

"You didn't fix her?" I said. "You didn't make her okay?"

"Genie . . ." Guanyin searched for the right way to put something that would never be right by me. "I can't make her *okay*. Sure, I healed her wrist on the way over. And I stabilized her heart. This time. But if you're asking me to make sure this kind of incident never happens again, I can't do that."

"Bullshit!"

My curse rolled down the hallway like a boulder chasing an interloper through a temple. It had so much heft to it that it made my throat sore as it came out.

There were probably repercussions for swearing in front of a goddess, but that didn't stop me. "You can do anything!" I yelled, keeping it under my breath this time. "You can step between planes! You can bend the laws of physics! You fixed Androu, didn't you!?"

I was referring to the past incident where the Six-Eared Macaque had infiltrated my school and kidnapped another of my classmates alongside Yunie. Poor Androu had suffered very real injuries. And Guanyin had fixed him.

"Androu was a healthy young person," Guanyin said. "I undid some damage that never should have happened in the first place and sent him on his way. Your mother can't be 'fixed.' She has a bad case of having lived *life*."

There was hardly any arguing with that. My parents were older than most of my classmates'. Mom had always been pretty upfront about the fact that they'd had a hard time having children; I'd snuck in under the deadline.

But Guanyin's statement was true in a different, more punishing way. For some people, living meant growth, becoming stronger, happier, fuller over time. In my mother's and father's cases, life had stripped their flesh down to the bone. The addition of health problems was like putting away the carving knife and bringing out the grinder.

"Your mother will always be vulnerable, Genie," Guanyin said softly. "Neither you nor I can change that."

I wondered how much of an atrocity it would be considered if I leveled this hospital around us.

"Genie," Quentin said, prodding my arm as I imagined air raid sirens and the National Guard rolling up to stop my rampage. "Your parents are calling for us."

Neither Mom nor Dad had met Guanyin, and they weren't going to. It had always seemed strategic to hold back that introduction, plus her general maturity made it harder to come up with cover stories. She could pass as my what, really? Teacher? Guidance counselor? Supermodel I befriended at the train station?

Quentin and I left her and went back to the lobby. Mom hadn't moved from her chair, and the way Dad stood off to the side made her seem like an empress on her throne. It was so typical of her. She wouldn't admit that she was sick, but she *was* willing to milk the moment for everything it was worth.

What *I* wouldn't admit was how painful it was to see my mom and dad as a unit. It was always accidents or impending doom that brought them in close proximity, as if their very existences were like naked wires. When they crossed, bad things happened.

The two of them deserved better. They should have been allowed to look at their daughter's face at the same time, in the same room, and be happy. Would it be such a friggin' problem for the Universe to let them be carefree together for once?

"Genie," Mom said. "I have something I need to tell you."

I tried to banish my gloomy thoughts and failed. "What, that you're fine?" I snapped.

"No. Something else. Promise me you'll listen, won't you?"

Huh. Hold on. There was a faintness in her voice that said for once, she'd dropped the act. She was letting herself be tired. Maybe she'd accepted the facts. This close call had pierced the reality distortion bubble that she normally generated around herself.

I always had the fantasy that one day my mother and I would lay bare our souls and finally say everything we meant to each other, with perfect understanding and ultimate sincerity. But not like this. I didn't want to buy a moment of revelation from her with a health scare.

"Genie . . ."

I steeled myself as best I could. I wasn't ready for this.

"Genie, I want you to go on your trip this weekend."

". . . WHAT!?" I shrieked.

"Keep it down," she muttered. "I don't want you to cancel it on my account. And don't you dare tell Yunie about this. She'll be worried sick."

A fake-out. I thought this was going to be her epiphany. That things had the infinitesimal chance of changing between us. Instead, surprise! There was another mask under the first mask the whole time!

"The *trip* is the last thing that should be on *anyone's* mind! How could you even *say* that to me right now?"

"Genie, just . . ." my dad said, a veteran soldier scarred by more battles than I, the newbie, could ever imagine. "I'm going to take a few days off to look after her."

"Even though I'm fine," Mom said.

"Yes," Dad said, playing both sides. "Even though she's fine. While you're visiting the school, there'll be someone at home."

I was skeptical. "Work'll let you do that?"

"I get vacation days," Dad said. "What am I going to do with them, go to Maui?"

I looked back and forth at my parents, before settling on my mother. *You think you're so clever, don't you?* I mentally seethed at her. *That this'll get me to shut up?* Dad looking after her wasn't going to help. For Christ's sake, he was the one who'd wrecked her blood pressure in the first place.

The very fact that they were resorting to this meant that she was bad enough to need proper medical supervision. She needed to stay at the hospital. Recuperating at home was a terrible idea.

"This is a great plan," Quentin declared.

I'd forgotten he was there. You could hear my neck screeching like a rusty hinge as I turned to look at him, the whites of my eyes showing like high beams.

"Hospitals aren't good places to be around," he said obliviously. "Bad feng shui. Better to rest at home and be comfortable."

I'd gone back in time. Everyone around me had reverted to the Dark Ages. What was next, a prescription of leeches?

"My parents could drop by," Quentin said. "You know. Mr. and Mrs. Sun?" He nudged me as if I'd forgotten whom he was talking about.

"Oh, that would be lovely!" Mom straightened up so fast she probably gave herself a head rush. "See, Genie? This is a fine plan. Quentin agrees."

"Quentin is not the last word in this household!"

Mom scoffed. "And you are?"

Oof. That was more than I could take. I was used to Mom stalemating me in arguments through sheer bull-headedness, but turning words on me like that was a low blow as far as I was concerned. I stormed out of the lobby.

■　■　■

Outside was too warm and humid for the air to be considered fresh. The designers of this hospital had the nerve to put a little patio by the doors with wrought metal chairs, as if people wanted to spend time here drinking in the ambience. I would have preferred a barber's pole with bloody bandages to serve as a warning: *If you are here, you are not well, and you need help.*

Quentin found me within a minute. "What's wrong?"

Where to begin. "Your parents?" I said. "Your *parents?*"

The deal with Quentin's parents, which took some getting used to even for me, was that they were shapeshifted clones of himself, formed from his own magical hairs. They had the appearances and personalities of two very polite businesspeople from overseas who were always traveling and completely neglectful of their son in that charming British boarding school way.

Quentin trotted them out whenever he needed to show he had a family. My parents adored his parents. If they had to choose two out of three among Quentin, his parents, and me, they would have pinned a note to my chest and tossed me to the curb.

I knocked my head against a brick column that supported an awning over the patio. "You're going to have your stupid walking magic tricks pop in to look after my mother?"

Quentin looked hurt. "I thought you liked them. You've asked me to have them keep your mom company lots of times."

"That was when she was *healthy!* She's going to try and entertain them! You *know* how much effort she puts into for guests! What do you think she was doing today when she collapsed?"

Quentin's lips parted as he realized what he'd done. "I'm sorry," he said. "I was trying to make her happy."

"Why did you butt in to begin with? She should be under medical supervision, not puttering around the kitchen!"

"I thought being involved was part of being a good boyfriend!"

Being involved *silently*, maybe. "You sided with my mother over me in an argument. You just took all your boyfriend points, set them on fire, and buried them in a dumpster under the floor of the ocean."

"I'm sorry," he said again. "I didn't mean to make things worse. You know I'd do anything for this family and—"

"*Quentin, you are NOT part of this family!*"

■ ■ ■

Ooh. Yup. Scientists and historians would look back to that moment and identify it as Peak Genie, where she had to be her usual hurtful, spiteful self, thinking she could emit her awfulness into the atmosphere the same as always without repercussions. Instead she'd barreled straight past the tipping point, sending the feedback loop spinning off its axis. She'd ignored the warning signs, and now the world was nothing but jellyfish and alkaline wastes.

Quentin pulled some kind of innate cool guy maneuver, taking a step back so that the shadow of the building fell across his face. I couldn't see his eyes as he spoke.

"You're right," he said, his voice flat and dull. "Sure. I'm going to leave before I do any more harm."

He walked away with his hands in his pockets and disappeared into the air using the most half-hearted Cloud-Leaping Somersault I'd ever seen him do. It was mostly calves.

I wanted to call out to him, but I was too dumbfounded by my own cruelty to speak. A flash storm had swept in and left recognizable debris pooling around my knees. A moment ago, my life had been relatively orderly. Now it was . . . this. I stared into the dark sky, wishing for a do-over that would never come.

Then I went back inside. I had to go check on my mom.

8

I WAS SCRUNCHED UP IN A FETAL POSITION. MY LEGS SCRAPED the back of the train seat in front of me. Someone had scratch-graffitied "Richard sux" into the plastic and the "sux" was rubbing my shin and making it itch.

I had a view from behind of a lady eating pad Thai, or something that smelled very much like it. Elsewhere in the car, a man in a fleece vest made loud guarantees on his phone that as the chief marketing officer of his company, he could order, nay, *force* his team to toughen up and deal with the unpaid overtime.

Yunie sat across the aisle from me, reading an honest-to-god paper book. We hadn't been able to find space next to each other. I was glad we couldn't talk right now. The slightest spoken word, and the story of how terrible I'd been to Quentin, would come blubbering out of my mouth and join the other assorted stains on the floor. It grew worse and worse the more I thought about it.

I was born from a rock. Never had parents, never did.

I'd thought Quentin had merely been explaining his origins to me that night we first had dinner at my house. I hadn't known him long enough to understand he'd been opening up to me.

59

His master Subodai had banished him. He'd first fought against, and then fought so hard for his little band with Xuanzang. If you looked at his story and considered him as a real person, then there was only one thing the Monkey King truly lacked. Family.

And I'd . . . I'd said *that* to him the other night.

The unlubricated screeching of the train and the cramped position I was in made it feel like I was sitting inside a trash compactor or a car crusher, the walls closing in around me. Each item of unfinished business thrown in here with me only hastened my demise.

Like the deal with Great White Planet and the Mysterious Demonic Threat he had talked about. I was very far outside my usual way of doing things when it came to that. In the past, if an unresolved issue or mistake ever showed its head, my instincts were always to run over and stomp it out of existence as soon as possible. Bring my full weight to bear on the problem to the exclusion of any distractions. It was how I knocked down and aced different subjects at school. The strategy worked in my academic life.

Not so much in my real life though. It had taken a while, but I'd realized I had to accept a certain degree of messiness in order to keep my wits about me. I'd *wanted* to agree with Guanyin and focus on one looming problem at a time. But this was a juggling act where I had to keep multiple balls in the air.

And my mom had tossed me a chainsaw in the middle of my performance.

I grit my teeth, thinking of her again. She was making me do this trip instead of staying home with her as some kind of punishment. She was screwing with me. She'd told me to enjoy myself, but she really wanted me to feel guilty about it the whole time. Or the whole thing could have been a test that I'd already failed. The right answer was ignoring her overt commands, throwing myself at her feet, and refusing to go at all.

It was guesswork as to what crime I'd committed. By necessity I'd been spending more time at volleyball, with Quentin and Guanyin. Maybe she'd been feeling neglected. Maybe I'd hung out with Dad too much, or not enough. It was impossible to tell because she wouldn't speak her goddamn mind. She wanted a psychic for a daughter. One who would cater to her every silent whim.

I was pissed off at Dad, too, which was rare. Had he and I presented a united front, we might have done the impossible and convinced Mom to back down. The one time I needed my father not to be easygoing, and we'd let our chance slip away.

An earsplitting metal howl made me look up. We were only a stop away from our destination. Even through the train window the surroundings already looked more collegiate. Instead of Santa Firenza's barren lot with yellow paint marking where you should stand to avoid getting run over, this station had overgrown boughs embracing wrought-iron fences. The parking lot contained Bimmers, Lexi, Teslae. In one section, loose leaves of kale lay scattered over the asphalt like flyers, evidence that a farmers' market had passed through here earlier. Despite what the map said, I was very far away from my home right now.

No, I decided. Enough. I wasn't doing this anymore. I wasn't going to be held emotionally hostage by my mother. She expected me to crawl back through our door, hobbled with guilt, having carried her in my mind every minute of the long weekend. Like hell I'd play along.

I stood up and banged my skull on the luggage rack overhead.

It was hard and loud enough that everyone in the car but Yunie looked over and winced. I ignored them.

I can make it four days without thinking about my mom. I'm allowed *to go four days without thinking about my mom.*

A tug came at my insides, my gut reminding me of other injured parties. I pushed the feeling back down with a vengeance.

And Quentin, too, for that matter.

9

I WOULD HAVE BEEN MORE IMPRESSED BY THE BLUE, SUNNY skies blanketing the campus had they not been the same ones I stared at from a couple of towns over. These stingy azure bastards were causing our drought. Screw these skies.

The families from New England and the Midwest, though, ate it up.

"I can't believe how hard it was raining back in Boston," one mother said, marveling, as if the West Coast weren't all the way across the country from the East Coast.

Well, get used to it, I thought. If the weather kept staying as pretty as this, we wouldn't have any more almonds, ever.

A bunch of visitors, me included, had clumped up near the campus entrance by an octagonal fountain with an aged cement dish for a spout. I'd already been mistaken for a current student several times. While we waited for our respective people to come and get us, small talk naturally gravitated toward *oohing and aahing* at our surroundings.

I could admit that the architecture was a big deal. It was absolutely, objectively, especially stunning. I'd seen pictures online, of course, but even the college's official website didn't do the sprawling sandstone buildings justice. The pinkish-brown archways that surrounded the courtyard we were standing in gave it a cloistered, peaceful feel.

It was the most spacious place I'd ever been in. The mission-tiled roofs and dominating chapel seemed to flatten the energy of the campus into a perfect, true plane. Where an Ivy League university nestled in a city might bunch its students into hamster habitats, here in NorCal we were, like, spread out and chill, man.

The green, ripe lawns sang with fresh-cut scent. Students floated through the pathways like platelets. Over the wafting breeze I heard the faint trills of a brass band playing "Louie Louie."

I shook my head and sneezed to break the spell. I reminded myself that despite this school's stellar reputation, it was not and had never been my first choice. I wasn't going to apply here.

It was too close to home. I had no desire to spend another four years in the Bay, riding the same train I'd just stepped off of. I wanted to see what snow looked like. I wanted to hear people say *mad* or *wicked* instead of *hella*. How was I going to evolve as a person if I was stuck in the same petri dish my entire life? I didn't want to be part of the control group. I wanted variables.

So no. I was only here this weekend to window shop. My goal was to see what *a* college might be like. This place would at least serve as a stand-in for the faraway campuses I couldn't afford to visit. I had told no one about mentally crossing this school off my list for fear of having to explain my complicated feelings. Quentin and Yunie still thought this place and I were a match made in Heaven.

A shame. It really was pretty. I felt the urge to flop backward onto the grass with my arms outstretched and take a nap.

"Stultifying, isn't it?" an unfamiliar voice said behind me. I turned around.

Yunie had returned with a tall (by normal standards), broad-shouldered girl draped in a hoodie the size of a poncho. She had a round, unmoving face as opposed to Yunie's expressive angles. Any lingering hope of a family resemblance was killed by the chunky glasses perched on her nose.

"Ji-Hyun," she said, shaking my hand. "Don't let the vibe fool you. On the surface it looks relaxed, but underneath it's a shark pit. This place will get as competitive as you want it to be."

Yunie must have coached her cousin on how to appeal to my base desires. "The way back to my place goes through most of the important stops, so if you don't mind dragging your bags for a bit, we can knock out the tour in one go," Ji-Hyun said.

It wasn't like we had a better proposal in mind. We wheeled our squeaky carry-ons behind her for a few paces before realizing we were being followed.

"Folks," Ji-Hyun called out to the other prospective students and their families trailing behind us. "I'm not an official guide. You need to wait by the quad."

"Can't we come with you anyway?" said one boy who'd picked up on Ji-Hyun's general air of knowing what she was doing.

"No," she snapped. "Beat it." The harshness of her tone caused the crowd to fall back.

Well, guess who *I* liked right away.

■ ■ ■

By the time we pulled up to Ji-Hyun's apartment, we weren't on campus anymore. The wheels on our luggage threatened to melt through their axels from friction.

Our final destination was a condo building shaped like a pile of cardboard boxes whose former owners had been too lazy to break down for recycling. Each residency jutted out, offset from the others, painted in alternating shades of beige. A dusting of prematurely dried leaves covered the street leading up to it.

Yunie wiped the sweat off her forehead. "Did we really have to look at two cafeterias and three different libraries instead of something nicer?"

"Well, yeah," Ji-Hyun said. "We're talking about four years of your life here. A successful visit means figuring out whether or not you can tolerate the school in the long run. There's no point in showing you a landmark or a gallery you're never going to bother with again as a student."

We entered the apartment complex and walked up the narrow hallway to Ji-Hyun's place. Her door had been painted several times over, as if it had been formerly exposed to the elements. "This is me," she said. "Make yourselves at home."

The inward swing knocked over a shopping bag full of empty glass bottles. Yunie and I stared in horror.

Her kitchen was more beer can than floor. Flies made strafing runs over a tower of unwashed dishes glued together at unnatural angles by dried foodstuffs. The pullout couch that we were nominally crashing on lay buried under piles of clothes that encompassed the entire spectrum of the laundering process. Most articles were firmly in the "haven't started" phase and were transitioning into "never will."

We weren't paying a visit. We were passing through a portal to a plane of elemental filth.

"Ji-Hyun, you . . . have roommates, right?" Yunie said.

"Five other girls," Ji-Hyun said. She cracked open a beer that had appeared in her hand like magic. "It can get a little messy in here. That's why the party's down the hall this week."

We gingerly pushed our way inside. I trod like a fisherman on a deck, avoiding shadows and coils that might tighten around my ankle without warning and drag me below the waves.

"Do your aunt and mom know she lives like this?" I whispered to Yunie.

"This . . . I don't even . . ." My friend had gone numb with shock.

Ji-Hyun somehow found enough space on the counter to hop up and sit. "Another thing to know about college is that at any given time of day, there is always something more important to do than clean. Studying, partying, sleeping. Anything else goes by the wayside. Maybe indefinitely."

She let out a burp. "Microeconomics one-oh-one. Rationality at work."

"It's not rational to take out the trash!?" Yunie shrieked, holding up a dripping bag that had been long forgotten.

"Whoops, that one's on me," Ji-Hyun said. "Unless you want to repay me for my hospitality and take it outside?"

■ ■ ■

"I don't know how you're hungry after that," Yunie said. "I may never get that smell out of my nostrils."

"We still need to eat," I said. Besides the fact that we'd skipped lunch for the tour, I had the sinking feeling that we'd need a buffer in our stomachs for tonight's party.

Having abandoned our bags in Ji-Hyun's apartment to whatever beasts lurked among the wastes there, the two of us meandered along a downtown street full of shops and restaurants. Outdoor seating bled from cafes into the sidewalks. Heat lamps that hadn't been turned on yet stood guard over the tables, a grim reminder that the weather could still stab us in the back and go freezing at a moment's notice, the flipside of the Bay Area climate that no one ever talked about. Thin trees spaced themselves down the blocks, a token nicety that probably pleased the local dogs more than their owners.

This town was basically Santa Firenza with money. The boba may have come in reusable glass jars and there might have been more upscale ramen restaurants than the laws of common sense dictated, but it was still the same flat, zoning-restricted, Northern California pancake of a burb. Maybe what I needed out of life was to swap places with Boston Mom.

"Found a spot yet?" Yunie asked.

"Everything is so expensive," I grumbled as I checked another menu posted in a window. Seriously, what they charged for a taco in these parts was criminal. Had none of their customers been to the city before?

Out of ideas, I pulled Yunie into a coffee shop that also had sandwiches. The interior was faintly lit and wooden, stained dark and glossy like a British pub. A hodgepodge of worn-down couches that promised no butt support at all made up most of the seating. A number of bespectacled TA-looking types were buried in the cushions, tapping away at aluminum laptops. The line for the counter was disproportionately long compared to the square footage of the place.

"Grab seats before they fill up," Yunie said. "I'm assuming you want the Cuban?"

I nodded as I sidled through the gaps in the tables, trying to reach a two-top in the corner that hadn't been claimed by a single person and their backpack like all the others had. I bumped a charger that had been carelessly placed in the aisle, knocking out the magnetic dongle from its device.

The owner looked up at me with a frown, and then did a double take.

I'll have to get used to that again, I reminded myself. This wasn't my hometown school, where everyone had acclimated to my height over the years.

But the college kid's surprise was only fleeting, without the usual disdain or gawking that came after. He smiled and yanked the cord out of my path. "Sorry, I'm in your way."

"Yeah," I said. He was.

I sat down on the free armchair and sank so fast that I had to catch my skirt from riding up. I tugged it back over my knees and glanced around to make sure no one saw.

College Kid was hacking away at a long sentence, but still caught me looking at him. He bit his lip shyly and pretended to be engrossed in whatever idea he would lay down next, but the tapping of his fingers stopped.

"That's, uh, that's a striking color," he ventured.

"Huh?"

He waved his hand around his eyes. "The gold. That's not natural, is it?"

Oh. That. Quentin and I had long given up on masking my (ugh) golden true sight eyes with brown, and I'd completely forgotten they were such an outlandish hue. I should have gotten them touched up before the long weekend, but he and I—

Man. We were fighting, weren't we? Quentin and I were having our first fight. Hooray for couple milestones.

I pushed the notion aside for now, or else I'd start wallowing. "No, they're not natural," I said.

"Aw. I thought maybe it could have been a mutation of your OCA2. It would have been pretty special."

"I'd better hope my OCA3 picks up the slack then."

I was somewhat pleased with myself when the guy laughed. I was well aware that my image at SF Prep was cold and prickly, a giant cactus that no one could get near. But this was college-level banter I was succeeding at. I could set a better tone than I did those first few days at SF Prep where I was too hung up to talk to anyone besides Yunie.

"Genie, could you come here for a sec?" Yunie said, louder than she needed to.

"I'll save your spot," said the guy.

I extricated myself from the chair and joined Yunie in line. "Are you out of cash?"

"No, not that," she whispered. "That guy's a creep."

"What?"

She nudged the air with her chin. "I caught a glimpse of his laptop."

The line had moved to the point where I couldn't see what she was talking about. I debated in my head how wrong it would be to shoulder surf, and decided I could take the hit to my karma. I put my hand to my temple and beheld.

This was an especially egregious misuse of my powers. But I saw what Yunie meant. The guy I'd been talking to wasn't working. He was on some kind of chat app, the thread full of crude memes and gifs, including a few that I didn't understand how he wasn't being kicked out of the cafe for looking at.

ayyy im about to climb everest, he typed.

WUT went the person on the other end.

theres this alternative japanese chick at the rookery shes so tall her legs go to the ceiling

tatted up her arm and wears contacts

I looked down at my wrist. I'd forgone my sweatband in favor of long sleeves, but they weren't long enough. The iron Milky Way mark peeked out.

you know when theyre in the rebelling against daddy phase thats the time to strike

PICS

PICSPICSPICS

ill try to get her to lean over the camera when she sits down again

I blinked back to normal. Our order was up.

"We'll take it to go, please," I said to the cashier.

■ ■ ■

"You're looking a little shell-shocked there, Stretch," Ji-Hyun said.

We were safe back in her apartment. I didn't think I would ever call such a festering pit safe, but here we were. I hugged my knees to my chest, perched on top of a beanbag that had more dried stains than a Pollock painting. Yunie was taking her turn in the shower.

"Are . . . are guys terrible?" I said.

Ji-Hyun shrugged. "I hear yours is pretty good."

My guy's not human, I thought. And he'd needed a while to come around to the limits of acceptability. I supposed if I gave Quentin the benefit of the doubt, his early bad behavior toward me was weapon-related confusion and not him wanting to hit it and quit it.

Anyway, now wasn't the time to give Quentin the benefit of the doubt. We were *fighting*. And I *wasn't* thinking about him.

Ji-Hyun drained the last of her beer. I had no idea what count she was on. Over the short time I'd known her it had become clear she was a gigantic lush, albeit one that held her booze very well.

"I'd be lying to you if I said that kind of stuff never happens at college," Ji-Hyun said. "You said he might have been a bio major? I'm not terribly surprised."

"What does that have to do with anything?"

"There aren't as many women in STEM, so some of the dudes there get warped ideas about what's okay or not. It can get even worse when you enter those fields and they see you as encroaching on their territory. One of the other premeds in my study group insisted I be the one to make coffee runs."

"How do you handle situations like that?" I asked her.

"I encroach." Ji-Hyun wasn't a smiler, but her eyes gleamed with confidence. "That particular guy had to find another study group."

Yunie passed her cousin in the hallway, the two of them swapping turns for the bathroom. My best friend toweled off her hair in the drier climate of the common room.

"Ugh, I can feel the dirt seeping back into my pores as we speak," she said.

"From here or the sandwich place?"

"Both. What did you do to that guy's laptop when we left?"

I pointed at one of Ji-Hyun's empty beer cans on the counter. Once Yunie was looking, I flicked my finger. It shot out like a rocket, telescoping across the room, impaling the can. I pulled it back just as fast, leaving a bullet-sized hole in the brewer's logo. Exactly like it did in said guy's laptop screen.

I'd figured out this trick trying to turn my light switch off while in bed. But it could be weaponized, too. We'd had to make a very quick escape out of the cafe.

"Oh my god," Yunie said, giggling hysterically. "Didn't anyone see that? It was fast, but I could still kind of make out your finger for a moment there."

"Eh." I shrugged. "Who's going to believe them?"

10

THE PARTY WAS TECHNICALLY IN THE ROOM DOWN THE HALL, but functionally it had spread over the entire building like an alien spore. A pulverizing beat rattled the plates in the kitchen. Unintelligible conversation from the hallway trickled into the suite. As soon as Yunie and I stepped out Ji-Hyun's door, we'd be in the thick of it.

Before we did, though, Ji-Hyun lined us up at attention. She solemnly placed an empty red Solo cup in our hands and poured almost-as-red liquid into them from a pitcher that had long sweated away its ice. The ritual sureness with which she was moving silenced any questions we might have had.

Ji-Hyun stepped back and took stock of us.

"I promised your parents that I would keep the two of you safe," she said. "And I intend to keep that promise. You don't hesitate to call me if you need me, and you don't consume anything that I don't give you myself."

Yunie tried to say something, but her older cousin cut her off.

"*However*," Ji-Hyun went on. "In the real world, there won't always be someone looking over your shoulder, and it'll be up to you to use your best judgment. The way to keep your head is to learn your own limits without letting anyone else pressure you beyond them, including me. The two of you are smart girls. Do you get what I'm saying?"

We both nodded. Yunie took a tentative sip from her cup and made a face.

"This tastes revolting," she said.

"That's because it was mixed inside a picnic cooler," Ji-Hyun said. She drank directly from the pitcher and lowered its contents by an inch in one swig. "Now get out there and have fun."

. . .

The hallway was mobbed. Someone had rigged a light filter that switched from purple to green to blue and back again. Candy-colored people milled about in the square inches allotted them. The bassline was determined to reach all the way to my back teeth.

With Yunie presumably trailing in my wake, I pushed forward through the crowd, hoping that some cues on what to do would rub off and stick to me like lint drawn by static cling. Sure, I'd been to the odd house party thrown by one of my classmates, but there I could usually talk shop with a teammate or gripe about a teacher with a lab partner. That option wasn't available right now, so I just listened dumbly to as many people as possible.

If I had to say what the biggest difference was between the high school scene and college, it would have been the amount of facial hair on the guys. I mean, this was like a lumberjack meetup being held on a crab fishing boat. I imagined the boys at SF Prep being forced to turn in their razors at graduation, dumping them into a cardboard box.

But the second-biggest difference seemed to be the self-assurance wafting through the air, thicker than cigarette smoke. Everyone spoke like they had the utmost confidence in the way the world worked.

Like, they were *literally* talking about how the world worked.

". . . and that's why piracy doesn't represent a loss of incremental sales to the artist. Plus it forces them to go on tour more, so they connect more with their fans. I'm really doing them a favor by not paying for the album . . ."

". . . see, the Swedes parent their children the right way. They make them use knives at the age of two, and they keep them outside in freezing weather. Kids today are too spoiled . . ."

". . . yeah sure she's the CEO of the fastest-growing wind farm company in the world, but if you read that interview closer you can tell she's missing out on the political situation entirely . . ."

By the time I reached the end of the hall, I was fairly convinced that the only way college students could communicate was by taking turns explaining reality to each other. It was like they'd handed out operating manuals to life itself during orientation, and everyone was convinced their particular copy was the only error-free one in existence. If I had a dollar for every time I heard the words "It's all a big scam," I could have paid for a fake ID and a fancier drink.

I glanced over my shoulder to see Yunie chatting with a mousy-looking guy in a turtleneck who, while very obviously and painfully smitten with her, at least seemed to be listening intently to what she was saying while maintaining a respectful distance. She gave me a little violin-bowing motion with her hand that indicated she'd found a fellow musician. We traded "I'll be okay on my own" waves and I turned back, only to crash straight into another girl.

I looked down out of muscle memory and almost apologized into her collarbone. I awkwardly scanned up, and up. It turned out the reason I was having trouble finding her eyes was because they were level with mine.

Holy crap.

'Twas the unicorn. A girl who was just as tall as me.

"Genie, right?" she said. "Genie Lo?"

She shifted her cup into her left hand and stuck out her right. Her wingspan was so great that she had to tuck her elbow into her ribs to do it, or else she wouldn't have enough space.

Ah, the elbow tuck. How familiar a feeling.

"Uh, yeah," I said, shaking what I could grab of her fingers. "How do you know my name?"

"Ji-Hyun told me she had some guests and that one of them was a hot prospect. Kelsey Adekoya. I'm the assistant captain of the volleyball team."

Kelsey had short, dark braids and a wide, easy smile, but the peppy intensity in her eyes made me think I was staring at Jenny 2.0. Upgraded for the game with an extra half-foot of reach.

"Okay, I'm about to come off as weird, but I stalked your high school's website and looked up your stats," Kelsey said. "You're a *beast*. Please tell me you're gonna try out once you get here."

Once I get here. Like it was a sure thing. I didn't want to rehash the speech I gave to myself earlier about not coming to this school to a complete stranger.

"I–I don't know," I said instead. "I kind of assumed I'd have to drop sports due to workload." That much was true, regardless of where I ended up. I knew I was going to prioritize courses over athletics. And I'd probably have to get a part-time job as well.

"Aww," she said, making a face like she'd been gutshot. "You can be on the varsity team and keep up your grades at the same time. Just don't take so many credits, and you'll be fine."

My brain needed to process the idea of not pushing myself to the brink academically. How was I supposed to keep my life options open if I didn't at least double major? The concept was rationally appealing but still unpalatable, like cilantro.

Kelsey took my scrunched-up thinking expression as a signal to switch tactics. "You know, you forge lifelong connections on a college team," she said. "A lot of our alums hook each other up with jobs once they graduate."

"*Pssh*," someone said in my ear, disturbingly close. "If that's what you're after, you're barking up the wrong sport. Come play basketball instead."

I turned to see another girl crowding in on our conversation. Even though she was swaying a bit, I could still tell she only gave up a few inches to Kelsey and me. A rounding error at this scale, really.

Three giantesses under one roof. The revolution had begun.

"We have so many investment bankers in this year's graduating class alone," said the newcomer. "Basketball is the sport of leaders. Volleyball is what you do at picnics."

"Goddammit, Trish, wait your turn," Kelsey snapped.

"I've never played basketball before," I said.

"That's okay," the other, drunker girl said. "Ever heard of Tom Dinkins? He was a swimmer up until his senior year of high school, and then he became arguably the greatest power forward in the history of the sport. We can teach you handles."

Kelsey was desperate not to lose her momentum. "If it's connections you want, you can't do any better than the dean of our business school. She's former volleyball. You'd have an in on the number three program in the country."

Trish waved the statement off and nearly caught her finger on Kelsey's necklace. "An MBA doesn't mean anything these days. B-school is all a big scam."

My breath was feeling shallow. "I, uh, need another drink," I said, even though I hadn't had any of my first one. "Excuse me, ladies; I'll be back."

I wormed my way toward the staircase, fearful of an ambush by the school's "reaching things on the top shelf" team. If Trish and Kelsey were continuing their argument without me, I couldn't hear them. The music was louder now, the air stuffier. I needed some space.

On the way down the stairs I passed two different couples making out, or maybe the same couple twice; I couldn't tell under the beanie hats. I didn't stop once I reached the steps to the apartment. The atmosphere there was so cloudy and skunked that I had to walk around to the back just to clear my head.

There was a stoop that faced the pool, so I plunked down on it. The pool itself was much less impressive an amenity than it had sounded when Yunie and I looked up Ji-Hyun's address a day ago. Apparently the nearby buildings and townhouses all shared communal access to it, which meant it was difficult to get a single party to pony up for maintenance and lifeguard fees. Right now it was locked behind a surrounding chain-link fence. A sign told any would-be swimmers that they'd have to wait until the chemicals reduced the algae levels to the point where the water wouldn't sicken anybody.

That was okay. I wasn't planning on taking a dip. It was comforting enough to listen to the gentle sloshing from the night breeze. The smell of bleachy fumes was preferable to smoke at the moment.

The way Kelsey and Trish spoke to me like it was in the bag that I'd have the chance to play for one of their teams had exposed an uncomfortable truth—I didn't know what I was doing with this whole college thing.

Yeah, I talked a good game about getting in. But I hadn't spent any time thinking about what life would be like on the other side. Breaking through the gates had seemed so distant a concept that I never bothered to figure out what I wanted from the college experience itself, and now it was dancing in front of my face, asking me to choose.

I had made a big mistake, treating College with a capital C like a monolithic concept, a single finish line. When in fact there were tons of complications. Repercussions. The biggest of which boiled down to money.

I'd left it unspoken before, but the biggest reason why I couldn't see myself at this school was because it was expensive. Of course my family couldn't afford it outright. And the more I'd learned about the financial aid process from my college adviser, the murkier my choices became. Even a decent aid package might require my family to pitch in an amount that looked small to others but would be completely devastating to us.

Just get a full scholarship! said an inner voice that was some combination of the ignorant me of a year ago and terribly scripted movies about college.

Sure! I thought. The prize for being poor was that I'd have to compete yet again with other needy, motivated students for a limited pool of free money, a tournament within the tournament.

I'd have to look twice as exceptional and win the Quarter Quell. Easy peasy.

I laughed to myself. Who was I kidding? I wasn't that special. For crying out loud, by college standards I wasn't even that big. Full-ride scholarships didn't fall from the sky for semi-special wafflers like me who couldn't formulate a simple theory about how the world worked.

The door behind me opened violently and a boy stumbled out, kneeing me in the back of the head.

"Jesus, Axton, knock her over why don't you?" a girl yelled from inside, over the din of the party.

The boy caught his balance and smoothed the lapels of his jacket. "Maybe if you didn't push me," he said calmly.

"Maybe if you weren't such a shill, you prick!" a completely different voice roared, a guy this time. The door slammed shut as the exclamation point on the insult.

"I'm sorry you had to see that," said the boy who'd been booted out. He gave his hair the same treatment as his clothes, checking carefully that each gelled strand was in place.

Not that it had hurt, and not that I wanted him anywhere near me right now, but he could have at least made sure the person he'd run into was okay. Plus he'd interrupted my alone time at a really bad moment. When he opened his mouth to speak again, I shot him a look so harsh it could have finished sterilizing the pool.

The kid got the message that this doorstep was my territory. He adjusted his cuffs and did a little two-fingered salute at me before walking away into the night.

The fact that he had been wearing a ridiculously expensive outfit for a simple off-campus rager sent my brain on a return trip to the dark valley of money problems. I had been selfish the first time around, thinking only of myself and my tuition. Of course the higher priority was my mother. My family.

Guanyin's handwaving around my mother's health scared me more than anything else. The uncertainty that we would have to live with was an unwelcome, permanent addition to our family. The scene that had played out in the hospital was like a horrific inversion of birth, my father rushing to my mother's side while I held her close and waited for the terrible news.

Even if I worked while I went to school, I'd be saddling us with a burden that would be difficult for our combined efforts to manage under the best of circumstances, with Mom and Dad both healthy. Forget this school. Every single one of my first choices was expensive and out of state. I'd made a list for Santa like a greedy little brat, putting down a pony, a diamond ring, a castle in the sky, without thinking about the logistics.

The chlorine was getting to me. I closed my eyes and wiped a tear off my nose. Good children used their wishes on their parents' health and happiness. Or world peace. I hadn't been a good child.

"Shouhushen!"

I woke up from my reverie, thinking maybe I had imagined hearing that.

But no. The speaker was standing in the pool right there in front of me, where he hadn't been a second ago. He was knee-deep in a section where the waters should have reached his chin, as if he was standing on an invisible platform.

It was an old man. Not as weathered and wiry as the Great White Planet, but still rather bulky and strong, full of piss and vinegar, able to smack around a dozen whippersnappers half his age.

He wore a coat of exquisite bronze lamellar armor that accentuated his ramrod-straight posture. And he stood completely motionless, with only his eyes following me intently, as if he were a British guardsman sizing up my threat level.

There were too many windows facing the courtyard. "If you know *conceal*, you'd better do it *right now*," I said to him.

From what I had gathered, concealment was a fairly basic spell among spirits both great and small. Luckily this guy was no exception. He made a quick series of hand gestures, more formal and ornate than Quentin usually bothered with, and the telltale fuzz of magic descended over us, blocking him from mundane view.

The old man was a complete newcomer to Earth, I was sure of it. There was no human-looking character out of a historical war drama among the yaoguai under my supervision, and he didn't have quite the same ambience as a full-fledged god.

"You picked a bad time, buddy," I hissed. "I don't care who you are and how you got here, but I'm off duty. And this is one of the worst places on Earth to conduct business. Do you know how camera-happy people my age are?"

With a smooth, expert motion the man drew a sword from the scabbard on his hip. The handle glittered with jewels, but the blade he brandished at me was definitely not ceremonial. It looked sharp enough to cut the prow off a battleship.

"Respectfully, this matter cannot wait," he said.

11

I LOOKED AT THE SWORD, GLINTING IN THE LIGHT OF THE STREET lamps. *So it was going to be like that, huh?* I was supremely grateful for the threat. The Universe had detected my imminent meltdown and sent me a gift-wrapped jerk to beat the daylights out of.

But before I could complete my ritual pre-fight knuckle cracking, the man did something unexpected.

"Shouhushen!" he cried. He twirled the sword around so that the tip pointed toward his unprotected throat, holding part of the blade with his bare hand to do so. Rivulets of blood dripped from the edge where it bit his skin. "You must listen to my plea!"

The mood flipped like a crashing car. "*No!*" I shouted, waving frantically. "No no no! Don't do that. Easy now. Let's talk. Let's talk, okay? Start with telling me your name."

Big fat tears began to roll down his face, though his sword never wavered. "I am Dragon Ao Guang, Guardian of the Eastern Sea."

"Wait, Ao Guang? Used-to-own-the-Ruyi-Jingu-Bang Ao Guang? Ao Guang who's supposed to be hunting down a gigantic extradimensional menace right now?"

"Yes," he said, trembling. "I was entrusted by Heaven to seek and destroy the source of demonic qi that threatened the harmony of the cosmos."

Oh no. Oh hell. There was only one reason why the dragon general would have appeared before me, right here and right now.

"I failed," Ao Guang whispered. "I failed Heaven, and I failed the spirits under my command. My army lies in ruins and now every plane faces devastation!" The blade sank deeper into his skin, as if leaning on it was only thing keeping him steady.

My worst fears were confirmed. First thing first, though. I had to stop him from doing what old Chinese generals in history often did after a humiliating defeat.

"*Drop the weapon, soldier!*" I roared, doing my best Sarah Connor impression. "I want a full debrief, and I'm not going to get it from a dead dragon!"

I wasn't sure if Shouhushen outranked General of Heaven, but Ao Guang relented and shakily lowered his sword. He stumbled across the surface of the pool until he reached the concrete edge and sat down on a bench, his armor pieces jangling against each other. His sword clattered to the ground, and he slumped forward, staring at the space in front of his feet.

I entered the pool area, breaking the padlock on the gate. It was as much of an impediment to me as a Cheeto. I gingerly sat down on the bench next to Ao Guang and waited for his chest to stop heaving in and out. I hadn't noticed at a distance, but he was bleeding from a wound across his back that had slashed clean through a section of his armor.

"Tell me what happened," I said, gently this time.

"We were ambushed in a Blissful Plane not far from Earth," he said. "The enemy . . . we couldn't see it. My soldiers started dying like flies. It was as if we were being cut open by invisible blades. There was no one around us, no spells being cast. There was no one to strike back against! We simply perished where we stood!"

Ao Guang was deeply traumatized by the rules of battle being violated. "We couldn't see it," he repeated with a shudder. "It was like a . . . a *Yin Mo.*"

Yin Mo. An invisible monster, an unseen devil. I had to stop myself from demanding more details. The guy had just said he had none to give.

"It was a massacre," Ao Guang went on. "I managed to form up the survivors and lead a retreat. We had to get off that plane of existence entirely. In my haste, I opened a gateway to Earth, using the largest, most familiar concentration of spiritual energy as a beacon."

"My aura," I said. Back when supernatural hijinks first started happening in my hometown, the explanation was that as the Ruyi Jingu Bang, I was basically a gravity well for this sort of thing, pulling ambient weirdness into my orbit.

Ao Guang nodded. "Shouhushen, I am deeply sorry. I had to get my remaining men out of there. I would have gladly faced death on my own, but I couldn't throw their lives away so carelessly. I beg your understanding and forgiveness."

I reached across his shoulders and patted them reassuringly. "You did well." I could have learned a lesson or two about command and sacrifice from the old coot.

He froze at such informal contact and then broke out weeping again. "Thank you," he whispered. "From one Guardian to another, thank you."

Ao Guang suddenly leaped off the bench, picked up and sheathed his sword, and stood at attention. "The Shouhushen is as magnanimous as she is powerful!" he bellowed. "I swear my unyielding loyalty to her in life! In death, may my liver grace her table alongside the marrow of phoenix and juice of jade!"

"Uh . . . Thanks? I guess?" I'd never been offered someone's viscera to eat, but from context I took it as a nice gesture. "We can take care of you and your men in a few days. I just have to find a place that's big enough and far away from humans that—"

Ao Guang's attention was elsewhere. He spoke to the deep end of the water. "Emerge! Crab generals! Shrimp lieutenants! Fish soldiers!"

The surface of the pool began roiling. As if the area under the diving board had transformed into stairs, the vanguard of an army marched upward onto the deck, rippling into existence while water spilled from their shoulders. Soldiers dressed in less fancy versions of Ao Guang's armor tromped in unison, filing to the left and right and forming into ranks over the lounging areas.

"Hey!" I yelled over the din. "I didn't mean you could bring everyone right this instant! Stop!"

No one heard me. The soldiers were concerned only with maintaining tighter coordination than the Wicked Witch's guards. They had faces much more reminiscent of common yaoguai, with googly eyes, scaly skin, or crustacean mandibles.

And despite their marching discipline, they were in bad shape. The lucky ones nursed bandaged wounds, layers of cloth soaked through with dark blood. There were lost fins and claws left and right. Toward the middle of the pack, the weakest needed to hang on to their comrades to stay upright. It was like watching the aftermath of a re-enacted Civil War battle. All that was missing was the somber humming of "When Johnny Comes Marching Home."

"Eel messengers!" Ao Guang said. "Snail bannermen! Squid quartermasters! Seahorse stable boys!"

They were going to burst through the fence at this rate. Forget that, they were going to spill over the boundaries of the *conceal* spell.

"Excuse me," a voice said from behind me.

Oh no. I turned around to see that guy who'd run into me earlier, returning to the scene of the accident. "I wanted to ask you something."

As long as he'd stayed in the courtyard area, he would have only seen me, perhaps heard me babbling to myself like a theater kid doing a warmup. Ao Guang and his supernatural army would have remained invisible. But the boy had pushed through the gate I'd broken and collided with the edge of the cloaked zone. The magic stretched over his face like plastic wrap and then gave way, causing him to stumble through the thin air. He blinked rapidly. And then he saw the pool. With the full arrangement of sea creatures.

"Motherfuuuuu—"

His hand dipped into his pocket for his phone. I went for mine at the same time, a quick-draw match at high noon.

I won, hitting my panic button before the kid could record anything. Sometimes it was useful to have a goddess on speed-dial.

． ． ．

Guanyin cast her baleful gaze upon me, withering my life points from the outside in.

"It wasn't my fault," I said.

The pool around us was empty. Ao Guang's legion of fishpeople had been teleported away. It was one of the biggest feats I'd ever seen the goddess pull off. So much magic had been fired off in the last ten seconds that her fingertips were smoking like the barrels of a machine gun. They cooled under her crossed arms.

The human witness had his mind wiped of a few seconds, which was just as taboo and last-resort as it sounded. We didn't mess with people's memories if we could avoid it. Though we'd sent him stumbling away down the well-lit street to regain his wherewithal safely away from the apartment complex, he'd have the equivalent of a massive caffeine headache in the morning.

"I didn't have a choice!" I said to Guanyin. "Ao Guang was going to hurt himself, and his soldiers were barely holding it together!"

The goddess said nothing. She didn't need to. I knew what her answer would be.

The critical choice to make had been days ago. We'd ignored the signs that something big was about to go down. Had I stayed at home, we could have handled Ao Guang's arrival better than him blundering his way into Earth in a crowded location. And the fact that a Dragon General of Heaven got wrecked so badly meant the demonic threat the Great White Planet mentioned was existential. Guanyin, Quentin, and I, the supposed demon-fighting experts, failed to act on a white-hot tip, and now Earth was in peril.

All because I had to go to a party.

Hot damn. Guanyin had silent-treatmented me into giving myself my own scolding. What a pro.

I could have tried to explain to her that this trip was about other things than getting drunk. But it would have been a tough sell when the two of us could hear the music and shrieking from the windows where we stood. Enough time had passed that the attendees were a lot louder and more wasted by now.

Just as importantly, I wanted to explain how sorry I was that I'd made her bail me out yet again. I wanted to let her know that I didn't see her as a Get Out of Jail Free card with unlimited uses. I hated disappointing her like this.

But if I said any of that, I knew she'd snap at me that apologies were pointless because her feelings were irrelevant. Which would hurt *my* feelings. A lot.

I abandoned trying to find the magic words. "Did you let Quentin know what happened?" I asked instead.

Finally Guanyin deigned to speak. "He came along."

"Then where is he?"

I got my answer in the form of an uproarious cheer from the floor of the building where the party was taking place.

Uh-oh.

■ ■ ■

I could hear the rhythmic chanting from down the hallway.

"QUEN-TIN! QUEN-TIN! QUEN-TIN!"

Everyone was trying to get a look. I shoved and jostled past the gawkers hopping on their tiptoes, phones raised to take videos, until I reached the suite where the party was originally supposed to be contained to.

There, in a spacious kitchen, Quentin was doing a one-handed keg stand while the crowd drunkenly cheered him on. For what I guess was the extra challenge, he'd tilted the barrel on its corner edge and rocked back and forth like a unicyclist standing still.

It was a feat of inhuman balance, and child's play for the Monkey King. His legs kicked the air to the beat of the music as he chugged, and he didn't stop until the entire contents were gone.

Then he did something really stupid.

Upon finding he'd tapped the keg single-handedly, he hopped back to his feet. He picked up the empty steel barrel like it weighed nothing and slammed it against his forehead the way a bro might do to a normal beer can. The metal squeaked and groaned as it flattened into a disc under his might. Once he'd compressed the keg into a hubcap, he tossed it aside. It spun around and around on its perimeter, making wobbly noises, until it agonizingly came to a stop on the floor.

The entire party fell silent. People gaped at him above the screens of their phones, the nearest of which had still caught the whole impossible display.

Quentin pumped his fists into the air. "Haters gonna say it's fake!" he whooped.

The crowd screamed in delight. They resumed raging twice as hard after the shot of adrenaline he'd given them.

I reached out, snatched him by the collar, and dragged him away.

■ ■ ■

Getting Quentin back into Ji-Hyun's room required swatting away the adoring college girls who were getting unilaterally handsy with him as we scraped by. To his credit, he paid them little attention,

91

his eyes never straying from me. To his detriment was absolutely everything else about him.

I slammed him against the closed door, prompting a "*woo*" from the people just outside who thought we were sneaking off for privacy. I mean, we were, but not that way.

"Are you *trying* to set new records for being stupid?" I said, still gripping his shirt in my fist. I'd snapped a couple of buttons off it already.

"I've gotten blitzed off Heavenly Elixirs of Immortality," he said. "I'm not going to get drunk from a few sips of human beer."

"That's not the issue here! Right now there's dozens of people outside who now know you're stronger than a hydraulic press!"

He looked off to the side. "Who cares? They're never going to see me again. You'll be fine attending your classes here. I won't be around to cause trouble."

Ow. I mean, really, ow.

I was breathing, my lungs caving in and out, but it didn't feel like oxygen was reaching my brain. My throat was a solid lump. This was a continuation of our fight, only with me on the sharp end of the stick this time. And it hurt. A lot. Enough to make me let go of him and take a couple of steps back.

The root problem was that Quentin and I had never discussed how he would fit into my normal, human life. *If* he would. That uncertainty played a part in me losing my temper and implying he wasn't welcome in my family, and him now implying he'd ghost me once I entered college. I had to address this issue now, before it gestated inside both him and me into a creature neither of us could defeat.

Instead I came up spectacularly short. "They. Have. *Cameras!*" I screamed.

Quentin's eyes flickered, as if he was just as relieved as me to argue about a less important problem. "So there's a video shot by drunk people in a poorly lit room. If it gets uploaded to the internet it'll look like a viral ad for a beer company. Stop worrying about it."

He was pitching me softballs. Quentin sloppy, Genie uptight. I could have kissed him.

"We've got a meeting with Guanyin tomorrow morning," he said. "You might as well make the most of tonight. Otherwise your trip will be wasted."

"I was never here to party in the first place!" I said, indignant that he thought I needed the pointless ruckus outside. "Yunie and I are not even having fun right now!"

Right then, Ji-Hyun burst into the room with Yunie slung over her shoulders in a fireman's carry. The din of music leaked in through the airlock before Ji-Hyun kicked it shut again.

"WOOO!" Yunie shouted, swimming a crawl stroke in the air. "College rules!"

She was Asian-blushing so hard, she resembled an overcooked lobster. "Who wants to arm wrestle?" my drunken friend hollered. "Fight me!"

Quentin glanced at Yunie. I prepared to get blasted in turn by a judgmental frown, but instead he gave me a saintly smile, which was worse.

"Regardless of the circumstances, this is still your night out, and I'm being unfair by impinging on it," he said. "I'm gonna go."

"Where?" I scoffed.

"I've been invited to some more get-togethers. Fraternities and sororities, that sort of thing." He paused, oblivious to how popular he was and why. "Kind of a lot of sororities now that I think about it? Eh, whatever."

He went over to the nearest window and opened it. "Ladies," he said, nodding to us before rolling gracefully over the side like a scuba diver off a boat.

"Bye Quentiiiiin," Yunie sang, still draped over her cousin's shoulders.

"So that's your boyfriend?" Ji-Hyun said once he was gone. "He seemed nice. And hot. Like, damn, girl, there isn't a high-five big enough for you."

"You don't seem concerned that he jumped out your window."

"Nah, everyone does that in this building. Lets them avoid the walk of shame."

Ji-Hyun tilted Yunie onto the beanbag. "What's with this graveyard?" Yunie said. "We need some tunes going!"

"How much did she have?" I said.

"Just the one sip from before," Ji-Hyun said. "I guess tolerance doesn't run on that side of the family."

I watched Yunie head bang, supine, to some heavy metal song that only she could hear. I didn't know she was a closet air guitarist, because she was miming chords and arpeggios and everything. Transferable genius, I guess.

This had been one of the most frustrating nights of my life, and that included all the times I was in mortal danger. I'd been exposed as a big fraud. I didn't know what I was doing when it came to college, Divine Guardianing, or my boyfriend, whom I was supposed to have an *actual* spiritual connection to.

I snatched the last cup of liquid red grossness from the nearby kitchen counter and slumped onto a pile of laundry. Why I was able to do that without taking any steps in between the counter and the laundry was a mystery known only to my host and her equally slovenly roommates, but for the moment I didn't care. I took a big gulp from my cup and waited to feel buzzed.

After a few seconds, something became clear to me.

"I can't get drunk," I said out loud.

"Sure?" Ji-Hyun said as she plied Yunie with water in a manner that would not have made it past the Geneva Conventions. "No one's going to judge if you want to be a teetotaler."

That wasn't what I meant. I meant I literally could not get drunk.

The invulnerability and healing power of the Ruyi Jingu Bang had become a lot stronger in me these days, ever since my fight with Red Boy and Erlang Shen. Apparently it also applied to chemical attack now. I could feel my insides identifying and nullifying the alcohol like a toxic agent, which I guess technically it was, leaving behind nothing but painful lucidity.

Great.

I was now the entire world's designated driver. Woo indeed.

12

"NOT HUNGOVER?" GUANYIN SAID TO ME.

If the next World War were to be fought with passive-aggression, Guanyin would be left standing alone in the crumbling ruins of civilization.

"I'm fine," I said, not bothering with an explanation of my new-found alcohol immunity. I'd snuck out of Ji-Hyun's apartment in the early morning, performing my own walk of shame of sorts. I left Yunie an email explaining that I was running a supernatural errand, and that she should stay away from the pool at all costs.

Guanyin had brought Quentin and me to an office park near the college. It wasn't a branded bank-like tower of glass and metal like the ones off the highway. Nor was it a swoopy modern campus designed by big-name architects around the latest principles of human behavioral science. This building, like the many others that made up the unobserved dark matter of Silicon Valley, was a single-story plop of concrete allowed to spread over the ground without being wiped up. It shared the same aesthetics as a drive-thru restaurant.

It was day two of the already ill-fated long weekend, so no one was there as Guanyin, Quentin, and I walked up to the front door.

I could tell because a number of the walls were made out of glass, exposing meeting rooms to the outside in what seemed like an unwise privacy move.

Quentin and I occupied ourselves with not looking at each other while Guanyin jiggled the door handle. It was locked.

"What are we doing here?" I said.

"Conference call," she said.

"Couldn't we have done that on campus? Colleges have good Ethernet speeds."

"We're using a different network." She flexed her hand over the edge of the door. I thought she was going to cast some kind of unlock spell, but instead she gave it a short, crisp, one-inch punch that snapped the deadbolt. Previously I would have sworn that Guanyin was purely a leave-no-trace style of camper, but I guess we all had our lax moments. She led us inside.

The interior of the building was in worse shape than the outside let on. Half of it was undergoing renovation, concrete floors stripped bare of any carpet, exposed wires pathing along the walls, held up with industrial staples. The habitable portions were packed with twice as many desks as would be reasonable. Hopefully for the occupants' sake, they'd be allowed to move back once the construction was done. I could easily see the arrangement being made permanent given how expensive space was in this town.

Guanyin ushered us into one of the still-functional meeting rooms. In the center of a long table surrounded by knockoff mesh chairs was a conference bridge-style phone in the shape of a flattened pyramid. We took seats near it and she pressed a button for the dial tone.

"Come on. You're not going to tell me who we're calling?" I said.

Guanyin answered without looking at me, instead focusing on rapidly tapping out an interminable number that, if I had to guess due to the repetitions and high pitches, consisted solely of eights and nines.

"Heaven," she said. "We're calling Heaven."

. . .

Quentin decided that whatever was going on between us in our personal lives, we still needed to talk business. "The armies of Heaven have been defeated," he said. "These are circumstances so dire that a conclave of the gods is necessary. The last one was a millennium ago. We are on high alert here."

He didn't look like he was on high alert. In fact, he looked nostalgic for days gone by. I remembered he used to be a rebel. Sun Wukong, who'd invaded Heaven and trashed the place.

"You should be flattered," I said. "There hasn't been a threat as bad as you in more than a thousand years."

The fact that we could put our emotions aside was either an excellent or disastrous sign for our relationship; I couldn't remember what the magazines in the hospital waiting room had said. "It wasn't me that caused the last emergency," Quentin said. He pointed his chin at Guanyin. "It was her."

I looked at the goddess with confusion. Among the three of us she was like the babysitter keeping her two bratty children in check. The head of the spy agency and also its best agent. Why would she be a problem for Heaven?

Quentin caught the expression of puzzlement on my face. "You don't remember the story of her traveling to Hell and vomiting out free good karma to make it less of an awful place?" he said. "That was the most disruptive act in the history of the cosmos. The Jade Emperor considers it worse than the time you and I laid siege to his palace. It upended what he sees as the natural order of the Universe. He won't admit it, but in his eyes, she's public menace number one."

"I can *hear* you two," Guanyin said. She was still focused intently on the conference phone and banged it a couple of times with her fist. Telecommunications seemed as frustrating for her as it was for humans.

"So yeah," Quentin said. "One of the primary laws of Heaven is no traveling between planes willy-nilly. Ao Guang is one of the greatest sticklers you can imagine for the rules. And yet he tore a bleeding hole in reality to escape this menace. He wasn't this scared when I walked into his house and demanded the Ruyi Jingu Bang."

I winced. The last threat level more frightening than Quentin had been Red Boy, the demon with enough firepower to raze an entire city. Red Boy had nearly smelted Quentin and me into stone and iron. Only a lot of luck and an alley-oop from the Goddess of Mercy had seen us through.

By now Guanyin's numerical entry on the phone had reached robotic speeds. Her fingers were a blur. The hardware itself glowed incandescently, the plastic staying solid through temperatures that could have fried an egg. I could tell that powerful magics were being wrought through this mundane device.

Suddenly, she stopped.

Guanyin withdrew her hand carefully, like she'd put the final touch on a house of cards. Our connection was tenuous, almost explosive.

"*Wai?*" she said.

An airburst of static knocked the wax out of my ears. "*KSHHH-HHHHHai? Wai? Miaoshan?*"

It was a woman's voice on the other end. She sounded older than Guanyin. Rounder and less melodic.

"*Mama,*" Guanyin said. "*Shi wo. Ta ren zai nali?*"

Noticing my confusion, she pressed the mute button. "The Queen Mother of the West," Guanyin explained. "Not my actual mother."

I had done some basic god research since becoming the Shouhushen. Not a lot, but some. The person we were speaking to was the highest-ranking female member of the celestial pantheon. The Hera to us all.

"Miaoshan!" the queen said, using what must have been a pet name for Guanyin. "I don't hear your voice for so long and you don't ask how I'm doing? Just 'where are the others?' What happened to you on Earth? Did you lose your manners down a pit? One of those recycling cans I've heard about? Did you recycle your manners?"

Guanyin's eyes rolled up like drapes. "Mama, I'm sorry but I can't talk right now. You have to put me on with the others. It's important."

"So this is how it is," the voice on the other end wailed. "She doesn't even want to speak to me anymore. She pretends I don't exist to my face. Aiyaaa . . ."

The lamentations went on and on, but it sounded like the queen was functioning through them. In fact, it sounded like she was walking to a different room and taking along whatever communication terminal she was using. I didn't know what the metaphysical layout of the Heavenly Palace looked like, but right now I was imagining a small ranch house. We'd called the outdated cordless phone in the den.

"My other girls aren't so busy with their work that they can't spare a moment to talk to me," the queen bemoaned to no one in particular, but intentionally loud enough that we could still hear. "Where did I go wrong with this one?"

"She sure sounds like your actual mother," I whispered to Guanyin.

The Goddess of Mercy gave me a look so dirty that Quentin had to roll his chair back from the table. But I resisted it without flinching. There were only so many times she could do that to me without me getting used to it.

Suddenly the background noise coming from the conference phone changed in pitch from the echoes of a small domicile to the roar of a cavernous stadium. This new location was large enough to house hundreds or even thousands of voices, all of which were jabbering away simultaneously. The Queen Mother had stepped into the palace auditorium.

The ringing of a gong shoved its way through the background chatter. I'd heard such an unearthly bronze din once before, and it had announced the Jade Emperor's presence. I expected to hear his over-salivated voice. Instead there was another familiar speaker in his place.

"I call this emergency meeting to order," the Great White Planet said. "Order! Come to order!"

It took several more insistent gong strikes to tamp down the side conversations. Substitute teachers had it hard.

"If I could be allowed to finish my statement," the Great White Planet said. "Yes, it is true that the Dragon King of the Eastern Sea has been defeated."

"Ao Guang should have his spleen roasted for dereliction of duty!" roared a god that I'd never heard before. "There is no room for cowardice among Guardians!"

"Respectfully, Thunderer Lei Gong," the Great White Planet said. "Ao Guang made the difficult decision to perform a tactical retreat with his few remaining survivors. He can't be faulted for his actions in the face of an overpowering force."

That bit of sympathy made me not hate the Great White Planet as much as I did in person. Maybe he was a fairer judge than I'd given him credit for.

"Furthermore, we have confirmed that the source of demon qi is shifting between the Blissful Planes and moving closer to Heaven as we speak," he said. "Earth lies directly in its path."

"How long until it arrives at Heaven's doorstep?" a sibilant, aristocratic voice inquired. "Perhaps we can buy time by sacrificing the lesser realms of existence. If the foe is demonic in nature, it might sate its hunger on a kingdom's worth of humans. Or two."

Man, eff this guy, I thought. I had long been accustomed to Heaven looking down on Earth, but it had never thrown us mortals under the bus so blatantly before.

"Respectfully, Immortal Zhenyuan," the Great White Planet sighed. "I suggest we take action *before* humanity is needlessly wiped out."

"We can't do that without the Jade Emperor's blessing?" Lei Gong yelled. "Why are we holding these proceedings without him?"

"Because!" the Great White Planet yelled back, losing his patience with the interruptions. "When I went to request his presence, I found a barrier spell the likes of which I've never seen before placed over the gates to his personal keep! He's locked himself inside and won't come out!"

The gathering of gods exploded into chaos. They'd been abandoned by their leader. As far as I could tell, the ranting and screaming from the other end of the line encompassed all five stages of grief, delivered at maximum volume. Quentin gave a sharp bark of laughter, the kind of noise you might make if you saw your nemesis trample over an elderly person to get into the last lifeboat on a sinking ship. Guanyin merely closed her eyes and rubbed her temples, trying to meditate the painful inanity of the world away.

"Wow," I said. I could say little else. "These are the folks upstairs, huh?" I had often wondered how the spiritual sausage got made, and now that I was witnessing it firsthand, I was finding it as unappealing as I'd imagined.

"Try dealing with this on the regular," Guanyin said. "For centuries."

Right when the racket took on an extra flavor of panic, the Great White Planet decided he'd had enough. Instead of more gonging, sharp wooden cracks ricocheted through the air. I knew that sound from close-up experience. He was smacking his staff on the ground as hard as he could, using it as a gavel.

"That settles it!" the old man roared with surprising force. "I've held back on this for far too long! By the power vested in me by the celestial foundations of Heaven and the fundamental laws that drive the workings of the Universe, I declare a *Mandate Challenge!*"

At the words "Mandate Challenge," there was a pulse of invisible energy in the hall of the gods. I could tell, because it happened in the room I was sitting in, too. It felt like a sudden elevation change, a shortness of breath. The lightbulbs flickered. I wondered if seismographs could detect qi.

The other end of the line went dead quiet. I looked at Guanyin and Quentin. Guanyin let out a focused, interminable breath through her pursed lips. Quentin, on the other hand, was manically excited and had to cover his grin with his fist.

"What's a Mandate Challenge?" I whispered. "What does it mean?"

Quentin hit the mute button. "It means the biggest friggin' opportunity in existence," he said. "The Great White Planet just called out the Jade Emperor for not handling his duties in a time of crisis. He's declaring that the Throne of Heaven is officially up for grabs."

When the Great White Planet visited, I thought the old god had only been talking about the Jade Emperor's mandate to rule Heaven as a cautionary tale. To warn me extra hard against messing up on Earth. The conversation wasn't supposed to play out for real. For a moment I felt the lightness in my spine that happened any time I watched raffle winners being drawn, even when I hadn't entered. Technically anything could happen from here on out. Timelines were branching off in droves.

"So what happens next?" I said. "Does every god in that room, like, battle-royale it out? Last deity standing wins?"

Guanyin gave me a look of distaste for my violent suggestion. "No," she said. "It's less of a tournament and more of a quest. Candidates are elected by the assembled pantheon and head out to defeat whatever evil is threatening the cosmic order. The Great White Planet goes along and judges their performance. Whichever god acquits themselves the best in his eyes becomes the next ruler of Heaven."

Guanyin explained in a tone that let me know exactly what she thought of this method of determining regime change. *Boys and their games.* "It's that simple?" I asked.

"It's how the Jade Emperor got the job in the first place," Quentin said. "A long time ago, an ultra-powerful demon threatened Heaven, so he meditated for a billion years until he was strong enough to defeat it. Or so the story goes."

Huh. That was a far cry from the image I had of the Jade Emperor as a do-nothing windbag. A deep, rhythmic drumming broke the silence coming from the other end of the line. It started low and steady, a primal chant, and grew louder and louder.

"As I have witnessed the mandate pass before, so shall I witness the mandate pass now!" The Great White Planet was really picking up momentum, casting off the mantle of Hobbit Gandalf and going full-blown Lord of the Rings Gandalf. The windows of our conference room vibrated with force. "Gods of Tian! Name thy warriors!"

"Prince Nezha!" someone cried out, timing themselves with the drumbeats. The name was picked up enthusiastically by the assembly. "*Nezha! Nezha! Nezha!*"

The gods shouted with hypnotic unity, a sharp contrast to how disorganized they were before. This was serious business, like European soccer.

"Wow, they like this Nezha guy a lot," I said. "Who is he?"

"Front-runner," Quentin said. "He's young, popular, enough of a traditionalist that he won't rock the boat. Kind of bland, if you ask me." Quentin seemed impatient, as if he were waiting for the good part of a movie.

The calling for Nezha made way for a single voice, high and clear. I assumed it was the nominee.

"Thank you, my friends," Nezha said, the drums backing his speech. "I swear upon my own bones that I will never let harm come to Heaven!"

We had to wait a while for another round of cheers to die down. "Who else is worthy of the mandate?" the Great White Planet said.

"Guan Yu!" a group in the back roared simultaneously, as if they'd rehearsed it. "*Guan Yu! Guan Yu!*"

Quentin whooped so loud it hurt my ear. He did a full flip out of his chair, bumped a dusty ceiling panel loose, and landed back down in his seat butt-first. The impact burst the compressed air out of the height-adjustment column.

"Take it down a notch," I hissed at Quentin. "What's the big deal?" To me the name Guan Yu was associated with the red-faced, bearded man whose image was kept in the shrines of shopkeepers and restaurants. My parents had a small shrine of Guan Yu they'd placed behind the counter of their furniture store. I never understood what he was supposed to do, because he certainly never brought them luck.

"Guan Yu is the warrior god of integrity, brotherhood, and righteousness," Quentin said. "He works hard and parties harder. He'd make a great King of Heaven."

Judging by the crowd, Guan Yu had a smaller but equally fanatical cheering section. If this were a stadium, then Guan Yu was the favorite of the ultras and hooligans. Quentin pounded loudly on the table in support, as if they could hear him.

I waited for the god to step up and acknowledge his selection, but instead the applause petered out to an awkward silence.

"Where is Guan Yu?" whispered the Great White Planet to someone standing nearby, using the drums as cover.

"He skipped out because he 'hates meetings,'" Nezha muttered. "The last I saw, he was in the training pavilion drinking wine and seeing how many boulders he could smash with his forehead."

Oh dear. I was beginning to see why Quentin liked this guy.

Instead of naming more names, the split crowd shouted for their respective champions, forming two unyielding blocs. The Great White Planet hammered away with his staff until a semblance of order returned.

"All right then!" the Great White Planet shouted over the low-level buzz of background excitement. "It seems like our two candidates are obvious. Now, in accordance with my sworn duty, I declare that—"

I jammed my finger against the unmute button and leaned as close as I could to the mouthpiece of the bridge.

"I nominate Guanyin," I said.

13

I COULD ONLY GUESS AT WHAT THE CROWD REACTION WAS IN the glorious hall of Heaven. Because the two divine beings sitting in this office conference room with me right now were so mortified that their lifespans could have been shortened to a fruit fly's.

Quentin stared at me, his jaw slack and his eyes swimming with disbelief. His chair had been rolling to the side at the moment of my interruption, and he was too shocked to stop its motion. He gently traveled across the room until his armrest hit the wall next to him.

Guanyin, surprisingly, was even worse off. She looked like I'd taken a battering ram to her stomach. Her skin became pale and wan before my very eyes. At this rate she would fade to nothingness soon, chalk washed away by the rain.

The Great White Planet interrupted the toxic cloud of silence with a cough.

"I'm sorry, who is this?" he said.

Normally I wasn't good at improvisation, or old-timey declarative speak, but right now my voice had never been steadier in my life. The words came pouring out of my mouth like I'd been born to say them.

"I am the Shouhushen Eugenia Lo Pei-Yi, Divine Guardian of the Protectorate of California on Earth, Former and Current Ruyi Jingu Bang, Slayer of Demons, and Conqueror of Red Boy and the traitor Erlang Shen," I said. "And you damn well heard me the first time. I nominate Guanyin, Goddess of Mercy, to be considered for the mandate."

Nezha didn't realize he was on a hot mic. "Can she do that?" he whispered to the Great White Planet.

"The Jade Emperor hasn't officially been kicked off his chair yet," I answered before anyone else could. "I still hold *his* mandate to possess dominion over the spirits on Earth. That's an entire plane I'm the boss of. My word counts as much as any god. Or goddess."

I wasn't sure any of what I said was true. It likely wasn't. But if there was ever a time for me to go all-in on a bluff, it was now. The slight twinge of hypocrisy I felt for using the power of the Jade Emperor's name, when I openly thought he sucked, vanished so quickly as to never have existed. I had to use the tools at hand.

The shock on the other end of the line was so great there wasn't any outcry from the collected gods. The Great White Planet took the opportunity to try and downplay the situation.

"My dear, ah, with all due respect to the Lady of Mercy, she is not exactly suited to the risks of this endeavor," he said. "You heard me before when I said we face a great force of destruction. Mandate Challenges involve much conflict. Violence!"

I rolled my eyes. Guanyin was twice as useful in combat as me or Quentin. She'd carried us in that brawl with Red Boy and Erlang Shen harder than Superman propping up the Wonder Twins. I took the Great White Planet's feeble protest as a sign that I was winning. He was resorting to concern-trolling.

"If it's necessary, Sun Wukong, Great Sage Equaling Heaven, and I can provide physical support toward her cause," I said. "He and I aren't gods, so we shouldn't count against the party limit." Or so I imagined.

The Great White Planet took a bit of time getting down from the petard I'd hoisted him by. "We need to deliberate this," he said. "Such a matter can't be taken lightly."

Double standard much? I thought, given that the other nominees were made official by screaming really loudly. I was going to say so too, but we got disconnected. From our end. By a long, delicate finger, attached to the person I'd just declared fit to rule over all of creation.

"Quentin, give us ten minutes outside," Guanyin said while staring at me.

Quentin didn't take his eyes off me either. He got up from his seat without protest at being ordered around, frowning at me the whole while in case I made any sudden moves. It was like I'd turned into a live rattlesnake in front of him.

The click of the door shutting was the only sound. Guanyin waited for a few moments to pass before letting the blood rush back into her face.

I smiled at her. "You can thank me lat—"

The Goddess of Mercy screamed, leaped over the table, and tackled me straight into the conference room door.

The hinges popped off and we landed in the open layout of the office cubicles. I tried to crawl away from Guanyin, but she grabbed my ankle and pulled my lower half off the floor. We flailed away, wheelbarrowing, until she flipped me over and jumped on my chest. She was still screaming at the top of her lungs. We both were.

I knew what someone trying to kill me felt like, and this wasn't that. This was off somehow. Unfamiliar. Guanyin's hands needed to be higher on my throat if she really wanted to choke me to death.

"YOU IDIOT!" she screeched. She mashed my face to the side with the heel of her hand, hoping to friction-burn my cheek against the cheap carpeting. "Do you have any idea what you've done!?"

I could speak with only the tips of my lips. "Ge of ee!"

I groped around for a weapon and found a dry erase marker. I flicked the cap off with my thumb and scribbled furiously over her face, but the marker was so old and dehydrated that nothing came out.

As Guanyin bit my fingers, I felt that strange sensation again. Separate from the pain of her teeth sinking into my skin. I kicked up and flipped her over my head, sending her tumbling into a cubicle, but she anchored herself with a fistful of my hair.

"Ow!" I yelped. "Let go!"

She squeezed harder and reached behind her with her free hand, finding a bottle of hand sanitizer. It loomed over my face like water torture.

"Don't get that in my eyes!" I shrieked. They were perhaps the only vulnerable part of me.

To my surprise she listened and opted for shoving the nozzle down my collar. I screamed at the cold gel flooding my shirt as she vindictively pumped the handle. I pushed away at her face, getting my thumb tip inside her nostril, but she wouldn't relent.

That was when it hit me.

Yunie and I'd had a ton of arguments growing up. An inevitable consequence of being so close. But we'd never laid a hand on each other. I was always so much bigger that the lightest rough-housing would immediately lose its innocent edge. So as an only child, I never really knew what all-out fighting with a sibling felt like.

I did now. *That* was the strange new feeling. I was sister-fighting.

And losing badly. Guanyin was as lengthy as I was and possessed the massive strength that every god seemed to have, regardless of their magical specialization. And she was attacking me like someone who held the moral high ground. I couldn't hit her back very hard in that situation.

No, I had to sit there and take it. Even though I was new to this, somehow I understood the unspoken rule of sister-fighting. The aggrieved party gets to be more vicious.

It took emptying the entire bottle of sanitizer on me to sate Guanyin's rage. She threw the empty plastic container against my forehead, and it bounced away. Then she slumped back against the nearest cubicle wall and caught her breath. I stayed where I was, looking at the ceiling, and grinned uncontrollably.

"I believe the phrase you're looking for is 'Thank you,'" I said.

"You smarmy little know-it-all," she said, her voice hoarse. "You just had to act out in front of the assembly of Heaven, didn't you? You don't understand what you've done."

"On the contrary." I struggled to my elbows. "I know exactly what I did."

"Oh really?" Guanyin sneered. "You think because you talk to me you know what gods are like? You think you're privy to the inner machinations of the celestial pantheon because you sat in on one meeting? There are institutional forces at work here, and you just blew your nose all over them!"

"Okay, let's say you're right," I said. "The Jade Emperor and the other gods—I can't comprehend what goes on in their heads. They don't operate by human standards. I don't know what they're like. But I know *you*."

I sat up and faced her. "You're perfect for the job. You're competent. Strong. And most importantly, you give a damn. Why would I not want a ruler of Heaven I can understand?"

Guanyin closed her eyes and thumped her head back against the cubicle wall.

"*They* don't want me," she muttered. "Why do you think I spend so much time on Earth? They don't want me up there. You heard how they reacted."

"Yeah?" I said. "Well screw them. What do *you* want?"

She tensed up so hard I thought she was going to explode like a grenade. But then she relaxed and glared at me. I smirked, knowing I had her.

"Okay, I'm sorry for not checking with you first," I said. "That was very uncool of me. But if you truly don't want to be in charge, if you don't even want to *try*, then withdraw. Call the other gods again right now and tell them you don't want to be part of the Mandate Challenge."

Guanyin snorted and looked to the side. "You know if I'm stuck in Heaven, I won't be able to babysit your dumb ass on Earth."

My grin spread even wider. The seed of possibility had been planted in her mind.

"I didn't do it to make my life easier," I said. "Or yours. If you're waiting for me to regret it, you might as well stop time right now, because it's never going to happen. Ever. There is no one in this world or the next who should be in charge more than you."

Guanyin sighed. The fight had gone out of her. "Shut the hell up," she said. "And answer your stupid phone. That buzzing is driving me nuts."

Yunie, I thought. I pulled out my phone only to find I was wrong. I had no call. And the buzzing got louder and louder.

Someone's shoes entered my view. They were Quentin's nondescript black oxfords, which met our school's dress code. He'd never bothered to swap them out for another pair.

Quentin looked askance at the destruction that Guanyin and I had wrought in the office. Ten minutes were up. And on his ears, my enchanted demon-alarm earrings were vibrating so violently that it looked like he might take off and fly at any moment.

"Hey, so if you're done with whatever you're doing, someone's about to get eaten," he said.

14

IT HAD BEEN A LONG TIME SINCE WE'D DONE ONE OF THESE. AN old-fashioned hunt. Quentin's earrings went off whenever a demon got really close to a human, which usually meant impending dinnertime for the yaoguai. We were on a clock.

And what made it even worse was the direction we needed to head was right back toward the college campus. I cursed up and down at my negligence. *Yunie*.

One of the things I'd learned about my friend was that she had an unbelievable amount of spiritual energy for a human being, rivaling Xuanzang from the days of yore. Which meant she stood out among a crowd as the absolute tastiest person to eat for a yaoguai bent on consuming power. For the sake of speed, Quentin and I left Guanyin behind with the mutual understanding that we could handle a basic hunt on our own.

Muscle memory took over hard. Acquire target. Get on Quentin's back. Jump. Land. Start punching. It was so ingrained that Quentin and I found ourselves right back at Ji-Hyun's apartment without thinking.

But the demon that had set off the earring alarm wasn't a vicious beast about to devour my friend. It was a little iridescent blob that floated in the air, pulsating over the doorframe of the building like a party balloon. And the human it was drifting too close to was that Axton kid who'd walked into the pool and interrupted my talk with Ao Guang.

Quentin and I approached on foot cautiously. Appearances could be deceiving, so we didn't let our guards down. We must have looked like a pair of doofs, stalking along the concrete sidewalk in plain view. A stiff breeze ruffled the grass and we paused like savannah cats.

"Oh hey," said Axton, waving. He didn't seem any worse for wear after the brain-scrubbing that Guanyin had given him, though he was oblivious to the creature hovering over his head. It rippled between hues of pink and purple and blue like a mood light. I focused my true sight until I saw the aura of concealment around it.

Best to pretend nothing was wrong until we could separate them. Spooking the human might set off the yaoguai. "Hiiiii," I said. "Did you forget something from the party?"

"Yes," Axton said. "You."

Uh-oh. Bad start.

"I shouldn't have left things like that," Axton said. "Not with someone as special as you. I had a feeling after we met, so I asked around the people who were at the party and came looking for you."

Just what I needed. Another asshole like the one in the cafe. Only more persistent.

Even better, I had with me my hot-tempered, preternaturally strong boyfriend who possessed a murder record hundreds of demons long. I glanced at Quentin to see how badly he was reacting to Axton's statements, to see how much damage control I'd have to do.

Not much, apparently. The shapeless demon blob had meandered off to the side and descended closer to the ground. Quentin was busy trying to approach it like it was an escaped chicken. He cooed at it with his palms out, trying to beckon as nonthreateningly as possible. It made a bizarre scene given that anyone watching us wouldn't have known what he was looking at.

He could at least be a little jealous, my brain leaked out before I grabbed the thought and stuffed it back inside my skull. "Look, Axton, is it?"

"Ax," he corrected.

Whatever. "Ax, I'm not interested." If I had been hit on more in my life maybe I would have softened the rejection. Or maybe not, because why the hell did I need to?

He gave a smooth chuckle. "You misunderstand. Are you Eugenia Lo, creator of Monkey King Jumps to Heaven?"

Ax pulled out his phone, not to get digits, but to show me the app store. My little nothing game was on his screen. Under the icon was a subtitle saying *Built by Eugenia Lo*. When Rutsuo helped me fill out the developer submission form, I was too lazy to come up with a video gamey business name like Playwonk or Gamenamyte like the rest of the apps, and simply put my real name out of standardized test habits.

A mistake, if it let weirdos like Ax track me down. "What of it?" I said. "Last I checked I was between two solitaire rip-offs and a carpeting simulator."

Ax tapped his phone and showed it to me again. "Maybe last week. Right now, you're being featured in the 'Best Timewasters' category."

I hadn't known there were category filters you could change. Under Ax's settings I was number sixty-eight. Huh. Sixty-eight was starting to get into the same territory as legitimate games I saw my classmates playing.

I kept the conversation going mostly because it had caused Ax to move toward me and away from the yaoguai. Quentin had sidled around and sat down on the stoop next to the demon blob, the cool teacher going *Hey, I'm just here chilling in the same spot as you, no need to talk about your troubles unless you want to. Want to have a jam sesh?*

"Okay, again, so what?" I said. "What does my app have to do with you?"

"Eugenia, have you ever heard of the Nexus Partnership?"

I had indeed. It was one of many word-jumble brand names that was incomprehensible to Bay Area outsiders but familiar to anyone living in Silicon Valley. Hollywood had actors, DC had politicians, and we in the Bay had billionaire venture capitalists.

The local news ran breathless headlines every time one of them dumped giant wads of money into some stupid company or other. When people shook their heads at a startup with a misspelled word for a name wasting millions of dollars on free beer and Ping-Pong tables, they were overlooking the VCs who invested in dozens of such cash incinerators as part of a normal working Tuesday.

For every pair of grad student buddies striking it rich from a company they founded in their garage, there was a VC behind the curtain, taking their cut. On occasion, an especially powerful venture capitalist would buy a children's hospital or pick a disease to eradicate. You know. To be nice.

The Nexus Partnership was run by Wynn Ketteridge, a VC rich enough to make his name appear on a building overnight. I'd seen pictures of the guy in some blog article or another. He looked like a normal middle-aged schlub with thinning hair and a puffy vest, only with a thick aura of gives-no-Fs surrounding him. When you had that many zeroes in your net worth, you could look however you wanted.

"Aren't you a little young to be working for Wynn Ketteridge?" I asked.

"That's where you're wrong," Ax said with a big grin. "The Nexus has a . . . junior arm, so to speak. Entrepreneurs of college age or younger. I'm one of them."

Now I remembered what I'd been reading about Wynn and his company. This guy, this VC, had made a big splash by embarking on a crusade against college. I mean he really, really hated college.

A college degree, he reasoned in the many editorials he'd bought across every Bay Area newspaper possible, was a waste of time and money. You spent four years learning nothing that could be applied in the workplace. A better education could be had in the school of hard knocks, surviving in the free market by working or founding your own company.

Look at all the successful businesspeople who never used their major, Ketteridge pointed out. The world ran on software and hardware built by people who rejected higher education. How many geniuses had been stifled out of existence by professors made lazy by tenure, or squandered their lives by, god forbid, specializing in the humanities? Entrepreneurship was the only true education to be had.

It was such a Silicon Valley–style opinion that talking heads in forty-nine other states united for a brief time to laugh at him. But I happened to live in the one part of the country where certain folks drank up his message like water in a hundred-year drought.

And one of them was right in front of me.

"I have a proposition for you," Ax said. "Come work for the company I'm founding. I have a pile of Wynn's cash burning a hole in my bank account and a mandate to hire whomever I want."

Oh sure, not suspicious at all. Maybe he had a white van I could get into where I could meet a deposed overseas prince who needed my social security number. "What's your company called?" I asked.

He shrugged. "I haven't decided yet. It's my first time doing this, and I want my brand name to be special."

"Who else has joined?"

"No one. You'd be employee number one."

"What does this company *do?*"

Ax grinned. "I don't know. But it doesn't matter. Wynn invests in people, not concepts."

Hoo-boy. "So you've got no idea, no experience, and no one else on board," I said. "That sounds like a recipe for disaster."

His feelings were immune to my bluntness. "Maybe," Ax said. "But that's okay. Wynn's number one motto is that failure is the best teacher. There's no real consequences for taking risks other than learning valuable lessons."

Another Silicon Valley–slash–Bay Area attitude I'd heard a lot. *Fail fast! Fail over and over again! Fail like there's no tomorrow!*

"Take me as an example," Ax said with a faint smile that indicated he absolutely loved it when people took him as an example. "Before I met Wynn I was trying to build an audience for my online

120

video channel. So I crashed one of his parties and handed out business cards that looked like raffle tickets for a Lamborghini. I got the emails of a lot of rich and famous people that way. The guests were pissed off when they found out there was no car, but Wynn liked my style, so instead of calling the cops he brought me into the program. Had I been afraid of failing, I never would have come this far."

The entitlement on this one was as thick as the Earth's mantle. Though maybe he and I were more similar than we appeared. I mean, I'd tried to upend the entire celestial pantheon this very morning. The stunt I'd pulled even shocked Quentin, the king of outrageous stunts and—oh god, I'd completely forgotten about Quentin and the yaoguai.

I glanced around and they were gone. "Ax, we gotta wrap this up," I said, shifting my weight side to side impatiently. I must have looked like I needed to go to the bathroom.

"All right then, here's the bottom line," he said. "I'll pay you a salary of a hundred thousand dollars a year if you drop out of school and come work for me."

I stopped dancing in place and clenched my jaw to keep it from hitting the pavement. I took a deep nose breath, blinked slowly, and stayed silent for a while, long enough to make Ax laugh.

He probably thought that as a poor person, I couldn't comprehend the sheer amount of money he was waving in front of my nose, like a medieval peasant witnessing a match being lit by a time-traveler for the first time. *Golly gee mister, I didn't know numbers went up that high!*

In truth it was the opposite. I was taken aback because I knew exactly how much money one hundred thousand dollars was. When I was younger I'd heard snippets of frantic conversations, late-night arguments, screamed obscenities between my father and mother that were about sums of money roughly in that range. A hundred racks was the size of a common small business loan, the kind that had wrecked my family.

And more recently to the point, it was enough to cover an ambulance ride, a few ER visits of varying severity, ongoing courses of heart medication, and general health costs for a non-smoking man and woman of my parents' ages. There was no particular reason why I'd looked that information up several times over this long weekend on my phone. No reason at all.

"Why would I have to drop out?" I asked. I'd thought the entrepreneurship for young people that Wynn Ketteridge blathered on about meant a side gig you did as an extracurricular, instead of debate team or chess club.

"Wynn wants to make sure that his protégés are completely committed to his philosophy," Ax said. "So you'd have to burn your bridges and publicly declare you're rejecting the concept of higher education. I dropped out of this very school myself. I sneak back on campus regularly to recruit for the program. As you might have guessed from last night, the message is lost on a lot of people."

Ending my academic career before it truly started? "I—I don't even go here," I murmured. "I haven't begun applications yet."

"Even better," Ax said, unfazed that he'd been talking to a high schooler this entire time. "We could call a few local reporters after you complete your apps and get into a few good schools. Make a big story about you saying no to every single one. It would be great publicity for the foundation."

Like Trish and Kelsey, Ax had no problem warping me into the future where I already got in to a school as exclusive as this one.

And the trip was making me nauseous. Either they knew something about me I didn't, or maybe you lost your memory of what the struggle was like once it was over.

"I can see you're on the fence," Ax said. "I've never met a better candidate for the program than you, so how about this? You have until the end of the long weekend to decide. After that, the offer's gone forever. You'd be blacklisted from working with any member of the Nexus Partnership ever again."

I frowned at him. "You're going to give me *less* time to make an important decision *because* you like me?"

"It's a negotiating tactic that Wynn teaches us. We use it when we really want something. You're a unicorn, Genie. A pretty girl like you, who can code? And a minority to boot? You could be the next face of the program."

I wanted to tell him that his deadline was dumb and unfair. And to break his nose for how sexist and racist his other comment was. But before I could do either, a greasy, crumpled-up paper bag landed at our feet.

"Ax, you don't even go here!" a girl shouted from the third-floor window. "Get the hell out before I call campus security!"

Ax backed away from the building with his arms upturned and a big smile on his face. "First they laugh at you, then they ignore you, then they fight you. And then you win."

■ ■ ■

I ran up the stairwell of Ji-Hyun's apartment building, taking the steps three by three. For now, I had to set aside the conversation with the guy in designer jeans who had the nerve to unironically compare himself to Gandhi using quotes that weren't historically accurate in the first place.

I knew I would find Quentin on the roof. Not through any sort of magical detection, but because I knew his habits. Whenever he needed to scramble, disappear, or be alone, he always clambered straight up.

He and I had done the same in my school the first time my Ruyi Jingu Bang powers had manifested themselves. Or really, he'd done the climbing while I panicked and screamed the whole time because my arm had turned into a gigantic stretchy noodle.

Was it weird that I missed those times? Back then, I only had to worry about my town getting eaten and burned by demons. There was no time for existential crises about my future.

The door to the roof had been locked. In my hurry I accidentally snapped it going through. Whoops. On the other side, though, among the ventilation housing and some forgotten rusty deck chairs, was Quentin. He held the shining mass of ectoplasm in his arms.

As I approached, it snapped into the form of a cube. "It's okay, it's okay," Quentin said to it soothingly. "She's my friend."

I suppose I could have been annoyed that he'd referred to me as just "a friend," but then again, this was a supernatural cube, not an Oscars acceptance speech. "What is that?" I said. "I've never seen a yaoguai like that before."

"It's not a yaoguai." The corners of the block softened back into a blob as he gently jounced it. "It's a formless spirit from another realm. A being of pure meditative consciousness. I guess Guanyin's alarm doesn't make the distinction between non-god unearthly creatures."

For whatever reason I didn't like him criticizing Guanyin right now, even if he was stating facts. "All right, so how did it get here?" I snapped.

The spirit turned a deeper shade of crimson. Quentin leaned back and crooked his head toward the direction of the pool. "I think it followed in the wake of Ao Guang's retreat. It's *scared.* Formless spirits aren't supposed to feel emotions, but this one is terrified."

It shuddered against him. He pressed his ear closer to the skin of the creature. "Is it . . . saying something?" I asked.

Quentin frowned deeply.

"*Yin Mo,*" he said. "It's screaming *Yin Mo.*"

▪   ▪   ▪

We thought the spirit might be more comfortable inside, so we went down the stairwell to Ji-Hyun's apartment. We knocked on the door and she let us in, not questioning Quentin's presence or why he, to her, appeared to be holding a big bag of nothing against his shoulder, like the parent of an invisible baby.

"Yunie's sleeping it off," Ji-Hyun said. "So, you know. Volume."

"Do you have someplace Genie and I can talk?" Quentin asked her.

She led us into an empty bedroom draped in tie-dye sheets and posters that were completely blank, presumably blacklight designs. The nubs of scented candles littered the desk and windowsills. A pretty impressive wine cork collection had been started by the occupant. It was only a few more bottles of rosé away from a complete pushpin board.

"About what happened earlier . . ." Quentin said after Ji-Hyun closed the door.

"What about what happened earlier?" I said. "I thought you wanted to discuss how there's a hole in the fabric of existence next door that's leaking ghostly amoeba."

"No, I wanted to talk about how you mucked up the Mandate Challenge!"

Oh, nelly. We were going to go there, weren't we? I sucked in air to oxygenate my arguing muscles.

"We were straight on course to having a better leader than the Jade Emperor, and then you derailed the whole train!" Quentin said. "There's no telling what'll happen now!"

His lack of faith disturbed me. "Quentin, I don't want a better god, I want the *best* god," I said. "The fact that you don't consider that to be Guanyin is either very wrong or very telling. After all the times she's saved your ass in this era and the last, you're really saying you'd rather work for your bro from Party Central over her?"

Bro code dictated that Quentin defend his friend's honor. "First off," he said. "Guan Yu is a tactical genius. Just because he likes to have fun doesn't mean he wouldn't make a great King of Heaven. And second, you're forgetting that Guanyin is *my* closest friend, and I trust her to make her own decisions, unlike you!"

I couldn't tell what made me more angry, Quentin calling someone other than me his closest friend, or him claiming more of Guanyin than I could. Both felt deeply wrong.

"Sometimes the people close to you don't share everything!" I said. "Sometimes they want things they don't tell you about!"

"Yeah," he said, looking extra hurt. "Like the fact that you're considering not going to college?"

The spirit in his arms flailed its pseudopods and turned as purple as a Concord grape. Quentin maneuvered his face out of its thrashing like he was avoiding getting smacked by a toddler.

"That's right," he went on before I could say anything, as if he'd found damning evidence that I'd been cheating on him. "I heard the whole thing with you and that Ax guy. When we first met, you would have slapped someone across the face for suggesting you give up on your education. And now you're going to throw away your dream for money?"

"Quentin, to a very large extent, *college* was about money! The whole point of getting my degree was so that I could make more money as an adult! I may not be able to wait that long anymore!"

I hadn't had time to weigh Ax's proposition before, but now that I was talking about it out loud, it sounded less like a fevered delusion and more like a real option. My family needed money, didn't they? I needed to take care of my family, didn't I? Well, now I had the means dangling in front of me. The only requirement was that I sell out my core identity to take on an unbelievable risk because a complete stranger told me to. Simple as that.

The ironic thing was that I was incredibly lucky—privileged—to have this choice. If I didn't live in the one part of the country that sailed on a sea of bloated promises, swollen wallets, and computer code, I would never have gotten close to such a big pile of cash in such a short amount of time. Hooray for the Bay Area.

"I can't believe this," Quentin said. "Since we met, our lives revolved around school! We scheduled demon hunts around it! In the course of one weekend, you're going to decide that none of that mattered?"

I pointed at him. "When we met, *you* were an insufferable asshole! Things change, people change, and if you're going to imply that *I'm* the only person not allowed to change, then you'd better get the hell out right now because I'm not here for it!"

The blob suddenly shifted into a tetrahedron, then a sphere, and then a spiky sea urchin shape. Quentin tried to keep it still.

"It's reacting to your emotions!" he hissed at me. "Calm down!"

"And not yours?" I whisper-shouted back. "*You* calm down!"

Quentin paused and then bit back whatever he was going to say. *Not in front of the blob!*

We glared furiously at each other while he gently patted the spirit, comforting it back into its amorphous, pale-hued state. "I'm going to find a safe place to put this thing," he said. "Call me once you've defeated whatever Genie doppelganger I'm talking to right now." He opened the door and walked out of the bedroom.

"That doesn't even make sense!" I yelled at his back as he left the apartment. I had the distinct feeling the blob had sided with him over me during the argument, and it pissed me off.

Ji-Hyun looked at me from the kitchen. She was stirring a Bloody Mary with a celery stalk.

Ah, hell. We hadn't used a *silence* spell, and she'd heard the whole thing. *Silence* was the first piece of magic I'd ever seen Quentin do, and we'd forgotten. Our negligence was getting out of control.

"I'm not going to judge you two for arguing over a video game, if that's what you're worried about," Ji-Hyun said. "I know they can get pretty intense, and if that's what you two center your relationship on, then that's what's important to you."

I didn't follow her until I realized that was how she'd interpreted our nonsense words. King of Heaven. Demon hunts. It probably sounded like guild drama in an MMORPG. I knew a couple of friendships at SF Prep that had ended over such issues.

"But you need to learn how to fight with each other better if you want your relationship to succeed," she said.

"I thought successful relationships meant never fighting."

Ji-Hyun chose to drink half of her brunch cocktail before explaining. I waited.

"That's not the case at all," she said. "Everyone fights. The important part is being fair to each other while you're doing it. The two of you are good at expressing what you feel, which is nice, but you're crap at acknowledging why you feel it. I give you a flat C."

The rules of hospitality prevented me from telling the older girl off. Instead I narrowed my eyes at her.

Ji-Hyun pointed to herself with her celery. "Burgeoning doctor, remember? I have a full complement of Intro Psych courses under my belt."

She bit the stalk with a crunch. "I really should be charging you money for this advice."

15

"I CAN'T BELIEVE YOU'RE DOING THIS," I SAID. "YOU WERE AT death's door this afternoon."

"I feel better now," Yunie said. She craned her neck in the mirror as she put in her other earring. Music pumped faintly through the door. It was coming across the pool, from the other building in the complex. The festivities had shifted location. To the other side of the spirit-vomiting waters.

"Ji-Hyun isn't partying tonight," I said. "She's with her study group."

"Yeah, her study group at the grad center bar." Yunie made the tippy-drinky motion with her hand. "I'm not going to have anything. Or at least I'm not going to have anything out of a Solo cup ever again. Yeesh."

I couldn't believe that my friend, or anyone else for that matter, had the endurance for this. I'd once chased a horse demon twenty miles down Highway 101 in the dead of night without breaking a sweat, but trying to be social throughout last night's party had crushed me into a marble.

A knock came at the door. It was too genteel to be Quentin, and Ji-Hyun would have let herself in, so I assumed it was one of her ghost roommates, who theoretically existed and yet were never here.

When I opened the door I got a surprise.

"What?" Guanyin said, reading my face. "Is now a bad time?"

When I couldn't muster a response, the goddess stepped inside and closed the door behind her discreetly. If the filthiness of Ji-Hyun's apartment bothered her, she didn't let it show.

It was surprisingly difficult to process this visit. Guanyin came on official business or in times of desperate need. She didn't show up out of the blue, like a mortal who needed to talk.

"I need to talk," she said.

Wow. Okay. I looked around for a clean place to sit and saw Yunie staring at us.

The wrongness of this situation jumped an order of magnitude higher.

"Hi," Yunie said. "You must be Guanyin."

"Yunie," the Goddess of Mercy said with a fixed smile. "I've heard so much about you."

And then that was it. They didn't say anything else or shake hands. I provided zero conversational help.

It was because I had absolutely no plan for a meeting like this. In fact, it was explicitly never supposed to happen. Guanyin was breaking the promise she'd made to me to keep anything supernatural as far away from Yunie as possible. And the goddess herself counted.

While I knew Guanyin could be trusted to the ends of the universe, she represented so much magic walking around that it was as if the guy holding the suitcase of ballistic missile launch codes had strolled into the apartment. It was technically safe, but I still didn't want it near my human friend.

Yunie tapped her foot, a musician waiting for her entrance.

"So you're the person taking up all of Genie's time," she said with what was supposed to be a joking lilt.

Oh dear.

"She and I do important work together," Guanyin said after a pause. "Of course, it's all very behind-the-scenes, but regular people like you benefit."

Ohhhhhh dear.

Guanyin's number one concern was humanity, of course, but her complete lack of bias toward individuals sometimes made her come off as cold. Like she thought people were interchangeable. That was . . . an incompatible philosophy with Yunie's worldview. And self-view.

"I mean, it must be important work," Yunie drawled. "She comes back with her clothes torn, like she's been attacked by wild animals. I once saw her arm looking all metal-y. I hope that with everything she does, she's not in any danger. That she has enough support."

Guanyin let slide the implication that she wasn't giving me enough help. Or maybe she didn't let it slide, because there was another awkward silence. The goddess towered over my friend as they stared at each other.

Is that what the height difference looks like when I stand next to Yunie? I thought. *Damn.*

Guanyin smiled again. "Could you give us a moment alone, dear?" she said to Yunie.

Yunie's nostrils flared. She didn't "give people moments alone" with me. Even Quentin knew not to ask her that. When my boyfriend needed to talk to me in private, he waited until Yunie lost interest in us and drifted away like a cat moving on to a different toy.

I made a helpless face at her. She frowned and went outside.

"Our agreement, remember?" I whispered at Guanyin once Yunie shut the door. "Work and her are never supposed to meet!" I slashed my hands up and down through the air to make a visual of the separation.

"I remember," Guanyin said dryly. "You remind me quite often. Of all the things you're supposed to be diligent about as the Shouhushen, that's the only one you've never let your guard down on."

"For good reason. You said you needed to talk?"

Guanyin nodded. "I received an update from Heaven." She paused. "I'm in. I'm in consideration for the Mandate."

I refrained myself from grabbing her and lifting her into the air as she'd done me. Her head would have punched a hole in the ceiling. Instead I grinned wildly at her and clapped with my fingertips.

"Tomorrow morning the other gods and I are going to gather at Ao Guang's rift and go through it the opposite way," Guanyin said. "The unfortunate reality is that whatever defeated him is likely to chase him through the same pathway he retreated along."

I winced. "And that path ends here." An enemy strong enough to provoke an upheaval of the cosmic order had a red carpet leading to Earth. Forget "Earth"; it was right next door, in the pool. There was more at stake here than who got to rule Heaven. If this Yin Mo made it past the party of gods, then humanity was in deep trouble.

Guanyin patted my shoulder reassuringly. "It'll have to get through some of the finest warriors of Heaven."

"And you." Guanyin as the last line of defense was more reassuring to me than placing my trust in some disembodied voices. "You didn't check in on us when Quentin's alarm went off."

"I trusted you to take care of it on your own. I need to do that more." She fidgeted nervously, making me confused and worried. After some hand-wringing, Guanyin mustered herself, looking more vulnerable than I'd ever seen before. "I also need to thank you."

So that was it. "Hmmmmm?" I said smugly, wanting to enjoy this moment for as long as possible. "I thought from the way you reacted, you didn't want to be in charge of Heaven."

"Of course I want to be in charge of Heaven," Guanyin snapped, finally bursting through the wall of embarrassment. "Every god wants that. Nezha tries to be a selfless golden boy, and Guan Yu pretends he's too rough around the edges for the office, but they both want it. I bet even the Great White Planet wishes he wore the crown himself, rather than having to anoint a new mandate owner time after time."

"They're all on my watch list, by the way," I said.

"What?"

"My watch list for secretly being evil and betraying us," I clarified. "After what happened with Erlang Shen? Any god we meet, I'm on the lookout for the slightest hint they're evil. As soon as they do, BAM! Ruyi Jingu Bang right to their kneecaps."

Guanyin sputtered silently, but as far as I was concerned my logic was flawless. Fool me twice, shame on me.

"You're getting me off course," she said. "The point is, very few gods approve of me or my methods. It's not only the Jade Emperor that I've antagonized. When you nominated me, you couldn't have known my history with the other gods, the way they speak to me, the compromises I've had to make simply to deal with them."

I saw the strongest god I knew slump her shoulders. I thought of the many times in the past where instead of unleashing her full power, she had to work around rules and limitations imposed by the Jade Emperor. That had to be more exhausting than using her talents to the fullest.

She rubbed at her eyes with her fingers. "When you constantly hear that you can't do something, or that your goal is out of reach, that it's wrong for you to have ambitions, and you hear that message over and over again . . . you start to believe it yourself. That's why I blew up at you earlier. I couldn't reconcile the truth of what you were saying with the lies I'd accepted for so long."

When she dropped her hands she looked like herself once more. The Lady of Infinite Capacity. The veil had been lifted.

"I thought I lacked the guts to pursue what I wanted," she said with a smile. "But you reminded me that I still have plenty to go around."

Inner Me was deliriously happy, bouncing off the walls at the way she'd come around. A Universe led by Guanyin, where mercy and action and good sense reigned. The vision was sweeter and more intoxicating than any drink Ji-Hyun could have mixed in her bathtub. Outer Me shrugged, playing it cool.

"We all need a boost from time to time," I said. "You know, you were pretty mean to me before, calling me a smarmy know-it-all. While you're here, I think you should apologize for that, too."

"Don't push it. You still are one." She reached behind her and produced a small, cloth-lined box.

"What's this?" I said.

"A gift." She opened the box so the contents faced me. Inside, lying on top a miniature velvet pillow, were two little oblong lumps of dark, glittery metal.

I picked them up. They should have been cool to the touch, but instead their temperature matched mine so closely that I could hardly tell I was holding them. The lumps were flat on the bottom, the short side. I turned them over.

One piece of metal had "Lo Pei-Yi" carved into it, in reverse. The other had the characters for "Shouhushen." I was embarrassed to see that the correct way to write my title was different than the way I'd been imagining it. I had to brush up on my Chinese.

"These are chops," I said.

"As you mentioned over the phone, you're the Shouhushen of California on Earth," Guanyin said. "We should have established your seal of office right away. This is long overdue."

She swept aside a nearby pile of trash with her arm to reveal a coffee table that I didn't know was there. With another sleight of hand, she yanked a scroll from thin air and rolled it flat on the glass surface. Next to it she put a small pot of waxy red ink.

My fingers shook as I hefted the first stone and dipped it into the ink. It was only a practice run on blank paper, and yet I was terrified of messing up my first-ever chop stamp. Pressing and lifting the lump of metal made a sticky, satisfying Crayola noise.

I didn't look at the results until the second seal was also finished. Once I was done, two bright crimson squares of highly stylized characters sat at the bottom of the page.

The Shouhushen Lo Pei-Yi. In the future, once I used them on official documentation, the stamps would be a symbol of my identity and authority. They would represent my word and my will.

This was a momentous occasion. You couldn't do business in parts of Asia without a chop seal. In some way—actually, in a very large way—this was Guanyin telling me that I was finally real. I'd arrived.

The goddess peered at my signature with more effort and interest than I thought she would have spared for a test version. Maybe it was a little crooked. I could work on it.

I examined the seals themselves. Usually fancy chops were made from jade or chicken-blood stone, a red mineral that was pretty, if unfortunately named. But these were extremely heavy and dense, almost unnaturally so. The contrast between the black metal and the golden flecks—

"Wait a sec," I said. "These aren't—they're not made out of . . . *are* they?"

Guanyin tucked the paper away before answering.

"They are," she said, looking me in the eye. "They're the same cosmic iron as the Ruyi Jingu Bang. You could say that, in a way, these chops don't only represent you. They *are* you. I couldn't think of a better material to make them out of. The most precious metal in the Universe, in my opinion."

I was speechless. This was more than a gift.

I made a big show of carefully putting the seals back in their case. Once they were safe and secure, I threw my arms violently around Guanyin and hugged her with all my might.

"Genie!" she coughed in surprise. "You're squishing me!"

Eh. As I knew from our previous fight, she was tough. She could take it.

16

IT WAS UNCOMFORTABLE TO LOOK AT THE APARTMENT COURT-yard the next day and know it was a staging ground for the most important gathering that would take place in this epoch. The surrounding buildings blocked out the stained pink and orange hues of the morning sky, looming over me like gray monoliths. There were a lot more people than I had been expecting up and about. Mostly fitness buffs, running on the sidewalks in T-shirts and shorts. A couple of older folks, maybe faculty, taking unhurried strolls.

"Are you sure we won't be seen?" I asked Guanyin.

The goddess stood next to me, surveying the area. "I've got concealment operating around us three layers thick, barriers impregnable to mundane means, and a web of silence that could muffle a shuttle launch. And if a human who isn't you randomly wanders too close, they'll feel the sudden urge to find the nearest bathroom."

She winked. "That's a unique little spell I cooked up myself."

I smiled at her cleverness. "Where's Quentin?"

"Here," he said behind me. I turned to see him grumpily holding a large coffee toward me, a big scowl on his face.

That was incredibly sweet of him, especially since I hadn't asked for it. It did my heart good to know that even though we were fighting, and we *were* still fighting, that my boyfriend was the least petty person I knew. He was all big heart and shouted emotions, with none of the silent, spiteful cruelty that I tended to—

I nearly spat my sip of coffee out. "There's a ton of sugar and cream in this!"

Quentin shrugged. "They must have messed the order up. I wasn't paying attention."

Okay, so he was becoming petty. The student was learning from the master.

"Nothing for me?" the Great White Planet said, suddenly appearing to the side.

I'd been in this business long enough to stop caring when and how gods appeared on Earth. The Jade Emperor, the one time I saw him, needed to be announced with pomp and circumstance. Guanyin descended from the sky like the saint she was. And the Great White Planet got his jollies from popping in and out of nowhere; it was his prerogative. I couldn't be surprised anymore.

"Boba shops don't open this early," I said. I chugged my erroneous caffeine to get rid of it faster and chucked the cup into a nearby trash bin. It left a disgusting film of sugar on my teeth.

"Just as well," the Great White Planet said. "Bribing a judge during a Mandate Challenge is a crime punishable by dismemberment."

He didn't seem amused by his own joke. Perhaps he was still salty over what I pulled during the conference call. "You look upset," I said, daring him to voice his disapproval of Guanyin to my face.

"I am," he said. "An extremely serious problem has arisen. And the blame can be laid squarely at your feet."

Quentin threw his hands in the air. "See?" he said to me, not waiting to hear what the issue was. "I knew this wouldn't go down smoothly. When you screw with the process, bad things happen."

As if to prove him right, a pair of bright red hands suddenly burst from the ground under Quentin's feet, grabbed him by the ankles, and dragged him under the surface of the earth.

"QUENTIN!" I screamed. I dove for the small sinkhole he'd left behind and clawed frantically at the loose soil.

Guanyin might have been yelling something behind me, but I couldn't hear her with the blood pounding through my veins. I had only one thought, a name out of my nightmares.

Red Boy.

The demon who had nearly incinerated the entire Bay. Red Boy had scorched Guanyin's arm into a mass of scars and mine into a smelted attachment of living iron. He'd nearly killed Quentin. The only way I'd defeated him was by burying him deep under the airless Earth, and he'd escaped somehow to deliver the same punishment upon us.

The lawn behind me exploded. Rubble and dirt showered down, a rock the size of a paving stone thudding off my back. Grit got in my eyes as I tried to make out what was happening.

Quentin had reemerged with his assailant, their battle taking them back above the surface. He and the red man grappled at close range, not wanting to give the other an inch of room to maneuver. They smashed each other's backs with their fists as they snarled and laughed and—

They were laughing. The terror clouding my eyes began to fade, letting me see for the first time that this man who'd attacked Quentin was a good deal taller and thicker than Red Boy.

And more clothed. Red Boy had been nearly naked except for a loincloth when we'd fought. But this new guy was wearing a panoply of silken robes that could have put Ao Guang's ensemble to shame. Quentin's fist-pounds had knocked most of the dirt off, and the gilded embroidery underneath gleamed like the sun itself.

He also had the biggest, densest beard I had ever seen on a living creature, human or not. His jungle of facial hair was so aggressive and bountiful that Quentin was nearly swallowed whole by it.

"MONKEY!" the man roared, loud enough to unsettle nearby birds into flying away. "YOU SON OF A BITCH!"

Quentin freed himself from the man's follicles and shoved him to get some space. "Guan Yu! You old bastard, I knew it was you!"

"Lies! I waited there five hours for that prank, and it was worth it to hear you squeal!"

The two of them slammed their arms together in a thunderclap of a handshake. They did it the old-fashioned way, each gripping the other's bulging wrist. It turned into a contest of strength immediately. They grinned at each other over the tug-of-war, and it seemed like the air itself would snap in two from the torque they were exerting.

"What's the matter?" Guan Yu snorted as Quentin budged a millimeter. "Gone soft? Too many peaches?"

Quentin pushed back, reclaiming the ground he'd given up and then some. "That's pretty funny coming from a soldier who hasn't fought a war since porcelain was invented."

A small shiny object pinged into the air and landed near my feet. It was one of Quentin's cuff buttons, popped off from the sheer power of their flexing. Given more time, their biceps would have caused a critical meltdown.

"It's a draw!" Guanyin said, stepping forward in between them and laughing. "It's a draw. Please, or we'll be here until the next eon passes."

Guan Yu let go of Quentin at her behest and bowed solemnly toward the goddess. Then he gave her a big smile, and an even bigger hug. "My lady, you are looking as radiant as ever."

Guanyin bore his affection with aplomb. They stood on opposite sides of the Mandate Challenge, but it was clear they were on warm terms at the very least. "It's good to see you too, General," she said, patting his back.

Guan Yu put her down and noticed me standing nearby. "And who is this human child?" he asked.

I was going to make a sarcastic comment about him being behind on the news, but I remembered he hadn't been present in the hall of the gods when I made my declaration.

"My name is Genie," I said, going with the short version. "I'm the Ruyi Jingu Bang." I extended my hand and prepared myself for another squeeze-war.

Instead Guan Yu took hold of my fingers like they were made of glass and bowed again. I was mildly disappointed that I wouldn't get to feel how strong he was. I needed to know if I could take him if things got ugly.

The warrior god straightened up and looked at me with a similar sense of probing interest. "Most curious!" he declared at an ear-splitting volume. An ear-splitter, this guy was. "I had heard tales that the As-You-Will Cudgel had taken a new form. But I never would have believed it until seeing you with my own eyes."

He stepped back, curled his tongue, and let out a whistle that made the Tarzan yell of his speaking voice sound like a church whisper. Even Quentin and Guanyin flinched at the inhuman shrillness.

High above us, a slice of lightning formed in the air, growing bigger and bigger, until an elongated shape fired downward out of it. The projectile slammed into the ground in front of Guan Yu, sizzling from friction. It looked like a metallic green staff, as thick as a parking meter pole and three times as tall, until he gripped it by the still-smoking haft and pulled the rest of it free. The earth revealed a broad, yard-long blade that glowed like a lightsaber set to dim.

It was a gigantic *guandao*. A halberd. A big-ass sword attached to a big-ass stick. Guan Yu hefted his weapon over his head and peered at it. It didn't catch the nascent sun's rays so much as Hoover them up and spit them back into your eyeballs like a cobra.

"The Green Dragon Crescent Blade," he pondered, stroking his beard with his free hand. "My companion of many centuries. If it ever reincarnates and leaves my side, I should certainly be up the proverbial creek."

He held it between us as if I could translate for him. "What say you, Madam Shouhushen? Is there a spirit in there who needs to be let out? I would hate to exploit an unwilling armament."

"Maybe?" I didn't remember the details of my past life as the Ruyi Jingu Bang or know what the rules were for weapons reincarnating. But I did appreciate Guan Yu's consideration for his blade. "I think if it glows, that's a sign that it's connecting well with whoever's wielding it. So it's probably not unhappy right now, in any case." In staff form, I had apparently glowed as Sun Wukong approached for the first time, and the guandao was certainly shiny.

Quentin seemed jealous that his buddy was paying more attention to me than him. "Helmet check!" he shouted. He leaped up and slammed his skull into Guan Yu's. The warrior staggered back before whooping and returning the blow with his own cranium.

I watched the two friends run at each other like a pair of mountain goats. It was almost hypnotic, a Newton's Cradle made out of Chinese gods and testosterone.

"I, uh, I'm not seeing King of Heaven material here," I whispered to Guanyin as the grass trembled from the dome-to-dome contact.

The goddess shrugged. "Guan Yu's actually a good egg. He's forthright and moral to a fault. He's just . . ."

"Kind of Quentin-y," I said, finishing her sentence. She smirked at me.

This time the Great White Planet played referee. "Enough," he said. "Before this interruption I was in the middle of explaining a matter of grave importance."

Guan Yu leaned on top of Quentin's head, the two of them catching their breath. "We're listening," he said.

The Great White Planet muttered to himself under his breath before continuing. "As I was saying, I have bad news regarding the nomination process. After the sudden injection of unorthodoxy by the Shouhushen, a rash of poorly considered ideas took hold in the assembly. Names of candidates began flying left and right. It was utter chaos."

"Stop right there," I said. "My decision to back Guanyin had good reasons behind it. And if you compare her to chaos, we're going to have a problem."

The Great White Planet threw up his hands in concession. "Noted," he snapped. "Yet the fact remains that many gods, including prominent ones like Lei Gong and Zhenyuan, began to question what made a candidate worthy of consideration for the mandate.

Was it raw power like Guan Yu's? Unshakable compassion as displayed by the Lady of Mercy? Or should more old-fashioned constraints like lineage take precedence?"

Quentin frowned. "So they don't want Nezha anymore?"

"No, Prince Nezha is still in the running," the Great White Planet said. "He's arriving with the final nominee right now."

To the side, on a pristine patch of lawn, a ring of fire bloomed. Little gouts of sparks and ash chased each other round and round in a circle, building up speed. The growing flames stayed in their lane, ignoring the rest of the flammable grass.

The inside of the hoop filled with a soft yellow light. As it raised by an underground platform, a young man floated upward into view.

He was stunningly pretty, even for a god. His long hair flowed with silken ribbons, and his exquisite robes were cut tight and sleeveless to reveal lean, well-muscled arms. He had a delicate, troubled expression on his face that twisted his pouty lips with concern.

This guy is totally Yunie's type, I thought.

"Prince Nezha," the Great White Planet said, forgoing any introductions with the rest of us. "Did you bring him?"

"I did," Nezha said in the same smooth tenor that I recognized from over the phone. He reached down below his feet and grabbed something heavy.

A foul smell of brimstone and caged animal filled the air. I heard the metallic jangling of chains. With a grunt, Nezha hoisted another man onto the lawn, bound tightly like a prisoner. The circle of fire closed behind them.

The second arrival was filthy and unshaven, and his bird's nest of hair fell over his eyes. His clothes were rough-spun and stained.

What I had thought were chains were instead strings of iron, baseball-sized prayer beads that looped around his neck and shoulders, trapping his wrists together in front of him.

But despite his stooped posture and mass of bindings, the man still radiated an air of menace that was not only chilling, but familiar. He raised his head. The fine, handsome lines of his face showed through the layers of dirt and scraggly facial hair, and pitch darkness couldn't have masked the gleam in those eyes.

"Behold, the final candidate in the Mandate Challenge," the Great White Planet said bitterly. "The Jade Emperor's nephew, Erlang Shen."

17

"HELLO GENIE," ERLANG SHEN SAID.

I ran forward and kicked him in the groin. I didn't get as much strength into it as I would have liked, but I still managed to elevate him a couple of inches off the ground.

The other gods were slow to react, but I knew better. You couldn't let enemies as dangerous as Erlang Shen get their footing. A word would turn into a sentence would turn into a lie, and then before you knew it you'd have flying demon bombs threatening to eradicate the nearest city. It had happened before.

Erlang Shen doubled over. "I see you're as mild of disposition as ever," he gasped.

I was going to grab his head and knee him in the mouth next, but a pair of burly arms held me back. "Hold on there, child," Guan Yu said. "He's helpless. It wouldn't be right."

That was easy for him to say. Guan Yu hadn't been dicked around by Erlang Shen and his plot to conquer Heaven by using me as a weapon. I cursed Guan Yu's stupid warrior's code of righteousness that prevented me from tearing the traitor god apart limb from limb while he couldn't fight back.

"What is this bullcrap?" Quentin shouted at the Great White Planet.

"I explained everything!" the Great White Planet said. "Were you not listening a moment ago?"

"This is a trick!" I said. I tried to mash my big toe into Erlang Shen's eyeball.

"If it's a trick, then it's being played on me as well," Erlang Shen said as Nezha dragged him backward, farther out of my reach. "Do I really look like I'm the one in control at the moment?"

"Everyone CALM DOWN!" Guanyin yelled.

In this case, "everyone" mostly referred to me. I stopped struggling. Guanyin motioned with her hand at the Great White Planet, indicating that he needed to take another turn speaking.

"As I made clear," he said. "Despite my strident recommendations to the contrary, a number of influential members of the pantheon decided that the best successor to the Jade Emperor would be someone who shared his bloodline. But the Jade Emperor has no children. Erlang Shen is his next closest relation."

"That doesn't make any sense!" I said. "He was going to overthrow Heaven itself! He's a traitor!"

"In the Jade Emperor's absence, the narrative played out a little differently in the minds of the court," the Great White Planet said, making a face at having to relive the memory. "Most of his crimes took place on Earth, far away from their sight. So it was easier for Lei Gong and the others to interpret his actions as a hero's mistake on the way to redemption through the Mandate Challenge. After all, who better to replace the Jade Emperor than someone who'd earnestly tried once before?"

"*Tamade!*" Quentin shouted. "I knew they were stupid and hidebound, but not that stupid!"

"On the contrary, Erlang Shen's backers are feeling very wise indeed." The Great White Planet snorted. "After all, true masters of the Way find wisdom in the counterintuitive and illogical."

I wanted to find these geniuses who thought Erlang Shen's personal journey was more important than Guanyin's record of service. And I wanted to show them with my fists exactly how much I hated them. "The only reason why his crimes aren't such a big deal to the gods is because *we* kept the fight from reaching their doorstep!" I said.

"I know, right?" Erlang Shen said. "I was going to slaughter the other gods like cattle, and now they're praising me for being a visionary! To think that I could have simply waited for my moment to claim the throne. The troubles of being ahead of your time, eh?"

Guan Yu caught my fist from behind again. He had good reflexes for a big guy.

"Look, I'm as surprised as you by this turn of events," Erlang Shen said. "One moment I'm in Diyu having my intestines twirled around a white-hot metal fork as one of the infinite tortures that await family betrayers, and the next I'm being hauled to Earth for my shot at unlimited power. It's very disorienting, so you could be a little more sympathetic to my situation."

"I'll kill you," I said coldly. It was less of a threat and more of me matter-of-factly stating a solution to my current problem. I'd done it once before, and I wouldn't hesitate to do it again.

"You can't," the Great White Planet said. "No lethal harm can come to him while he's in those restraints. And like it or not, he is an official candidate to receive the mandate. He must accompany us to face the challenge if succession is to be legitimate."

I felt like weeping. I had gone through several low points during my career as a demon hunter and then as the Shouhushen, but this was the most I'd ever felt like straight-up quitting. I'd have preferred to march Erlang Shen straight into the assembly of Heaven and let the monster loose. Every god would have seen exactly how wise they were in an instant.

I looked at Guanyin. If someone was going to stop me from declaring war right now, it was her. She'd tried to warn me about the frustrations of dealing with the celestial pantheon, but I hadn't listened.

The goddess was amazingly, astoundingly calm when she should have been more enraged than any of us. She wore her cool, logical face, a Vulcan calculating the most amount of good.

"Well, we're not leaving him here on Earth unsupervised," she said with a final shrug. "He could hurt someone."

And that was it. As if that were the only important thing, preventing harm to dogs and children that wandered too close to Erlang Shen, like he was a sharp stick. *He could take someone's eye out!*

She saw me staring at her. "What?" she said. "I'd rather he be surrounded by a group of us somewhere far away from Earth than keeping him on the same plane as humanity."

Guanyin didn't spare a word for this injustice inflicted upon her. Only others mattered, as usual. I couldn't tell if I loved or despised her for it right now.

"Then Quentin and I are coming with you," I said. "There is no way I'm letting this bastard out of my sight until this business is over and he's back in Hell." I shot a look at the Great White Planet to see if he had any objections that I could summarily overrule. If he did, he held his tongue.

Erlang Shen's throaty chuckle added the punctuation mark to her decision. "Oh, this is going to be fun," he said. "But now that the matter's settled, I have a different question. Why is this uniformed gentleman approaching as if he can see us?"

I turned slowly, keeping an eye on Erlang Shen. He could have told me my own name and I would have treated the statement as a trick.

But sure enough, a security guard was hustling over from across the lawn, on the double. Several people on the sidewalk were watching our motley gathering, whispering and pointing to each other, and at least two were in the middle of uploading video selfies with us in the background. Dawn had turned into morning while we'd been arguing, and the apartment courtyard seemed to have come to life.

An uncomfortable silence passed through the group as the white-shirted guard slowed down at a cautious distance. He began muttering into a shoulder-mounted walkie-talkie as he approached.

"What happened to our spell-cloaking?" I said.

"Ah! It's possible I broke its effectiveness when I summoned my weapon through the boundaries," Guan Yu declared, without a hint of shame for his actions. "The Green Dragon Crescent Blade is mighty indeed."

If I pushed on my eyes any harder they were going to pop out the back of my head. "So . . . we were visible this entire time."

"I also could have broken the concealment," Nezha added in a helpful voice. "I did travel from the waiting room of Hell directly to Earth."

Erlang Shen threw his head back and howled with laughter. He nearly toppled over before Nezha caught him by the chains and righted him.

The guard was close enough to hear the squawking of his radio. "Central, we have a possible four-eighty-two," he whispered into his shoulder. As he looked up, his expression changed from suspicion into a neutral smile.

"Hi folks," he said. "Do you care to explain—"

"*Family visit*," I said.

"*Student film*," Quentin said at the exact same time.

The guard glanced back and forth between us. I put up a finger to say *let me handle this*. Quentin crossed his arms in a huff. He liked being the one to make up stories.

"A student film, about a family visit," I said. "That's why some of us are dressed weird."

"And who is us, exactly?" the guard said.

"Granddad," I said, grabbing the Great White Planet and shoving him forward. The old god looked supremely offended at my rough treatment, but it wasn't like he could dock me personal points on the mandate.

"My uncle from the country," I said, pointing at Guan Yu, whose reflexive beard-stroking added a fitting air. I waved at Nezha holding up Erlang Shen. "My cousins. Also from the country."

Erlang Shen snickered at my lack of improv skills, but Nezha gave me an earnest thumbs-up of encouragement.

"And, uh, my siblings," I said for Quentin and Guanyin combined. Anyone who was dressed in modern clothing was not from the country and Guanyin almost always blended in flawlessly. "They're helping with a movie I'm making about . . . the dichotomy between traditional Asian values and modern sensibilities. Hence the fashion divide."

The guard nodded in understanding. "Well, thank you for that explanation," he said. "You're all detained until the police get here." He pulled out a pencil and notepad.

"I said it was a student film! You can't outlaw a student film!"

The guard pointed at Guan Yu with the eraser end. "He's carrying a weapon. We have strict rules for props and cosplay around campus. Not to mention there's a giant hole in the lawn."

"That hole," I sputtered, "is CGI."

"Don't even think about running, unless you want this upgraded to felony vandalism. I need each of your names. You can start with 'Granddad' if you want."

A giant paw came down on my shoulder. "I can see you're in distress, Shouhushen," Guan Yu said. "Allow me to assist!"

The guard was startled by the sudden motion of Guan Yu's great bulk. "Sir, step back now," he said. The guard dropped his writing implements and reached behind his waist for possibly pepper spray, a Taser, or, god forbid, a gun.

"Forget!" Guan Yu bellowed. A tiny arc of lightning sprouted from his free hand and crawled over the stunned guard's skull, knocking his cap off and leaving a trail of soot over his bald head. The poor man's eyes rolled toward the sky, and he collapsed on the grass.

"There," Guan Yu said proudly. "He won't remember the last month or so."

"A month?" I shrieked. Guanyin's work on Ax had been surgical down to the second.

"Well, hopefully that long," Guan Yu said. "I admit I'm a little rusty."

A boy and a girl sitting on a bench across the courtyard had sprung to their feet and were yelling in approval of what they'd seen. They might not have understood exactly what had happened, but they appreciated figures of authority getting dunked on. Their followers *had* to see this.

I gestured toward our audience. "You—you Earth noobs understand why this situation is bad, right?"

"Of course!" Nezha said brightly. "The position of Shouhushen requires a delicate balance of action and discretion. Unguided revelations about the spiritual world to mundane humans are not only embarrassing, but potentially very dangerous."

He pointed his finger at the couple. "*Forget!*"

A solid beam shot from his hand. It flew across the lawn and knocked the boy clean off his feet, sending him tumbling backward over the bench to the ground. The girl stared at the empty space he no longer occupied, and screamed.

I had to admit I was impressed by Nezha's aim. But for all his precision, he was just as oblivious as Guan Yu.

"So . . ." Guanyin said to me as her competitors for the mandate gleefully chucked spells left and right, the cries of terrified people filling the air. "It felt like any muscle I moved would have made the situation worse."

A *forget* spell the size of a grapefruit whizzed by my head, fluttering my hair.

"Sorry," Quentin called out. "Trying to get in on this action."

"Can we just go?" I said weakly. "Through the rift or whatever? I can only deal with so much. I don't think I want to be on this plane of existence right now."

Guanyin patted my shoulder. "Maybe that's for the best." She snapped her fingers. "Hey! Train's leaving the station!"

The gods got their last few licks in with their technically harmless spells. The lawn was littered with slumbering people, like there'd been a gas leak. This was a catastrophic break in the masquerade that Heaven nominally tried to maintain.

"Is there a category for subtlety?" I muttered to the Great White Planet. "Because if there is, I hope you're taking notes."

"Don't tell me how to do my job," he said. "But yes, there is. Despite what you may think, I'm not oblivious to your champion's talents."

■ ■ ■

Guanyin led us into the pool area. Backtracking along Ao Guang's route to Earth meant ignoring the chemical levels and jumping in.

"Wait," I said, barring the entrance with my arm and causing a pileup behind me. "We shouldn't be letting Erlang Shen near water."

I couldn't see him roll his eyes, but I knew he was doing it. "These wouldn't be very good restraints if they let me use my godly powers," he said. "Though the fact that our journey begins with my personal element means the Universe favors me as the eventual victor."

The Great White Planet was actually writing that BS down in his notebook. "Seriously?" I yelled at him. "He gets points for a coincidence?"

"There are no coincidences when it comes to a Mandate Challenge," the Great White Planet said. He tucked the notebook back into his robes. "And every little action counts. I have to go first so that I can judge your entries from the other side." He smoothed down his robes and slid into the water feet first with nary a disturbance to the surface. As soon as he was completely under, he vanished like cotton candy.

I was starting to grow suspicious of our judge's fairness, but no one else was bothered. "You heard the man," Guanyin said. She smiled at me before diving in with the grace of a striking cormorant.

I couldn't help but feel that prior to our little pep talk last night, the old Guanyin would have waited for the rest of us to go in front of her, shepherding each god through like she was loading a peewee hockey team into a minivan. New Guanyin led the way and didn't wait for slowpokes. It was a subtle difference, but one that made me immensely happy.

"She's going to get points deducted for that," Erlang Shen commented. He seemed to know more about the mandate process than the rest of us, which only made my alarm bells ring louder. "It's discourteous to push your way to the front of the—"

I smashed my palm into Erlang Shen's face, shoving him into the pool so that he flopped in without dignity.

Quentin and Guan Yu chuckled. Nezha gave me a worried look and jumped in after Erlang Shen.

Guan Yu whapped Quentin hard in the solar plexus. "Splash check!" he roared. He leaped into the air, not toward the water, but the diving board. The springy plank bowed to the breaking point under his weight and propelled him skyward, reaching half the height of the surrounding buildings. At his apex, he curled into a cannonball and plummeted into the deep end.

The splash he made was like a depth charge. Quentin threw up a casual barrier spell to keep us dry as the water rained down. I was surprised there was any liquid left in the pool.

I expected Quentin to answer the challenge immediately with some flashy attempt to best Guan Yu, perhaps climbing the stairs to a nearby roof and cliff-diving in that way. But instead of following his friend, he paused.

We were alone, just the two of us. It was a good opportunity to talk about whatever we wanted.

"I'm about to be the first human being to visit a different dimension," I said. "I feel like this is a momentous occasion. I'm like an astronaut."

Apparently what I wanted was to joke around like normal. It felt like ages since we'd spoken without being mad. My mother had gone to the hospital less than a week ago. Distance from Quentin had messed up my sense of time.

He grimaced. "Yeah, but astronauts don't have to fight the living embodiment of their deepest personal terror in order to get to outer space."

My jaw dropped. "*That's* what's required to cross into another plane?"

"It's either that or voluntarily give up a portion of your soul," he said, scratching the back of his head. "The Screaming Hand forces you to choose."

I stared at him. He maintained a solemn expression for as long as he could before he cracked and burst into a chuckle. "I'm sorry," he said. "I was messing with you. That was mean."

I was both pissed off and secretly delighted that he wasn't stonewalling me. Why couldn't it stay like this forever, us messing with each other? Why did we have to trade in a perfectly good compact relationship for a larger model with more baggage? In hindsight, I would have taken a million Quentins dive-bombing my bedroom window if it meant property destruction was our biggest problem.

"But in all seriousness," he said. "Blissful Planes are weird. They're like certain spots on Earth, only exaggerated and simplified at the same time. Things go from geographic to conceptual as you travel through them. Your head could go a little fuzzy."

"Thanks for letting me know," I said. I meant it without sarcasm. Mind trips seemed to be the theme of this weekend.

Quentin wasn't done though. "Genie, we should talk," he said. "I'm afraid of what'll happen if we don't."

So was I. I knew exactly what would happen if we couldn't figure ourselves out. I'd witnessed the slow-motion crash that was my parents, and Quentin and I were falling into the exact same pattern. Starting out angry and finding new reasons to stay angry. Waiting for things to get better instead of making them better. Letting an outside event become a wedge between us.

I'd had the ultimate "What Not to Do in a Relationship" guide in front of me for years, and I still couldn't figure a way out of this trap. For all I condescended toward my parents, I was no better at opening up to the boy I—

I shook my head. "We've lingered too long," I said. "Let's go. The others are waiting."

Quentin's disappointment was palpable. I felt the leaden weight of it on my shoulders as I escaped through the portal to another dimension.

18

TRAVELING TO ANOTHER PLANE OF EXISTENCE TASTED LIKE cyan. It smelled like a stubbed toe. I detected notes of lighthouse, iambic pentameter, and general relativity.

I stumbled forward as if I'd stepped off a moving walkway too quickly. The first part of me to regain consciousness was my skin. It itched and burned all over.

A heavy object collided with my back and threw me to the ground. My hands found fistfuls of dirt. I crawled around in circles and blinked furiously.

Someone grabbed me by the armpits and hoisted me to my feet. It was Guanyin. "What happened?" I yelled, dizzy from the journey. If we had even made a journey. "Are we in the right place?"

"We're in the right realm of existence," Guanyin said, pointing me by the shoulders. "A dimension that's neither Heaven, Hell, nor Earth."

As my vision came back, I saw we were standing in the middle of a scrubby desert that stretched all the way to the horizon. The pool was nowhere to be found, and my clothes were dry.

"Welcome to the Blissful Planes," Quentin said as he dusted

himself off. I assumed he was what knocked into me from behind when I didn't get out of the way fast enough.

The Blissful Planes looked like Utah. The hard-packed sand around us was littered with striated orange monoliths of stone. The nearest ones looked like Earthly buttes and karsts, but farther in the distance they took strange, loopy, cursive forms, like the terrain had been designed by Dr. Seuss. I did not want to walk too far in that direction. It was likely going to screw my mind up with non-Euclidean geometry. I'd read enough cosmic horror fiction to guess.

Looking upward confirmed the weirdness. I could see like it was daytime, but there was no light source to be found. And the sky was pink. Not pink as in sunrise watercolors, but pink as in solid salmon across the board.

"I think this is a touch too whimsical for me," I said, feeling queasy. I glanced back in the direction it felt like we'd come and saw an irregular patch of warm yellow glow hovering at eye level in the air, like a lens flare. I assumed it marked the terminus of the portal we'd taken.

"It's not easy for human brains to process unearthly surroundings," Guanyin said, echoing Quentin from earlier. "Do you want to go back?"

I shook my head. Not this soon into the challenge. I looked for the rest of the traveling party. They stood scattered in a loose group, groaning from the rough ride.

"Well, that was certainly uncategorizable," the Great White Planet muttered. He took deep breaths as he leaned heavily on his staff. "I hadn't realized that Ao Guang had torn such a crude rift to Earth."

"If this realm is where he fought the Yin Mo, he would have been at a severe disadvantage," Erlang Shen said. He sniffed the air. "His forces are aquatic in nature. This place is as dry as a bone."

The traitor god jangled his chains. "Speaking of which, can I have some water? I haven't had a drink since Hell."

"Make it yourself," I snapped.

"I can't *make* it," he said, annoyed. "On Earth I was drawing on the abundance of liquid in my surroundings. I'm only asking for a mouthful."

"Yeah, right, so you can craft a shank or a lockpick?" I said. "We don't have any water to begin with. Now shut up before I shove your head down your own neck."

"If you did, at least this infernal beard might stop itching," he muttered. He tried to scrape his chin with his shoulder. "I don't know how Guan Yu manages it."

At least some of us remembered we were in this dimension for reasons other than chit-chatting. Nezha stepped in front of the group and heroically gazed into the distance.

"Behold! I sense the demonic qi that plagues Heaven on this realm. . . ." He operatically swept his arm toward the funkier-looking rock formations. "In *that* direction."

His statement was for the benefit of the Great White Planet, who already had his judging notebook out. The old god gave a little shake of his head. Apparently that was too much of a gimme to be worth anything.

"I've got a better way to find our enemy with more specificity," Erlang Shen said, making Nezha scowl. "Genie can do it."

The gods turned to me. "She has true sight," Erlang Shen explained to the others who hadn't known me for long. "Finding a powerful source of demon energy would be a snap for her."

It was technically true, but hearing him mansplain my own abilities made me want to claw my eyes out from sheer spite. *"Hey!"* I yelled at the Great White Planet, who was scribbling away. "Do *not* give him points for that!"

"He thought of the idea," the old man said without looking up from his writing. "And he's why you're here to begin with. You and the Monkey King are neutral parties. Guanyin doesn't automatically receive the benefit of any good you do, nor does Guan Yu from Sun Wukong."

My temper flared at him, for boosting Erlang Shen and also for noticing the all-too-real split between me and Quentin. "Genie," Guanyin said, sensing my blood heating up. "It's okay. You helping us out will only be a good thing in the long run."

"Fine," I sulked. I went over to where Nezha was standing, and he got out of my way before I shouldered him aside. I faced the direction where the landscape got weirder and held my fingers to my temple.

And shrieked.

The purple light that bombarded my eyes was like a flashbang going off in a dark room. I fell on my rear in surprise and tried to press the sting out of my retinas.

"Yaoguai!" I shouted. "They're right there!"

"Where?" Quentin said.

"Everywhere!"

The area had looked clear and pristine when we'd arrived, untouched by any living presence. But the moment I'd had true sight on revealed that less than a hundred yards away, the landscape was absolutely covered with the telltale purple glow of demon qi.

Nezha tried tilting his head. "I don't see any yaoguai."

I knew what I saw. Less than a hundred yards away, there were so many sources of demonic energy that they blended together in a Pointillist mass of light. And they were shining stronger than any of the monsters I'd fought on Earth.

"I can settle this," Guan Yu said. He stepped forward and raised his halberd. It quickly started to glow brighter and brighter. My horror truly sunk in once I realized he was doing it on purpose.

"Foul creatures!" he roared at the empty space, waving his luminescent weapon like a road flare. "If you are out there, be warned that you stand in the presence of Heavenly gods, as well as your mortal enemies the Shouhushen and Sun Wukong, who each have slain scores of your kind in the past! You would do well to consider the circumstances before making any aggressive maneuvers! Now show your ugly faces, cowards!"

There was a moment where nothing happened. And then, as if they'd taken Guan Yu's advice to heart and carefully tallied our numbers and strength, the yaoguai revealed themselves.

Powerful individual cloaking spells shimmered and melted away. Irregular shapes unfurled and stretched to their full height. I saw animal limbs and bird talons and tree boughs waving ominously at us.

Yaoguai. Hundreds of them—maybe a thousand.

And not just any garden variety. These were heavies. Many were bigger than Yellow-Toothed Elephant or radiated the magical power of the Six-Eared Macaque. Or both. The yaoguai of the Blessed Planes belonged on a different level than the ones I babysat in the forest. Those demons were high school. *These* demons were NCAA with options to go pro.

And with their concealment magic, they'd caught us in a perfect ambush. We'd blundered into an army of the unseen. The Yin Mo.

Because there were so many yaoguai, and because a lot of them had so many eyes, I could nearly hear them blink in unison. They stared at our numbers, verifying how outmatched we were. Gods or not, we were so far up the creek we could have drunk from the source.

Their faces twisted open to reveal glistening fangs and ravenous tongues. A howl went up through the demons' ranks, and the ones in front began a measured jog at us, the kind that turned into a full-out charge.

Guan Yu would not be beaten to the punch. "Battle commences!" he said with glee. He took off for the opposing horde by himself.

"Tactical genius, huh?" I yelled at Quentin over the noise of the demons' animalistic baying.

"Quit turning this into a contest!" he snapped at me, before running off to help his friend.

Bad air between us or not, I had to go prevent my boyfriend from being killed. I joined Quentin and Guan Yu in their charge. We didn't want to receive the attack flat-footed.

Nezha fell in beside me. "Uh, Erlang Shen?" I yelled, trying to remind him that we had a prisoner that needed watching. I knew Guanyin had stayed behind, but I wanted at least two gods on him at all times. The Great White Planet didn't count.

"He can't keep up in those restraints," Nezha said happily, completely missing my point. "He'll have to miss out on the glory!"

I was going to kill these idiots, assuming the yaoguai didn't beat me to it. It was too late to go back. The tsunami of demons made our little god squad look like surfers paddling into a hurricane.

While the vanguard of burliest yaoguai came straight at us, maintaining eye contact and hurling threats at the top of their lungs as they came closer, the rest went for the left and right as fast as they could, trying to outflank us, trailing streams of black blood and ooze in their wake. With their numbers they could have surrounded us almost immediately, but they hobbled and limped along without trying to shut the jaws of their trap.

Something didn't add up. And I had near zero time to figure out what. I zoomed in on the nearest demon stragglers.

They were injured. In some cases, mutilated, slashed up by sharp blades just like Ao Guang and his spirit soldiers. I hadn't noticed it earlier due to the wonky shapes that yaoguai came in, but these demons already had their asses kicked by the same force that attacked the army of Heaven.

They weren't the Yin Mo. They were fleeing the Yin Mo.

"Stop!" I screamed as I sprinted ahead of my group, my lengthening legs giving me the speed advantage. "Everyone stop!" I increased in size as I ran, planning to become a mountain in the middle of the battlefield that would keep the opposing forces apart.

That would have been cool and impressive and gotten everyone to listen to me right away. Instead, I tripped like a clown.

Growing while running threw off my center of balance, and I faceplanted in the dust, tumbling head over heels from the momentum of my still-increasing mass. I heard terrified screams from the yaoguai who might have thought I was trying to roll over them.

Luckily I skidded to a spread-eagled halt before I turned anyone into paste. Out of the corner of my eye I saw that Quentin and the gods had stopped charging, possibly out of sheer embarrassment for me. It was a good thing phones weren't common with this crowd. On Earth I would have been turned into a meme before I could catch my breath.

"Okay," I said, my voice booming over the alien landscape. "Everyone just give me a second here."

The good thing about being this size was that compliance was immediate. Not a peep came from anyone as I got to my truck-sized feet and cleared the debris from my clothes. What appeared to me as pebbles lodged in my waistband were more like boulders that crashed to the ground, sowing more fear in my audience.

"Sorry!" I said. "Not trying to hurt anyone—I'm coming down, okay?"

The yaoguai and gods gave me plenty of space as I reduced to my normal size. They were clearly more afraid of my incompetence and lack of control than anything else, but whatever. I got the effect I wanted.

"Who's your leader?" I said to the demons. "Who'll speak for you?"

I saw the sea of demons part ways around one of the toughest-looking warriors, who was pretty much a straight-up werewolf with no extra bits. He glared at me with suspicion, his lips curling to reveal dagger-like fangs. His muscles ripped under a hide that was scarred and pitted from countless fights.

But as I approached the gray-furred beast, he held out his hand in what I thought was a strange palm-up salute. He got down onto his knees and pressed the back of his knuckles to the earth. At my look of confusion he pointed to the dirt in front of him.

There was a moving speck on the dusty ground. I had to get down on my hands and knees to make out the features of a thumbnail-sized ant yaoguai.

For his size, the little guy was pretty brave. The tiny demon stared at me, only inches from my nose, pure defiance in his compound eyes. Four of his arms were crossed in front of his thorax.

"Why did you stop?" the yaoguai asked in a wizened, disproportionately deep voice. He could have narrated a nature documentary about himself.

"Why did you start?" I said.

One of his antennas served as an eyebrow, raising slightly into the air. Reluctantly, he gave up his information.

"We . . . had heard this place contained a rift that would let us escape this plane," he said. "But tears in the fabric of reality are inherently unstable. We weren't sure the rumor was true until you arrived. Once you and the gods made your presence known, we had to act quickly or lose our chance."

"You're not here to fight, are you?" I said. "You're running from the Yin Mo."

Tiny snorted, which shouldn't have been possible without a nose. "Several of us were here to fight. We thought the gods were coming to close our one way out, so our vanguard was willing to sacrifice themselves to hold it open. Our bravest and strongest were prepared to die so the rest could make it to safety."

I glanced around. The wounded demons leaned on one another for support, or simply gave up and sat on the ground in miserable huddles. Their earlier ferocity had been born of desperation. They were scared and broken, much like the remnants of Ao Guang's army.

This was a pivotal moment. I swallowed my hesitation. "Maybe we can work something out," I said. "Do you know who I am?"

Tiny was cautious. "Someone powerful and dangerously clumsy?"

Okay, ouch. "I'm the Shouhushen of California on Earth. There might be a way to get you off this plane to safety *if* you do exactly what I say."

Both of his antenna swung wildly in the air, ruining his poker face. "Why—why would Heaven make that offer?" he said.

"It wouldn't. *I* would."

Tiny's mandibles stretched open and shut with a click. He beckoned Clean Werewolf over. The large demon leaned down so his ant boss could whisper in his ear. The wolf's eyes went wide with shock before he flinched, likely from Tiny yelling at him not to give too much away.

Wolf Guy straightened up and disappeared into the crowd with a sense of purpose. It made me think that he was passing the message along to other trusted lieutenants, so that frenzied excitement wouldn't overcome the crowd. If that was true, then I had to hand it to Tiny. He was a pretty good leader.

Wait a second, I thought. *Tiny's a "she." Ants are led by queens.*

The little yaoguai, who definitely had the proportions and wings of a pre-laying queen now that I remembered my bio, regained her composure. "How do we know we can trust you?" she asked. "We have no assurances."

Maybe the fact that I haven't squished you already, huh? I wanted to retort. But I held my tongue. I had to remember that demons weren't used to kindness. Especially not from me.

Shrink, I said to myself.

The world around me grew bigger, grains of sand becoming pebbles, rocks becoming boulders, and the yaoguai surrounding us turning so large that I could hardly tell them apart against the backdrop of the sky. I stood up, no longer needing to crouch to see the ant.

Tiny, at eye level, turned out to be pretty gross. Her carapace was covered in sticky hairs, and her body twitched constantly. But despite her alien appearance at this scale, she seemed astonished that I'd willingly join her down in the dust.

"Well then," I said in a squeaky, mouse-lung voice. "I guess we'll have to negotiate like equals."

19

THANKFULLY TINY RECOGNIZED MY GESTURE OF SHRINKING AS just that—a gesture. I was allowed to resume my normal size for our peace talks. Since we had to stand around like jerks without furniture, it felt rather like a middle school dance where everyone clumped in opposite corners and occasionally sent ambassadors to neutral ground in order to discuss who liked whom.

Sun Wukong, the Goddess of Mercy, and the Shouhushen represented our side, though Quentin wasn't doing much other than trading glares with the wolf bodyguard accompanying Tiny. The two snarled and flexed at each other in a contest of macho posturing while the rest of us worked.

"I don't understand," the leader of the yaoguai said. "The Earth end of the rift is in a *what*?"

"It's like a . . . a nursery for grown-up children," Guanyin said, doing her best to describe the college experience in a way the demon would understand.

"You can't eat them," I said.

Tiny gave me a look like I was being a condescending fool. "I assumed that was implicit in any bargain we struck."

"Well, I'm making it explicit. No human consumption. Don't touch anyone or anything."

"You're going to have to provide your own concealment," Guanyin said. "There's too many of you for me to hide at the same time."

"Shouldn't be a problem," Tiny said. "We got the drop on you lot, didn't we?"

Part of me was really annoyed with the demon's sass, and part of me liked the hell out of her attitude. Between her and Yunie, maybe I had an affinity for feisty small things.

"Look, the forces under my command are all powerful enough to restrain our hunger and stay invisible to the human eye," the ant queen said. "But not indefinitely. Without a strong enough divine presence on Earth, this truce of ours could go sideways fast."

She pointed at the other gods who'd been so eager to spill demon blood. "Deny it all you want, but I know that if there's one slipup on Earth, the wrath of Heaven'll come down on my people no matter who's to blame. I'm as worried for their safety as you are for yours."

There was a grim pause. She wasn't wrong.

"Then we'll all simply have to hope there aren't any slipups," Guanyin said.

■ ■ ■

Before we set the plan into motion, Guanyin popped back through the portal to Earth, both to use herself as a guinea pig to make sure the rift would hold, and to make sure the other side was as clear and safe as it could be. Perhaps she'd set up a ruse and tent Ji-Hyun's entire apartment complex for fumigation.

She was gone long enough for me to get worried, but then she reappeared through the warm glowing rift, leaping back into this plane. She gave Tiny as enthusiastic a thumbs-up as could be warranted in this situation. The first of the demons, the most seriously wounded, went through the portal under Guanyin's watchful eye. It was nothing as dramatic as jumping into a pool. Each demon stepped into the light and disappeared. That was it.

I stood some ways off, next to the Great White Planet, who scribbled in his notes. "She'd better be getting a metric crapton of points for this," I said.

"Not as many as you're hoping for," he said. "If these yaoguai aren't the threat that beat Ao Guang and forced the Mandate Challenge, then helping them saves us a costly fight. But it doesn't count as a victory. The biggest 'crapton' of points will go to whoever lands the killing blow on the Yin Mo."

Screw you, old man, I thought. It seemed like Guanyin had to do twice as much for half the gain in this quest.

I mean, we were witnessing a miracle here: a queue of yaoguai snaking away into the distance. Tiny did indeed have a crew of trusted helpers. Her network spread the news of what was happening, and after letting the crowd have a moment to celebrate, they quickly tamped down the joy and hustled the mass of demons into a formation resembling a line. Stations were established at regular intervals to keep everyone in order.

Yaoguai. Lining up. I thought I'd never see the day.

"They're going to betray you, you know," Erlang Shen said.

Behind me was the group of sulky boys who hadn't gotten to throw down like they'd wanted. Erlang Shen was lucky he was sitting on the ground, or else he would have been close enough for me to club him across the face like I was inclined.

"Your original gang that you broke out of Diyu hasn't," I said.

He looked astonished, then amused. "You let them *live?*" Erlang Shen said. "That's rich. Demons can't be trusted or redeemed. As soon as the hunger for human flesh takes hold of them again, they'll revert back to snarling beasts. No one can escape their nature."

"Shows how much you know," I said. "They're living quiet lives in the forest now. The Californian Dream of homeownership. Growing wolfberries behind white picket fences." Sure, there was a minor insurrection now and again, but I wasn't going to admit that in front of him.

"I hope you're right, for your sake," he said with a shrug. "I'm assuming whatever tenuous little peace you've arranged requires your constant presence. And if you haven't noticed, the Shouhushen, the Lady of Mercy, and the Monkey King are here now, in this godforsaken in-between place, away from Earth. An opportunity for misbehavior now that the watchdogs are gone."

I couldn't think of a good retort. I'd seen what college kids did away from their parents. Hell, Yunie and I were supposed to be getting up to trouble this weekend. An uncomfortable sense of urgency gathered in the pit of my stomach. I wondered if Quentin's alarm earrings that detected dangerous proximity between humans and yaoguai got reception in this realm of existence.

Don't let Erlang Shen get in your head, I thought to myself. *Everything will be fine. Guanyin will make it so.*

Quentin could have backed me up, if he and Guan Yu hadn't bailed several minutes ago to run off and play dodgeball with chunks of sandstone the size of hay bales. It annoyed me that Quentin couldn't preserve some level of solemnity for the monumental task that Guanyin and I were performing, and it annoyed me that I was annoyed with him. I still couldn't master my feelings and reactions when it came to him, not even with the benefit of experience.

Nezha snapped me out of my reverie. "I have to say, you were a sight to behold back there."

"What are you talking about?" I said. My vision was bleary and I needed more coffee.

"When you grew to such a mighty size," Nezha said enthusiastically. "It was magnificent. It reminded me of long ago, when you tussled with the armies of Heaven. I was part of those forces."

Oh yeah. Sun Wukong and the Ruyi Jingu Bang's first rampage. "Look, I gotta tell you, people keep bringing that up, and I don't remember." To me, it was an embarrassing baby story, nothing more.

"That's a shame," Nezha said. "You personally thrashed me pretty soundly in single combat, so I was hoping that you'd recognize me. Here, does this help?"

He struck a pose as if to fend off a blow from above and made a wide-eyed face of abject terror. A citizen about to get stomped on by Godzilla. "There," he said. "That's what I must have looked like to you at the time."

Okay, that was kind of funny. Nezha had an easy, humble charm about him that, along with his pretty-boy looks and flawless posture, made him resemble a Regency suitor. The most eligible bachelor in Fitzfordshire.

"I guess I'm pretty scary when I grow to that size," I said.

"Oh, that's not even your ultimate battle form," Nezha said. "The most powerful shape that Sun Wukong took that day was that of a three-headed monster the size of a mountain, with six arms, each pair of hands wielding a Ruyi Jingu Bang of its own. That's what scared Heaven more than anything. That a weapon of infinite power could be suddenly tripled."

This was confusing. I'd never tried to get legal rulings on my exact power set. I'd always chalked up any inconsistencies in the legends to mistakes on the part of whoever had written them down.

"How were there three of me while there was only one of Sun Wukong?" I said. "I thought I was dependent on him for any duplication tricks, like when he makes hair clones of us."

Nezha shook his head. "Those other two of you weren't mere clones in this case. They were you, indistinguishable and matching in strength. None of us had seen such a feat. My father, the Pagoda-Bearing General, and I theorized for days after the battle. Our best guess was that the trio of you formed a gestalt consciousness that could act independently while experiencing three separate viewpoints at once."

That was a bit much for me to handle while I was watching a conga line of demons disappear through a portal under a bright pink sky in an alternate dimension. I just sort of swayed in response.

"My father could explain it better," Nezha said eagerly. "I would love to introduce you to him sometime. We could help you gain a greater understanding of your capabilities—"

"Uh-*ohhhh*," Erlang Shen interrupted in a singsong voice, like a child who'd spilled his milk on purpose. "Someone's got a crush."

Heads turned toward him.

"What?" Erlang Shen said. "He thought about you constantly, and he wants you to meet his parents. That sounds like a crush to me.

"I think you've got an in," he said to Nezha. "She's got a predilection for anyone who can help her grow stronger."

Nezha turned bright red and stomped off to join Quentin and Guan Yu. I felt bad for the poor young god. "Do you have to be so insufferable all the time?" I snapped at Erlang Shen.

"You don't get to tell me how I talk to my friends," he scoffed.

I gave him a skeptical frown. So far he'd done nothing but antagonize the other deities.

"That's right," Erlang Shen said. "Nezha's my friend. He picked me up from jail. Who else but a true friend would do that? You forget that I had a life in Heaven before our little escapade on Earth. I was extremely popular in the celestial pantheon.

"For example," he said, pointing with his chin. "That one next to you was my mentor for centuries."

The Great White Planet froze, his pen never completing its journey to the next line in his book. I felt the river of blood in my veins reverse course to flow uphill. I'd been played for a sucker.

"What, the old man never told you?" Erlang Shen said to me. "The so-called impartial judge of the gods used to tutor me in a great many subjects. History, policy, debate. Why, one might have assumed he was grooming me for leadership of Heaven."

My hands floated upward of their own accord, seeking to throttle the Great White Planet. "You son of a—I *knew* you were biased! You set this whole thing up to free Erlang Shen and make him the winner!"

"*I did no such thing!*"

The pen snapped in the Great White Planet's hand, and he threw the shards to the ground. He faced me with ink on his fingers and tears in his eyes. "I did no such thing! I argued my heart out to keep the traitor in Diyu where he belonged!"

I slapped true sight on to flood them both like an interrogation lamp. "Yeah? Convince me!"

"He's telling the truth," Erlang Shen said. "Despite our past, no one hates me more than my former *sifu*. You should have seen the look in his eyes when he learned that I'd turned on the Jade Emperor. He advocated for the harshest possible sentencing in Hell. He despises the fact that I'm here now."

"You betrayed more than your uncle!" the Great White Planet cried. "You betrayed my teaching and my trust! And for what? Power that could have been yours anyway, but for your rashness and your hate!?"

If either of them had been lying under my true sight, bubbles of molten metal would have poured from their mouths. The ability worked on gods. But their lips were clean. The Great White Planet wasn't tilting the scales in favor of Erlang Shen. And the two of them really did have a history full of pain and anguish.

A few minutes ago I would have done anything to get Erlang Shen to shut up. Dredging up the past seemed to do the trick. I could tell the genuine disappointment and disgust of his former mentor had seeped through Erlang Shen's armor. The two of them were silent for a long time.

Guanyin came over. She noticed the atmosphere and wisely ignored the other gods. "Genie, can I speak to you for a moment?"

I walked off with her toward the portal, glad to get some distance from this giant pile of baggage. We watched the yaoguai, erstwhile enemies, vanish through the rift in an orderly fashion instead of trying to tear our throats out.

"I need to tell you a couple of things," Guanyin said. "The first is that I am so, so proud of you."

Hearing that from *my* personal divine mentor after what I'd witnessed between Erlang Shen and the Great White Planet was like eating a mouthful of sugar after sucking on a lemon. The sweetness in contrast was almost too much.

"That was a fine display of leadership with the yaoguai," Guanyin said. "You took control of the situation and snatched peace from the jaws of disaster. You've grown and adapted so much."

My heart wanted to burst out of my chest. As a certified teacher's pet and academic brown-noser, I was a connoisseur of praise from authority figures. This was the best vintage I'd ever tasted.

"I averted bloodshed!" I said. "That's like *your* move!"

"I know, right?" Guanyin said. "You're doing amazing, and I really mean that. The other thing I wanted to tell you is that I have to drop out of the Mandate Challenge."

20

THE SKIES FELL OUT OF THEIR MOORINGS. THE SEAS TURNED black, Guanyin had brought the end times.

My face didn't show it, nor did hers. The two of us had cemented our expressions to the point where it looked like we were having a funny, lighthearted conversation, like women in stock photos. All we needed were some salads.

"You are the one person whose ass I wouldn't kick for saying that," I said. "In fact, I'm not sure I'm *not* about to kick your ass for saying that."

"Genie, look around you. Half of these yaoguai are a hair away from death and will require major healing magic. Earth is about to have more spirits in it than have been seen in a millennium. The other end of this rift is packed full of some of the least aware human beings I've ever walked amongst."

She let out a measured breath. "The ant was right. It's going to take a divine presence on Earth to handle this situation properly. Our agreement with the yaoguai doesn't mean we get to put them out of sight and out of mind. They need care and attention. I have to stay with them for who knows how long, which means dropping out of the Mandate Challenge."

Okay. This was a problem to solve. That's what Guanyin was posing to me. A farmer was trying to cross a river with a fox, a chicken, and a bag of grain. I simply needed to be good enough, fast enough right now. Shouhushen my ass off.

"No big deal," I said, psyching myself up. "Quentin and I can go back while you stick with the group."

"Genie, I don't know if you, me, and Quentin *combined* can deal with this cleanly. For Heaven's sake, it's hard enough for me to keep this portal open right now. If it closes while someone's partway through, it's going to snap them in half."

I wrung my hands out, trying to stay loose and keep my brain oxygenated. "Okay," I said. "This is bound to be simpler than it appears. I can fix this."

"No Genie, you can't. Neither can I, or Quentin, or any of the gods here. This is a simple matter of priorities. If we want to save lives, then I have to take the hit."

My efforts to breathe ground to a stop, leaving nothing but tightness in my lungs. I'd been so wary of a god betraying me, and it turned out to be Guanyin.

In mummified silence my eyes fell on the portal. Werewolf was next to it, but instead of jumping through himself he spent a moment nuzzling the sleek, long-lashed fox whose turn it was. He whispered goodbye in its ear and dutifully hustled back to his guard post farther down the line.

The fox caught me looking and blushed through its fur. It gave me a timid wave of its paw before vanishing through the gate.

I opened my mouth, needing to count through the steps that made up speech. "Why is it always you?" I choked. I wanted to pound my clenched fists against her chest. I wished I was in my childhood bedroom so I could scream my lungs out with the right context. "Why do you always have to be the one making the sacrifice?"

"Because that's what stepping up and taking charge truly means," Guanyin said gently. "This is the only lesson I ever needed to teach you. You can't win every battle, no matter how powerful or clever or perfect you are."

She laid her arm over my shoulders and pulled me in close, providing a screen for my sniffling. "Sometimes you just have to take your losses," she said.

She was trying to soften the blow by comparing this to a single meaningless game. But in my mind, the analogy didn't work. We weren't surrendering a game, we were voluntarily forfeiting the whole season. We were giving up an entire future.

I couldn't process this. Backing down was not how I operated. The contradiction threatened to turn me into dust.

I was so distraught, in fact, that it took me a while to notice the faint sound of screaming in the distance.

21

SOME OF THE YAOGUAI, THE ONES WHO RESEMBLED EASILY spooked prey species, whipped around to look back down the line. I heard it again. There were definitely screams, coming in louder and longer.

"Go find out what that is," Guanyin said to me, forcing calmness into her voice. "I have to stay here and keep the portal stable." She turned to the yaoguai. "Eyes forward and keep moving!"

I jogged down the column and snapped my fingers at the other gods. They'd all heard the noise with their sharpened senses. The horsing around was over, and any lingering feuds had to be set aside. Quentin, Guan Yu, and Nezha with Erlang Shen in tow formed a new battle line next to me. The Great White Planet followed behind us.

Our party turned the heads of demons as we passed. They knew as well as we did that something was terribly wrong.

Suddenly, a pulse of fear came rippling through the line, coming from the back like an electric current through a cord. I could see fur standing on end, teeth beginning to chatter, a frightened whisper taking hold of the crowd.

"Stay in line and keep going!" I yelled at the demons, echoing Guanyin's command. "It's the fastest way through!"

But the gears of panic were in motion. They couldn't be stopped. It took only one phrase to kick them up a notch.

"*Yin Mo!*" a demon screamed. "It's here!"

The swell of terror made me think of an explosion captured on high-speed video. The demons who'd heard the name of their tormentor ran straight into the ones who hadn't, causing a pileup that started slow and picked up speed. The conclusion made its way through the line, each yaoguai learning from the one behind it. The Yin Mo had come.

■ ■ ■

The line of demons had dissolved into a tide once more. We had to fight through the onrush of terrified yaoguai, elbowing them left and right to make way. I had to stop a couple of times to help demons that were getting trampled. They bled on my hands and sleeves from their injuries but kept running for their lives. They had no choice.

It was utter chaos. Hell broken loose. I didn't want to think about what was happening at the front, where the portal was within tantalizing reach of the panicked survivors.

I nearly tripped over the first body. It was a long-necked turtle the size of a Great Dane, with a shell that looked like it was made out of diamonds, and yet it had been sliced cleanly in two.

Quentin caught me as I stumbled. "Why hasn't it poofed into ink?" I shouted in his ear.

"That's only what happens on Earth!" he said. "Anything dies here, it's *dead* dead!"

The poor turtle. And it was only the first victim we'd found.

As the crowd cleared out, more and more corpses littered the ground. Animals and monsters of all types. Big and small, young and old. More than a few bodies cradled each other, as if they'd tried to shield each other, or be together in death. Every single one of them had been cut clean through by some kind of unimaginably sharp blade.

It was a slaughterhouse. A killing floor. Scores of demons whom I'd promised help, massacred. I thought it couldn't get worse until I saw a corpse that had been slashed open from the front instead of the back.

It was the werewolf. He'd faced the unseen enemy in a futile attempt to buy time for the others. He'd died upright, on one knee, like he'd been trying to summon his strength for a final desperate counterattack. A Guardian until the end.

Hot tears welled up in my eyes. My fingernails bit into my palm, gouging into my skin until they met resistance and the pain vanished. I glanced down at my hand. It was glittering black. My arm was turning iron on its own, rage seeping into my fist.

Good, I thought. Because before this day was over, I was going to put my hand straight through whoever did this.

The world had suddenly become quiet. There simply weren't any more living beings around, other than the gods of the mandate. The landscape was barren, devoid of movement and sound.

"There's no trace of the enemy," Guan Yu muttered. He gripped his halberd tighter. "No footsteps, no blood, not even any errant strokes. It's as if the yaoguai fell apart of their own accord."

"Someone tell me what this is!" I screamed. "Who did this?"

"*I did*," a woman's voice whispered right up close in my ear.

I jumped and spun around in the direction of the voice. "Did anyone hear that?" I said.

The only answer I got was another unfamiliar sound. One of the stranger, more bizarre auditory experiences I had been party to. Quentin crying out in pain.

A red lash bloomed on the back of his white shirt from shoulder to opposite hip. He fell to the ground and bled and bled.

Maybe time slowed, or maybe it was my poor reflexes like those the Great White Planet had criticized me for, but I didn't move. The sensation of wrongness I felt in that moment went bone-deep, into my marrow. It paralyzed me.

Quentin had never taken a wound like that since we'd been together. It wasn't the right kind of wound for him to take. The fight with his evil doppelganger, the Six-Eared Macaque, had busted his face up in an amusing, hockey brawl way. His near-death experience with Red Boy's purifying flame had briefly petrified him, but that was almost like he'd been immortalized, preserved for the ages.

This was different. My boyfriend turned out to have rawness and pumping blood inside him. He had been breached.

"Look out!" Guan Yu roared. He knocked me to the side with his bulk and spun his weapon in a helicopter twirl. The edge of the guandao sparked as if it had made contact with another blade.

There was a sharp little zipping noise. Behind me, a rock the size of a trash can slid into two pieces, the top half skiing down the bottom half at an angle. It had been sliced through.

"Get down!" Guan Yu said to the rest of us. "As low as you can!"

He strode forward, somehow having determined the direction the attack was coming from. The warrior god began weaving his polearm through the air. His eyes were heavy in concentration, nearly closed, and he breathed deep through his nostrils.

More sparks flew from the business end of his halberd, each one accompanied by a *clang* and a ricochet whine. He deflected the invisible, slicing projectiles to the left and right, up and down, creating as much of a safe zone as he could for us.

But his task was monumentally difficult. Bloody slashes appeared on Guan Yu's burly arms when he was a microsecond too slow. He could only protect so many angles. The other gods and I had to throw ourselves to the deck and belly-crawl into a wedge behind him.

The Great White Planet, prone on the ground, scribbled furiously with a fresh pen, doing his duty like a war correspondent under heavy fire. A puff of dust thudded into the sand near my head. I pulled up close to Quentin and curled my body around his.

Nezha was already working on his injury, and I sent a prayer of thanks to him that the young god knew how to do healing magic. "Looks worse than it is," Nezha said to Quentin. He wiped his forehead with the back of his hand, his fingers and palms covered in blood. "If you weren't Sun Wukong, the cut would have been deeper."

"Thanks," Quentin coughed. "Genie, let go. I'm fine." He tried to get to his knees, but I grabbed his head and mashed it back down to the ground. Like I believed him. What was with everyone close to me declaring they were fine after nearly dying?

Eventually the ricochets started to land farther and farther away. "Heh," Guan Yu muttered, oblivious to his own dripping wounds. "I have your pattern figured out."

Whoever was attacking us seemed to agree. They took one last potshot at Guan Yu, which he blocked easily, and then they stopped.

Quentin glanced up at his warrior god friend, and then at me. "See?" he said with a weak smile. "Tactical genius."

I was as angry as I was relieved. "Do you have to joke every time you get hurt?" I said.

We dragged ourselves to our feet. We'd weathered the storm, but just barely. The deadly barrage of what I could only guess were invisible blades from afar must have been what murdered the yaoguai. Ao Guang's people, too. No wonder they'd been scared of the Yin Mo, a completely unseen death.

"General," Nezha said to Guan Yu. "You're bleeding."

"I lack the time to bleed," Guan Yu growled. He gazed at a dot on the shimmering horizon. "Our enemy approaches."

Someone or something was heading our way. Erlang Shen, who had hit the dirt with the rest of us, inch-wormed his way to a kneeling position. "I think, as a precaution, you should take off my restraints," he said. He flexed against the bindings, making a little jangle.

"Shut up," I said. I zoomed my eyes in. My golden-eyed sight may have been magic, but at this level of magnification, spotting a target without any landmarks nearby was as hard as getting a telescope to land on the exact right star in the sky. I dialed in, catching bits and pieces of a blurry shape, over and undershooting as I tried to compensate.

A delicate breeze blew in my face. I blinked to shield my eyes from dust and lost my focus.

"Genie!" Quentin said.

"Don't distract me! I almost had it!"

"Genie, it's right in front of you!"

I was going to yell at him that backseat true sight drivers needed to shut their traps, but he turned out to be right. The thing I'd been trying to spot was now only fifty yards away, visible to everyone. I'd missed it travel more than a mile in the time it took for a gust of wind to pass.

It was a woman.

She was square-shouldered but lithely tapered, her frame suggesting the tightly bundled power of a dancer. She was wearing a form-fitted suit that covered her from neck to toe. The underlayer was made out of a fine black weave that looked like it could stop bullets. Over her muscles and vitals were rows of matte armor scales. They were hinged like vents and flapped slightly open at random intervals to let small hissing jets of steam out.

Her face was covered by a mask that was part ninja's and part scuba rebreather. The top half hid her eyes behind mirrored lenses, and the jaw section had a series of valves that forebodingly looked like they could be cranked up past eleven to provide some terrible spike of power.

She resembled a warrior sent back in time from three centuries into the future. The whole getup was unbearably badass. It was honestly the most badass-looking outfit I'd ever seen.

Too bad I'd have to wreck both it and the wearer. "Who are you?" I demanded.

In lieu of an answer the woman slowly, languidly cocked her wrist, pointing at each god, Quentin, and me in turn. She was making a show of counting us. One, two, three, four, five, six.

"*No more?*" she whispered.

Judging by her voice she was the one who'd spoken directly in my ear before, despite being so far away at the time. Even now I shouldn't have been able to hear her so easily given her soft, ethereal tone and obstructed mouth, but her words tunneled straight into my brain. I almost looked to make sure she wasn't standing right behind me, her hands gripping my shoulders.

"Why are you doing this?" I said. This wasn't a parlay like with the yaoguai. The time for that had long since passed. I merely wanted to understand the monster I was about to take down.

She didn't respond. She held her ground like she was waiting for something more interesting to happen.

We were at an impasse. I glanced at the gods to try and see how I should be reacting. They were perfectly still, with the bridled tension of duelists unwilling to make the first mistake. Personally, I took the woman's inaction as our moment to strike.

"We could rush her," I whispered. "There's more of us. I could—"

"*Don't!*" Quentin said harshly. "We don't know what we're dealing with yet."

The standoff was broken by the sound of feet digging into the sand. Guanyin came running up to join us. I could tell from the pain on her face that there'd been carnage near the portal. She wouldn't have come unless the rift had closed early.

We didn't have time to confirm it though. Guanyin's arrival triggered a response in the strange woman. Our opponent reached up to the side of her mask and flicked its latch with her long, delicate fingers. As she removed the mouthpiece, it made the puffing noise of air pressure being equalized. The goggles were next, but she kept her eyes closed as they came off, like she wasn't ready to face the daylight yet.

She was beautiful on the level of a goddess. Her thin face and expressive mouth gave her a sad, lonely composition out of a Baroque oil painting.

"Take off my restraints," Erlang Shen suddenly yelled. "Do it now!"

Asshole wouldn't stop screwing around, even at a time like this. I could hear shuffling in the dust, which was probably Quentin fanning out. Quentin moved to flank her while her eyes were still closed. I knew my partner's tactics well. We had our disagreements in our personal lives, but in battle, we were a well-oiled machine, always knowing what the other was—

"*Tian a!*" Quentin yelled.

That wasn't what he said before a fight. I risked a glance back at the group and was completely stunned at what I saw.

The divine beings standing on my side weren't moving into attack formation. They were backing away. Guan Yu, Guanyin, Quentin, all of them. There was fear on their faces. Outright fear.

Nezha was trying to get his body in between the woman and the Great White Planet. Gaining points was not the goal here. He was ready to sacrifice himself to protect the old man.

Guan Yu hunched over defensively with his weapon held in front of him, the massive god determinedly making himself as small of a target as possible. Guanyin, who could stop time by looking at it funny, was mumbling to herself, fingers kneading the air, powering up for a defensive spell bigger than I'd ever seen her cast before.

"What is going on?" I said. "Someone answer me!"

"Take off my restraints!" Erlang Shen screamed, a hysterical edge in his voice. "The clasp on the side of my hip! Break it!"

I didn't have time to make sense of his statement before Quentin, *Quentin* of all people, who had been mortal enemies with

Erlang Shen long before the rest of us, who had hated him before it was cool, reached over and smashed the locking clasp that kept him powerless and imprisoned.

The individual beads of iron that served as Erlang Shen's shackles dropped to the ground. They'd been linked together with some kind of binding magic. It was gone now. I could feel a ripple of power emanate from the god, blood coming back to an unused muscle. Erlang Shen flexed his hands before his face with an incredulous expression.

"*Why did you do that?*" I shrieked at Quentin.

"Because we're going to need his help!" Quentin said. "That's Princess Iron Fan!"

Maybe I had heard the name before, but in the shock of the moment I could hardly remember my own. "Who is that?"

Erlang Shen could have seized the opportunity to run, or attack us, or simply take a celebratory stretch after being bound for so long. But instead his first action as a free man was to take a stance and clench his teeth like a Viking coming to terms with Ragnarok.

"She's Red Boy's mother," he said.

22

THE WOMAN OPENED HER EYES. AT FIRST THE COLD, SOLID GRAY color filling her sockets made me think she had them rolled back into her head, or that maybe she lacked irises entirely, but tiny wisps and tendrils of fog began to bleed from her face like weightless tears. The shape of her eyeballs was made up of two spherical vortexes, spinning in place to keep their cloudy vapor contained.

Her eyes weren't living tissue. They were miniature roiling storms, thunderheads inside her skull. If this was Red Boy's mother, then she was part yaoguai and part weather system.

Princess Iron Fan inhaled through her nose. The clouds in her eyes unfurled and shot forward.

The ground between her and us unzipped, ripped open, disemboweled itself, the flying guts of the earth marking the progress of a wind unlike any I'd ever seen. To call it a straight-line hurricane that threatened to blow us off our feet was selling it laughably short. It was a solid mass—a writhing, angry wyrm that promised to tear us apart where we stood.

I used the split-second we had left to throw my hands over my face. The Great White Planet was right; my reflexes were terrible, and I had to pray that the invulnerability of the Ruyi Jingu Bang would save me.

The impact didn't come. I looked up to see the wind parting around an invisible sphere surrounding all of us. Guanyin. The goddess was really leaning into her just-completed barrier spell with every ounce of her might, her center of gravity far beyond her toes.

"I'm gonna need you big strong fighter types to think of something quick!" she shouted at us. "I can't hold this forever!"

The gale outside peaked, sending giant cracks into the protective magic that spiderwebbed all around us, turning the shield opaque with damage. "Genie, get down!" Quentin yelled. He threw his arm over me and plowed his other hand into the ground.

"But what about—"

The barrier shattered. Guanyin, who had held the spell to the very end to buy us time instead of protecting herself, went flying into the air along with the shards of her magic.

"No!" I screamed. I tried to break free of Quentin's grip and go after her, but even with the wind dying down, catching a face full of it was nearly enough to snap my neck. Quentin had to catch me again by the wrist like I'd fallen off a sheer cliff face.

I dangled sideways, helpless, until Princess Iron Fan's attack subsided. With the air still once more, this was our chance to fight back. But instead of getting a unanimous rally from our side, I had to bear witness to one of the most disheartening sights I could have imagined.

Erlang Shen, the god who'd nearly destroyed my world and my life, had dropped to the ground and was crawling away on his hands and knees as fast as he could. He was so desperate to stay low and out of sight that he was practically huffing the earth like a pig, scraping the gravelly sand with the side of his head.

After his big to-do about his restraints, I had expected more from him. Hell, I'd expected more from Erlang Shen as an enemy in general. It felt like his cowardice reflected poorly on me, the person who'd handed him his biggest loss.

At least Guan Yu was still game. He stepped up, pointing his blade at Princess Iron Fan. I was worried he was going for a too-obvious bull rush, but his motions took on a delicacy I hadn't expected from the burly god.

"Have a taste of your own!" he shouted.

With a clean stroke that started from the soles of his feet and flowed all the way through his perfectly synchronized joints, Guan Yu slashed the air toward the yaoguai. A green, crescent-shaped slice of energy flew out of the guandao's cutting edge. A laser bolt, curved sideways.

Princess Iron Fan wasn't impressed by the mimicry of her technique. Right before she was eviscerated, she batted away the visible light with a flick of her wrist, using a cushion of air to avoid contact. The glowing slash went angling off to the side the same way Guan Yu had deflected her long-distance blades of air.

I detected a faint, mocking smile on her face. *Anything you can do, I can do better.*

Guan Yu didn't quit. And he never stopped the motion of his weapon. He sent a barrage of projectiles at Princess Iron Fan, each one culminating from a different point in the smooth, almost artistic form his motions produced. The yaoguai was forced to use both hands now. She parried the attacks left and right until the ground around her had been slashed to ribbons.

A bloodcurdling war cry sounded behind me. At first I thought a sound as frenzied and hungry for battle as that could have only come from Quentin, but it was Nezha, his eyes glowing with eagerness to fight. The young god stamped his heels, and two spinning rings of fire, spoked like chariot wheels, sprouted from his ankles, elevating him into the air. He clapped his hands together, and when he pulled them apart, a long, deadly pointed spear appeared out of nowhere like a magician's scarf. Nezha arced skyward and couched his lance at the yaoguai.

"Genie!" Quentin said. "Give me a bump!"

We'd talked about this maneuver once before. As a joke. On a lazy afternoon, not too long after we'd saved the city from Red Boy and were still drunk and infatuated on the fact that we'd gotten together, the two of us had snuck up to the school roof for a cloud-watching session. With my head in Quentin's lap, my lips still warm from his, I'd posited that as high as he could jump on his own, he could get still more power if I gave him a boost from the ground.

I set my hands. He backflipped and landed with the balls of his feet on my laced fingers, and for the first time, I felt the true massive weight of the Monkey, born from a stone. Quentin was a friggin' tank.

I hurled him sideways, straight at Princess Iron Fan, at the same time as he kicked off my hands. My move would have been an illegal carry in volleyball, but it turned Sun Wukong into a cannon shell.

Nezha whooped again and dive-bombed the enemy, his spear pointing the way. Guan Yu sent a fresh volley of laser blades at Princess Iron Fan. Every attack was going to hit her at the same time.

Princess Iron Fan took in the entire scene and decided she no longer wanted to bother. She spun around on a pointed toe, the prima ballerina demonstrating her grace, and a tornado followed in her wake.

▪ ▪ ▪

The air that hit me from the side scooped me off my feet so precisely that it felt like telekinesis. Guan Yu was sucked up by the raging wind as well, the god's massive strength rendered meaningless with nothing to hold on to. He tumbled helplessly end over end, a dust bunny of beard and flapping robes.

I was spinning around like Dorothy's house, watching familiar objects fly by. Bushes. Rocks. Oh hey, the Great White Planet, wide-eyed with fright, clutching his staff as if it were a pool noodle keeping him from drowning. I'd wondered what had happened to him.

A sense of order began to form out of the debris. The struggling gods and I came to float in a rough line, held still by roaring pressure differentials. We could flail all we wanted, but there were no solid surfaces to push off against.

Princess Iron Fan did not suffer from the same problem. She floated up through the center of the storm, supported by pillars of wind. Seeing her lean against nothing, anchored like a kite, told me what to do. *Grow*, I said to myself. *Or stretch.* Just reach the ground somehow to gain traction.

Princess Iron Fan shook her head at me.

Before I could change more than an inch in size, she slammed me forward and back against the sides of a clear cage of air. She rattled me like a bug in a jar. I lost focus as my head bounced around, and I tasted blood from my nose and mouth. Only the sight of Quentin trying to reach me kept me from blacking out.

Once she'd knocked the ability to concentrate out of me, Princess Iron Fan examined her captives. Nezha was farthest to her right. She beckoned at him, and he slid over to her as if he'd been mounted on rails.

"What do you want?" he yelled, writhing helplessly in her invisible grasp.

"*I want the strongest,*" she whispered.

I was concussed, without a doubt. But I could still comprehend why, despite the howling wind, every word she spoke was perfectly clear. If she controlled air, she controlled sound. That was how she'd taunted me from such a distance.

Princess Iron Fan used her invisible grasp to stretch Nezha out like a rack, cutting off his cry of pain. She inspected him from both sides, head to toe, searching for an answer until she found it.

"*And it's not you,*" she said to him.

With both eyes, she blasted Nezha at point-blank range.

The young god was completely enveloped by the vortex of clouds. If he screamed, we didn't hear it. Next to him, Guan Yu bucked with every ounce of his might, trying to get closer to the deadly wind, as if he might be able to pull Nezha out of harm's way using his teeth.

Quentin was right. His friend was a good man. But Guan Yu's efforts were in vain. When Princess Iron Fan ceased her attack, there was nothing left where Nezha had been.

The demon didn't pick another victim from us immediately. She waited again, dissatisfied, until her winds brought one more figure into her floating gallery of targets. Guanyin, who'd been briefly separated from us at the start of the fight.

"*Ah*," Princess Iron Fan whispered. "*Better.*" She elevated the Goddess of Mercy and brought her closer like she'd done to Nezha.

"Wait!" I shouted.

I was still so dizzy that yelling made me want to puke. I swallowed down my bile and shouted the most distracting thing I could think of. "I killed your son!"

Princess Iron Fan pushed Guanyin away and looked at me. This entire time she'd been serene and imperturbable, but now her face was locked in a frown.

"Red Boy's your son, right?" I had no plan, no goal here other than to get the demon to focus on me instead of my friends. I fought the instinct to struggle and tried to hurt her back the only way I could. "I'm the one who ended him."

Princess Iron Fan jerked me closer, until her fingers closed around my neck. She could have applied more pressure using her wind magic, but I'd made her angry. I was getting in her head.

"Your son was a rat bastard," I snarled. "I *buried* him. I buried him in the dirt with only worms to keep him company. No air for his fire. And the last thing I saw in his eyes as I put him under, was that he was *scared and wanted his mommy.*"

I couldn't believe how evil I sounded. But Red Boy was a murderous wretch who'd nearly blown up an entire city. I'd had no regrets. Until now.

Princess Iron Fan took in what I'd said. Mulled over her options. And then she curled her tongue and whistled. A long, low tone that a human could have produced. A swirl of wind, a little doodle of a cyclone sprang into being above my head.

As she kept going, her whistle became shriller and shriller. The cone whirled faster and faster. She didn't stop for breath the whole time.

The narrow bottom of the white funnel began squiggling and extending like a living snake, searching for material to burrow into. It closed into a sharp spike the width of an ice pick and arced around until it found the right path. Straight toward my left ear canal.

Princess Iron Fan's whistle was now the high speed whine of a dentist's drill. I couldn't hear anything else. The tip of the cyclone reached closer.

The tiny spear of air caressed the outside of my ear, as if to taunt me one last time, and then dipped inside. I gnashed my teeth and screamed so that the last thing I would ever hear would at least be the sound of my own voice.

But then nothing happened.

I was too afraid to turn my neck to see, so I craned my eyeballs. The little storm that threatened to skewer through my earholes had stopped. So had the whistling.

When I looked back at Princess Iron Fan, she was recovering her balance, like she'd been punched. She angrily wiped something off her face.

It was water.

The demon straightened up, flicked her fingers dry, and glared at Erlang Shen.

The rain god hovered before her. He was both supported and shielded by a continuously flowing geyser of water that reached all the way back to an opening in the ground below. The vertical river encased most of his body, keeping him stable in the buffeting winds. The drops torn off by the storm were easily replaced with reserves from what must have been a massive underground aquifer.

"I found what I was looking for," he announced to us with a grin.

Princess Iron Fan's blank, vapory eyes took on an expression of rage. She suddenly thrust her hands forward, concentrating her energy into a single dimensionless point. At the same time, Erlang Shen mirrored her movements, down to the very last crook of his fingers.

It was more than simple mockery. His needle of water met her spike of air head-on, and in this clash of elements, the least compressible state of matter won. Erlang Shen's thin jet of water pierced its way through Princess Iron Fan's attack and straight into her body.

The yaoguai looked down at the rapier blade that had run her through, impaling her right in the heart.

Her imminent death amused her. Then it really amused her. Then it became downright hilarious. She tilted her head back and began cackling in laughter, her high-pitched voice echoing off the walls of the continuing storm.

In between her howls she managed to trade a few words to Erlang Shen. I couldn't hear them this time. But whatever she said was enough to make his eyes grow wide. Princess Iron Fan's suit suddenly ballooned out to spherical proportions.

Erlang Shen pulled a protective layer of water over himself like a fire blanket, right before the demon exploded with enough force to finally knock me out.

23

I CAME TO ON THE COLD, HARD GROUND. I COULDN'T TELL WHICH way was up. The dirt pressing into my back could have been a wall, not a floor. Maybe a ceiling.

I peeled myself off the surface and waddled around, trying to get my bearings in the haze cloaking my vision. I felt groggy, nauseous, but worst of all, hideously vulnerable. I had never lost consciousness like this before. Certainly not since embracing my identity as the Ruyi Jingu Bang. My knees were wobbly, my ankles twisty.

A big gray shape congealed in front of me. I didn't understand why it was so big until enough time passed for my brain to process that it was part of the geography. It was a mountain. I was wandering around the slope of a frigging mountain. That was why I couldn't get level and stable.

I looked up and saw the irregularities of the rocks and switchbacks converge over the distance into a forty-five-degree slope so perfect I couldn't judge how far away the peak was. The sky had switched from pink to an electric blue, like someone had highlighted it in a web browser.

Looking down gave me nothing, either. A solid carpet of marshmallow-y white clouds blocked any view of the ground. The vapor stretched into the horizon. I couldn't see any other peaks poking through the cloud cover other than the one I was standing on.

There had been no clouds and no mountain in the desert where we'd started. I was getting supremely fed up with how the rules of plate tectonics worked outside Earth. I had geological standards.

A groan coming from behind a nearby boulder told me I wasn't alone. I picked my way around the house-sized chunk of granite and found the only person who could have made this situation even better.

Erlang Shen lay on his back with his arm draped over his eyes like an artist's model waiting to be sketched. He appeared to be unconscious. I hadn't been the closest to him when Princess Iron Fan self-destructed, but the cocktail shaker of the explosion had mixed us together and dumped us in the same spot.

A wave of sheer despair took hold of me. I dropped to my knees and gripped my own elbows to stop from shaking. I couldn't handle what this implied.

We'd lost. Princess Iron Fan was the Yin Mo, and Erlang Shen had been the one to land the killing blow on her. By the rules of the Mandate Challenge, he was the new King of Heaven.

I felt dead inside—gutted and scraped of my vitals—as I realized this. The scales of the cosmos did not tilt toward justice. The good and the decent did not prevail. The Universe would throw chance after chance at the unworthy until they capitalized on it and stole everything from the rest of us.

I didn't know if Quentin and Guanyin were alive in the wake of Princess Iron Fan's explosion, but fate had decided Erlang Shen should be saved with absolute certainty. The circumstances that were required to get here—each precarious moment of stupidity and bad luck balanced on top of each other—made me want to weep.

You can do something about this, a voice whispered inside my head. I tried blocking it out, but it forced two small words through the cracks in my brain.

Kill him.

Erlang Shen was out cold and vulnerable. The Great White Planet was nowhere in sight. Whatever coronation or recognition that went along with declaring a new ruler of Heaven hadn't happened yet.

Kill him. Before he wakes up.

The natural forces of the Universe were corrupt. I saw that now. I couldn't reweave the fabric of events into an outcome that made sense. But I could lash out. Cut the cloth in defiance of the pattern.

I stared at Erlang Shen, trying to muster the will to murder him in cold blood. I knew he'd do it to me if our situations were reversed. He needed to die for the good of Heaven and Earth. He deserved to die.

And yet I couldn't do it. Minutes passed while I struggled against my skin to move forward, my teeth grinding in an attempt to kick-start my body into action. My resolve failed an infinite number of times.

I slammed my hands against the ground over and over and cursed myself. I was weak, too weak to do what was necessary.

■ ■ ■

Erlang Shen woke up to see me sitting off to the side, my head buried between my knees.

He scrambled away, conking his head into the nearby boulder. Like me, he realized how vulnerable he'd been. He glanced at his limbs, incredulous that I hadn't broken them.

It took him a few halting tries to sit up, like someone who'd planked too long the day before and now had the sorest of abs. "Well," Erlang Shen said as he planted one foot on the ground and leaned on his knee. "I'm waiting."

I found I could talk to him normally now. My grudges didn't matter. Nothing mattered. "For what?"

He frowned. "For you to thank me. I saved your life."

He would have to wait a very long time for that. "What is this place?" I said. My voice was dull. I was asking on autopilot.

He prodded the back of his head and looked at his hand like he'd been expecting blood. "I think it's a different Blessed Plane entirely. If I had to guess, with her last moments Princess Iron Fan hurled us through the boundaries of existence into a reality even farther from Earth."

"How do we get back?"

He gave me an annoyed look. "So full of questions, like I know everything. I don't think we *can* get back. At least not the way we came."

"I would have thought the new King of Heaven could go wherever he wanted." Drained of anger, drained of every emotion, I could call it like it was.

Erlang Shen didn't look as celebratory as I'd expected. "First off, I would need the Great White Planet to make it official.

In case you haven't noticed, he's not here. Secondly, I'm not sure if Princess Iron Fan was the source of the trouble to begin with."

"What do you mean? She killed all those yaoguai. She nearly killed Ao Guang."

"The last thing I said after I stabbed her was 'Thank you for the Throne of Heaven.'" He got up and stretched, grimacing as if the memory was embarrassing. "She laughed and said I hadn't earned it yet. That was right before she exploded."

I still didn't get it.

"The mandate winner is defined as whoever defeats the *ultimate* evil threatening the Universe at the time the challenge is called," Erlang Shen explained. "Princess Iron Fan was the Yin Mo, but I think there's something out there bigger than her." He pointed toward the peak of the mountain. "Take a gander in that direction with true sight."

I did as he requested, without the surge of revulsion at complying with my enemy. Was this what calm people felt like all the time? Weird.

But turning my eyes on the summit of the mountain revealed a troubling presence that managed to pierce the layer of indifference I was wrapped in. An energy signature like I'd never seen before. The qi of demons and gods was like an open flame, raw-edged and flickering in eddies and whorls.

The top of the mountain, on the other hand, held an entire sunrise of power. It was a solid halogen mass, a radial scorch in the atmosphere. I couldn't look at it for more than a moment. It hurt my eyes and defied my belief.

Erlang Shen watched me squint in pain. "I believe *that's* what Heaven originally detected when this whole mess started," he said.

Great. Princess Iron Fan had just kicked the snot out of us, and she wasn't even the final boss. I didn't see the point of playing this game anymore. I wanted to go home. I wanted to see my parents again. I wanted to see Yunie. I wanted to turn back time to when I had Quentin by my side and our only concerns were which state landmarks we wanted to irresponsibly jump to next.

"There's no 'we' here," I said to Erlang Shen. "If you want to climb up there and get killed by whatever's pumping out qi exhaust, then nothing would make me happier. I'd rather take my chances downhill."

"I'm fairly sure down that way is an infinite slope into a never-ending abyss," Erlang Shen said, pointing at the ominous layer of clouds. "And if your friends are still alive, and in this plane, our best chance of finding them is at the summit. We'll have better odds of surviving this cursed place if we stick together."

I thought about my options. He knew his way around the non-Earth realms better than I did. And he hadn't been lying about needing to climb to the peak, both to find the others and to complete the Mandate Challenge. I'd watched him with true sight. He really believed he hadn't won yet.

If I couldn't stomach murdering Erlang Shen when his guard was down, I could always grab him and jump off the nearest cliff, I told myself. We'd fall forever, fighting for eternity. I could punch him as much as I wanted then.

I hauled myself to my feet. The deadness hadn't left me, not yet. But I'd grind this out. I still had some fumes left in the tank.

He snorted at my labored efforts. "Good," he said. "I was beginning to fear you'd become a sniveling little *nuofu.*"

I gave him the Italian chin-flick in response. If he didn't know the gesture, he got the general meaning. Keeping him a safe distance ahead, where I could keep an eye on him, I followed Erlang Shen up the mountain.

24

I WAS STARTING TO BELIEVE THIS PLACE HAD BEEN INTENTION-ally designed to mess with us as much as possible. The mountainside, though studded with little nooks and crannies of gray-pink stone that made plenty of steps and handholds, was angled in such a way that forced us to crawl upward on all fours.

Trying to go faster by beasting it with pure strength caused the rock surface to crumble like talc, leaching away the extra force. I also had the idea to stretch my arm out, plant my hand on the mountain, and then ride upward like a ski lift as my arm contracted, but I couldn't shrink back to normal fast enough to make it worth it. The only thing I accomplished was looking like an idiot in front of Erlang Shen.

"This is stupid," I said after my failed attempts to cheat the system. "You can fly."

"Like I'm going to make myself an easily spotted target," he scoffed. "You saw what happened to Nezha."

I frowned at him.

"Get off your high horse," he said. "You knew him for a single morning. I already told you that Nezha was my friend."

He had, but I'd assumed he was making stuff up at the time. "Nezha was one of the few gods close to my age in centuries," Erlang Shen said with genuine bitterness. "After you exposed me for a traitor, he pleaded for mercy on my behalf. So don't you dare act like I'm incapable of feeling for him."

We climbed in silence for another minute. The memory of Nezha must have been really eating at Erlang Shen, because he spoke again, unprompted.

"If anything, you're the outsider," he said. "Getting involved in the business of the gods. You think you have us figured out. You understand us as well as the roach does the humans who're dropping crumbs on its head."

An errant step of his sent pebbles and dust cascading into my face and down my shirt. I scowled and moved over to the side where the path was less obvious but still manageable. The next kick upward I took brought me parallel with him.

Guanyin had said something similar once, about me not knowing what happened upstairs. I decided to tug on this string, partly out of interest and mostly because it seemed like a chance to get under Erlang Shen's skin for once.

"Yeah, well, sometimes you gods act as petty as the rest of us roaches," I said. "You created the mess with Red Boy because of a spat with your uncle."

He stopped where he was. I'd struck the nerve I was ostensibly looking for, but perhaps had dug too deep.

"A spat. With my uncle the Jade Emperor. Yes. That was why I did what I did. A *spat*."

Glancing at his face, I was taken aback. I knew that look, when your rage was so cold and ossified that it was part of the foundation the rest of you was built on. Poured into the concrete, invisible to everyone except those who understood the signs.

"I used to have a third eye," he said.

"What?"

"I used to have a third eye. For real. Right here, in the middle of my forehead." He pointed to his skull and made a little circling bullseye over his skin. "I was an honest-to-goodness tri-clops when I was younger."

I shouldn't have wanted to laugh at the image. A little snort came out. Erlang Shen almost smiled. Almost.

"My third eye granted me true sight," he said. "You think yours is special, but I can tell you right now that what you have is like being gifted a flashlight inside a *coffin* compared to what I had. I could see more than lies and faraway objects. I could see possibilities. I could see reasons. Futures. Threads of fate that might weave themselves into the most beautiful outcomes if only the right strands were tugged."

Erlang Shen closed his eyes, his two remaining regular ones. "There was a world I glimpsed, a timeline that was perfect. Heaven and Earth in alignment. Every human born would have been cared for, and every god would have done their part to make it happen. It would have been something out of Guanyin's most hopeful dreams."

I wanted to say something but hesitated. I had delighted, once, in the prospect of a better tomorrow under the Goddess of Mercy while lying on the cheap, scratchy carpet of an office building. It was a little frightening how much his words sounded like my own thoughts.

"I went running to the Jade Emperor once I was sure my gift had been developed enough," Erlang Shen said. "I wanted to help him, down to the sinews of my being. I thought we were going to do so much good together, my uncle and me bringing a grand new destiny to the cosmos. *My uncle and me!* Ha!"

The rocks he was holding on to began to sprout cracks under his fingers.

"The Jade Emperor looked at me like I'd drawn a knife and rammed it between his ribs," Erlang Shen choked out. "How dare I. How dare I try to stick my nose where it didn't belong. To suggest that his mandate-appointed rule could ever be improved. The very act of thinking that I could play a part in guiding Heaven and Earth was both treason and a stunning lack of filial piety. It had to be punished."

He clenched his teeth. "The Jade Emperor took my third eye from me. He ripped my flesh apart in a great big ceremony in front of the Court of Heaven. You would have thought I was getting a medal. Instead he lectured me in front of the other gods while I screamed on the floor of the Peach Banquet Hall, clutching a bloody crater in my skull!"

I winced and looked away.

"My special sight, gone forever," Erlang Shen said, his voice raw like scraped leather. "Don't you get it? The enormity of what he did? It wasn't just me he punished back then! By taking that vision of beauty, of what could have been, and destroying it, he hurt you, he hurt humanity, the gods, even the demons! He *cheated* us! He *swindled* us! *He robbed us all of a perfect future!*"

I heard the noise of rocks exploding under pressure. Without thinking, I reached behind me as quick as I could with one hand and grabbed Erlang Shen's arm before he fell down the mountain.

In retrospect the gesture was actually kind of pointless. We were still on a slope, not dangling dramatically off a cliff edge. Neither of us would have been greatly injured by a slight tumble. At best I'd saved us the time it would take waiting for him to catch up with me again.

But still. He and I clung to each other's wrists like our lives depended on it. We both managed to save our footing, so we ended up frozen in the apex of the world's most awkward ballroom twirl.

Erlang Shen tried to still his features back to his normal self, but the best he could manage was shame at spilling his guts. He relaxed there, letting me keep him upright, knowing I could hold him easily.

"And I used to have a trident," he muttered.

"What?"

"A magic trident," he said, deciding that petulance was a better emotion to show me than sincerity. "A unique weapon of my own, similar to Guan Yu's Green Dragon Crescent Blade. The Jade Emperor took that away from me as well. So if you were wondering why I had such a fixation on you as the reincarnated Ruyi Jingu Bang, it was because you were the closest thing to what I'd lost, in one package. A weapon and true sight."

I sighed deeply. In an unnecessary move that I'd only seen in action movies, I swung him like a pendulum. The momentum took him to the same elevation as me and he caught his grip on the rock face once more.

"So," he said, pretending like the last few minutes didn't happen. "Do *you* have any embarrassing family stories you feel like sharing?"

He was only covering for his lapse by being a smartass, but I found I suddenly did want to talk about my family. Overwhelmingly so. I needed the reminder of why I'd taken the ride that had eventually landed me here, far from them and Earth.

I resumed climbing. Erlang Shen kept pace beside me. We both kept our eyes on the mountain.

"When I was younger, there was this plush toy that came out one year," I said. I tested my next foothold and stepped higher. "Everyone at school had one. It was like a bear . . . deer . . . cat thing. I wasn't sure what animal it was supposed to be."

"Sounds like a yaoguai," Erlang Shen said.

"Ha! Maybe. I asked my parents for one, for my birthday. It was overpriced but they didn't say no. It was right after the two of them had opened the store they'd been working on, so they must have been feeling flush and confident. They must have been *so sure* they were going to succeed."

I'd never told Erlang Shen my personal family history, but you didn't need a third eye to see it wasn't perfectly happy. He was content not to interrupt my fairly trivial story and keep quiet for once.

"I was so excited when I tore off the wrapping paper," I said, still climbing. "Only to find it wasn't the right toy. My guess is that the shop wanted to hang on to as much stock as they could to see if the price would rise, so when my dad asked for one, they pawned off something similar on him or convinced him a different toy was better than the original."

I could imagine how my dad would have looked like an easy mark. "Sometimes parents do that, you know? They're not content to give you what you ask for and feel like they have to go the extra mile or think of something super special and different for you. When all you want is the basics."

"What did you do?" Erlang Shen asked.

"I just kind of froze. It was obvious from my reaction that I wasn't happy. My mother started yelling at my dad for screwing up, and my dad was yelling that he'd make it right. But he couldn't. They couldn't get a new one because both toys were expensive, and that was the moment where it dawned on me how strapped for cash my family really was. I was a child, and I didn't understand the concept of being poor. Until right then and there."

We reached a little flat terrace with enough room for both of us to stand. It seemed like a good place to take a break. Erlang Shen and I stood on the level terrain and wrung out our fingers. I wasn't done talking.

"It was also the first fight they had after opening their store," I said. "So for a very long time I assumed all the bad luck that happened afterward was my fault. I'd cursed their business with misfortune. Which meant their eventual split was my fault, too. Because the tiniest chains of events matter."

Erlang Shen shook his head at the ground, taking this anecdote about luck and fate and money very seriously. God or not, he was still Chinese, after all. "Family is the worst."

"No," I said. "You don't understand. I love my family more than anything. My mother took it out on my father because she wanted me to have my heart's desire. My father withdrew into a shell because he couldn't handle disappointing me. I am their whole world, and they are mine."

Erlang Shen looked up to see my index finger, doubled in length, pressing dangerously close to his eyeball. He jerked his head away in surprise, but my finger extended to follow him, threatening to pierce his brain.

"You put my mother in danger," I snarled. "And you tried to kill my father. So don't you *ever* get chummy with me, or I will make a corpse out of you and hang it on my wall, right above the spot where I've kept that wrong stuffed animal all these years."

Erlang Shen had done me a favor. The exhaustion, the sense of surrender that threatened to drag me down to the bottom of the sea lost its grip. Bringing up family had caused the shackles to break, allowing me to rocket back to the surface, buoyed by the one emotion that would always be there to provide me high-octane fuel.

The color drained out of Erlang Shen's face, replaced by a killer's pale calm. A glaze fell over his eyes, like a reptile's second lid closing itself before the attack. He cricked his neck, beckoning me to look downward.

In his hand was a small blade made of water he'd hidden somewhere on his person. The point of it was aimed right at my kidney. The encounter with Princess Iron Fan had illustrated to us the advantages of using our powers in smaller, subtler, more lethal ways.

For perhaps the first time ever, Erlang Shen and I stared at each other with something akin to mutual understanding. There was a measure of respect in his gaze. He was looking at someone as awful and hate-filled as him. Rage was our common ground, a lack of forgiveness our shared little plot.

He raised his hands, and the shank of water disappeared into his sleeve. I retracted my finger. We went back to climbing. If we ever ran out of mountain, there would be a whole lot of feelings and bloody guts strewn over the rocks.

"You would have done well as my weapon," Erlang Shen said.

His comment made me remember those wild, overwhelming days when Quentin and I first unlocked my Ruyi Jingu Bang powers together. After the first couple of critical missteps, Sun Wukong stopped referring to me as "his weapon." We became partners. A duo. I shuddered to think of the tutelage I would have received from the god next to me, a doubling of my worst traits instead of Quentin's warm affection.

"No," I said with absolute certainty. "I wouldn't have."

25

WE REACHED THE TOP OF THE MOUNTAIN RIGHT AROUND NIGHT-fall on this plane. It hurt to think of how much time we'd lost. By my rough calculations, the third day of my long weekend was over.

I couldn't check how long I'd been gone. I'd intentionally left my phone back on Earth, afraid it wouldn't survive a supernatural adventure. Maybe if I joined Ax, I could start affording replacements. I wanted to both laugh and cry, remembering my Earthly problems.

The peak, which had looked like a point from down below, was now a long-edged plateau that implied the very size of the rock formation had changed in the second we weren't thinking about it. I had the feeling that physics was getting looser with our altitude. I refused to look down the slope behind me, fearing that instead of clouds I'd see an unrendered, placeholding void.

I was still ahead of Erlang Shen and didn't want to wait, so I peeped over the side like a badger. There, I spotted the first good news I'd had all day. Quentin, Guanyin, Guan Yu, and the Great White Planet were sitting close to the mountain's edge, circled around a small fire.

I shouted incoherently like a shipwreck survivor. Vaulting over the top, I ran at them, waving my arms. Quentin was the first to his feet, but instead of coming to greet me, he stayed where he was like a statue, frigid and unyielding.

Way to ruin the moment, I thought. I collided with Guanyin instead and hugged her into the air.

"Genie," she said, rubbing her knuckles against my scalp.

"Were you waiting here for us?" I said. "How did you know where we'd be?"

"I had a feeling," Quentin said, his voice even more robotic than his stance.

Oh, right. Our "mystical connection that spanned time and space, forever linking our souls in the most intimate manner imaginable." Pfft. Whatever.

I put Guanyin down so I could take in our surroundings properly. Behind the other gods was a forest, thick and dense enough to house a horde of German witches. There were barely any gaps between the trunks, and the canopy seemed to replace the sky itself. Quentin and Guanyin were right; the geography here wiped its butt with Earth-based standards.

The Great White Planet stared at the woods with a face of extreme worry. "There's been many false starts to our adventure, but without a doubt it ends here, one way or another."

I didn't need to turn true sight on to confirm his statement. Being this close to the gigantic source of qi, I could feel the troubling energy on my skin in rhythmic waves, like something breathing on me. Rather than having to detect its presence, we had to mentally block it out so as not to lose our minds.

"Princess Iron Fan may have been the one who defeated Ao Guang and attacked the yaoguai, but whatever this phenomenon is, it's orders of magnitude more powerful than her," the Great White Planet said. "If it grows any stronger it could crush entire realms of existence under the mass of its energy."

He reached into his robes and pulled out his notebook. I thought he was going to scribble more in it, but he shocked me by tearing out his older pages entirely and crumpling them in his fist. The notebook was much thinner now, with only a thin sheaf of blank space remaining.

"I'm declaring that the Mandate Challenge is still ongoing," he said. He gestured toward the woods. "Whoever can safeguard Heaven and Earth and all the planes in between against *that* will be the victor."

"Oh come on!" Erlang Shen snapped. He was either protesting the Great White Planet's decision to cancel his previous victories or the fact that Guan Yu had the edge of his halberd pressed against his neck.

Good on Guan Yu for showing initiative. "What, are you going to whine when things don't break exactly your way for once?" I said to Erlang Shen. "Because that would be a pretty spineless move of you."

"I'm saying there is no fighting whatever 'that' is," he said, wiggling his fingers in air quotes, a gesture that was probably lost on the more traditional gods. "If whatever's out there is many times stronger than Princess Iron Fan, then we don't have any hope of beating it. I say better to leave it alone and hope it doesn't stir. Now that we're together, we can combine our powers to figure out a way off this blasted plane."

"We already tried opening a portal while we waited for you, and it fizzled," Guanyin said. "That energy source is like a dwarf star pulling us in and trapping us on its surface. Spiritual gravity, remember?"

Erlang Shen swore up and down. He was the one who'd explained the concept to me in the first place. Spiritual power attracted spiritual power like magnets, the smaller charge getting stuck to the larger. That was why yaoguai tended to cluster around me in the Bay Area. I couldn't imagine what kind of power was needed to immobilize Guanyin, Sun Wukong, and three other full-fledged gods.

"We can't get back to Heaven, and Genie can't get back to Earth, until we shut down the source of that qi," Guanyin said. "The only way out is through."

Erlang Shen grimaced. Part of it was that he wanted to call the game early while he was still winning. But there was another emotion behind his mask, one I recognized because I'd put it in him before. The god was afraid. He didn't want to confront the monster in the forest. By the looks on everyone's faces, no one did. I could tell they were thinking of Nezha, how the young god's power and immortality had failed him.

"Welcome to our world," I said.

The assembled divinities looked at me, confused.

"Now you know what we humans feel like," I said. I could smell the hospital disinfectant as I spoke and could see my mother's thin hands worry her nails as she tried to be brave in front of me. "We're afraid. We're vulnerable. We have no control over when death comes for us. Life isn't some grand adventuring quest where each setback is really a leap forward to victory. Sometimes you get set back into the dirt six feet deep, and there you stay."

I knew Guanyin already understood this. I was trying to deliver the message to Guan Yu and Erlang Shen in case one of them ended up the new King of Heaven. The Great White Planet needed to hear it, too, for the next time he tried to dungeon master a Mandate Challenge without concern for who might perish in the upheaval.

"So yeah," I said. "Welcome to the party."

Guan Yu chuckled. "Aye, the child is full of wisdom. What a paradise the Protectorate of California must be, under her reign."

I didn't tell him that California was jacked up beyond my control. "Are we forging on, then?"

"It would be prudent to rest and regain our strength first," Guan Yu said. "A good tactician knows when to exercise caution."

"I'm with the general," Erlang Shen said. "If you're putting me through the crap of having to win the Mandate Challenge twice, then I'm doing it at a hundred percent and nothing less."

I glanced at Guanyin. She made a shrug saying she didn't disagree.

"Okay," I said. "How do gods recharge?" I knew Guanyin sometimes mentioned needing to do so, but she'd never revealed the details. "Do you sleep? Meditate? Power down like robots?"

My curiosity earned me a round of annoyed stares, including Guanyin's. "I'll . . . give you your privacy and go take a nap over there," I said, pointing over my shoulder.

■ ■ ■

As I made my way to the far edge of the campfire's radius, Quentin blocked my path.

"We need to talk," he said.

I felt a surge of guilt rushing up my throat for how relatively little I'd been thinking about him since the Mandate Challenge started. During the mundane portion of the long weekend our only contact had been fighting, but at least it was contact.

I'd missed him on a visceral level. We hadn't touched in so long. Our usual method of traveling from place to place literally required squeezing each other's bodies. I could have that again, right now. The cost was simply opening up.

"Yeah," I said. "Don't you think what happened with Princess Iron Fan was weird?"

Guh. I was such an idiot.

Somewhere between now and our moment at the pool, Quentin had learned to hide his crushing disappointment with me. "How so?" he asked calmly.

His forbearance was disturbing, a bad sign. Quentin was supposed to be my equal in temper, not an emotionless statue. "What was she trying to do exactly?" I said, wincing internally. "If you think about her actions, it's like she was picking a fight for no discernible reason."

"You said it yourself. We defeated Red Boy. Maybe she wanted revenge for her son."

"That can't be it. You and me being there seemed like a surprise to her. She wasn't interested in us. If anything, she was overly interested in Guanyin."

Quentin shrugged. "She said she was looking for the strongest among us. And Guanyin's incredibly strong. Especially when you consider the reserves of good karma she's stored up over the millennia. I wouldn't be surprised if she represents the greatest total amount of spiritual power in one god."

He wasn't using this as an opportunity to bicker about the mandate and the merits of Guan Yu. Quentin not wanting to bicker? A huge red flashing light was going off. The seawater was rising around my ankles.

And yet I was still ignoring it, fiddling away on the sinking deck. "It doesn't add up," I said. "Especially when you consider all of us getting sent to this mountain-plane as a group. What are the odds of that happening? There's a piece missing here."

His arms rose and fell with a slap against his sides. "I don't know what to tell you. I really don't."

That came out with too many layers of meaning. I floundered for more things to say to keep him talking to me but left too big a gap. "You should get some sleep," he said, before he turned and slipped into the woods, disappearing behind the trees.

"Hey!" I said. "That's not safe! Quentin!"

He left me alone, gnashing my teeth in the fading light.

I thought about heading back to the others to lie down by the fire they'd made, but that wouldn't have settled the roiling in my throat. I wasn't going to give up like this. If it took me a million years of standing awkwardly in front of Quentin to result in a productive conversation, then that was what it would have to take. The two of us could fossilize together, our sulking faces preserved in amber for eternity.

But first I had to find him. It was growing darker fast, and the woods were a labyrinth of choices, trees obscuring the view past a few yards. Using true sight would have blinded me. I felt like a puck dropped down on a board embedded with nails in a carnival game. Random bounces would take me anywhere but to the prize.

In an act that was mostly fueled by spite, I half closed my eyes until I could barely see the ground under my lids and stepped forward slowly and surely, taking lefts and rights with complete confidence. If Quentin could find me by my aura, then I could find him by his. I refused to let him win that contest.

I knew it had something to do with how our energies interacted and amplified each other. Mine was like sound waves generated by an iron bell; his was a roaring golden torch. I'd learned this back when we spent most of our time training together. When it felt right, I opened my eyes again.

In a little clearing nestled in the roots of a large tree, the perfect spot for someone to meditate in the embrace of nature, was . . . nothing.

Quentin wasn't here. I'd struck out.

That I couldn't make our connection work the same way he could nearly broke my heart, until I remembered a crucial component: I wasn't the greatest expert in mystical auras, but I knew my boyfriend's habits.

I ran forward and kicked the tree. It vibrated from the impact. I heard a yelp come from above, and an object plummeted from the top of its branches. I caught Quentin in my arms, bridal style. He was still the heaviest thing I'd ever carried, but the strain was worth it.

"You jerk!" he shouted, his face adorably grumpy. I'd never held him like this before, but I was going to do it a lot more from now on. Whenever we were fighting, I'd just scoop him into my arms. I put a stop to his wriggling escape attempts by leaning forward and pressing my lips gently to his forehead. If I couldn't put words to my feelings, then I could act, and hope the translation was good enough.

"Put me down for a sec, will you?" he said. I relented and set him on his feet. He surprised me by turning me around and hugging me tightly from behind, pressing his face into my back.

It was like today was hold-each-other-weirdly day. "What are you doing?"

"Shut up," he said, his voice shaking so hard I could feel it through my skin. "I'm about to cry and I don't want you to see it."

I sputtered unintelligibly. This was new.

"Genie, I thought you were *dead*," Quentin said. "The last thing I saw was Princess Iron Fan about to murder you."

He took deep shivering breaths, and the back of my shirt grew damp. "After the explosion, it took me hours to pick up on your aura again. That was hours of me thinking you were gone forever. I nearly went berserk. Guan Yu and Guanyin *and* the Great White Planet had to restrain me from tearing down the mountain."

That seemed disproportionate. Not to humblebrag, but I hadn't been that scared for myself during the encounter with Princess Iron Fan because everything had happened so quickly. It wasn't the slow-motion horror of watching Quentin fall under the flames of Red Boy or seeing him suddenly bleed from Princess Iron Fan's assault. *Those* were the worst experiences of my—

Oh.

That was the terror I'd put him through. That gut-wrenching, would-rather-the-world-end kind of pain. Normally Quentin was the one who tanked more hits from our enemies, so seeing Princess

Iron Fan nearly kill me must have been a fresh kind of hell for him. If he'd felt for my safety what I felt for his . . .

I shook my head. I didn't want to think about him hurting inside that much. I reached behind me until I found his shoulders and squeezed him further into me.

"I thought I'd lost you," he said. "I thought I lost you again. And that the last memory we'd have of each other was being angry."

He spun me around so fast that it made me woozy. I lost my balance, and he caught me like a romantic pirate holding his swooning betrothed.

"Genie," he said, looking more desperate and vulnerable than I'd seen in any yaoguai fight. "Genie, I'm so sorry. I've been acting like a jerk. I got needlessly upset because you've been surprising me so much lately. When you named Guanyin for the mandate. When you talked about not going to college."

Each time he sniffled he sent a gigantic yank on my heartstrings. "Of course you're not obligated to only do what I expect, and I'm sorry for implying it," Quentin said. "It's just that all of these surprises sent me back to a really bad place, to when you first threw me for a loop by disappearing from my side as the Ruyi Jingu Bang. That was the first time I thought I'd lost you forever."

The confession came pouring out of him with ease. He'd beat me to Ji-Hyun's advice about self-examination. I shouldn't have been surprised. Sun Wukong had the power to learn fast, and I had the power to be an emotionally stunted doof.

I couldn't fall so far behind. "The only reason I'm surprising you is because I'm surprising myself because I don't know myself as much as I thought and that terrifies me!" I yawped.

It took my competitive unwillingness to let Quentin "win" at honesty to force the words out of me. Not healthy at all, but effective for now. The blockage had been loosened.

"Back when we first met, I had one goal," I said. "One. And now it's like life is getting way more complicated. The future's not a single checkbox anymore. And it's overwhelming me. I feel like I'm drowning sometimes."

I gripped him tighter—my personal flotation device. "*I'm* sorry. I've—I was such an asshole to you. Saying you're not family. But Quentin, you know what happened to my mom and dad. They are all I've ever witnessed when it comes to relationships and family, and I'd do anything not to follow their example."

He looked troubled. "Should I give you space? Should we not be a thing for a while?"

"*No!*" I said with certainty. "I want you close by. I—I need you close by. But we don't always have to be perfect together."

I pulled myself out of his arms and sat down in the clearing. He plopped down next to me. The two of us, not staring into each other's eyes, but facing the same direction, like a team. This was easier.

Ji-Hyun's advice was working. Quentin and I had finally gone down the path she'd told us to take. She was like a . . . drunk Jedi or something. I needed to thank her once we got home.

I threw my arm over Quentin's shoulder and rested my frame on his. It wasn't the most comfortable, given how dense and hard he was. Embracing him was always a little bit like trying to cuddle with a V8 engine block.

"What I mean is, I've learned there's going to be times where 'you-and-I' have to take a backseat to more important business,"

I said. "Like with the Mandate Challenge, for instance. There were plenty of moments this weekend where I forgot about you entirely."

"Gee, thanks," he muttered.

I smacked him on the shoulder. "And that should be allowed. We'll drive ourselves nuts if we try and live inside each other's heads. I get enough of that with my mother as it is."

He leaned on me. We sat there, enjoying the comfortable silence.

"I'm also sorry for how I treated you when we first met," he said after a while.

I looked at him, interested. It was true—he did owe me an apology for messing with me the first few days we'd known each other. "What brought this on?"

"I went to the wrong campus party and saw some stuff." Quentin shuddered. "Stuff too reminiscent of how I acted back then. I should thank Heaven every day that you still let me into your life."

He rubbed his thumb over his knuckles, making me believe he'd dealt with any issues he'd seen in the same manner I would have. I liked apologetic, worshipful Quentin. I couldn't resist teasing him while I held the upper hand.

"Sooo," I said, nuzzling his temple. "You don't like it when I surprise you, huh? That's very possessive and controlling. Maybe you haven't changed as much as you think."

I could feel him scowling through my skin and delighted in the way it tickled. "I assumed we were supposed to be completely in sync after we started dating," he grumbled. "I was told the best couples understand each other's thoughts and finish each other's sentences."

228

"Ha! Where'd you get that advice, an internet quiz?"

"Well excuse me for wanting to be romantic!" he said, his voice rising in pitch.

Oh, sweet banter. How I missed it.

"Quentin, I love you, but I don't want to merge with you," I said, tugging on his sideburns. He needed a haircut soon. "You're going to have to accept a surprise every now and then."

He paused. Then he looked up at me. His face had a wild, Cheshire grin smeared all over it. "Do you know what you just said?"

"That you're going to have to deal with surprises?"

"No. The other thing." I backtracked, puzzling over what he meant, until it hit me.

Oh god no.

"You said it!" Quentin crowed. "You said it first!"

I could feel the blood rushing upward through my neck and into my cheeks. "That doesn't count!" It wasn't supposed to be a contest between us—who said the three words of doom first. Except of course it was. It had been our unspoken battle to the death for a long time now.

"You will never live this down," Quentin said. "My victory stands for all time!" He shimmied along the ground in a butt-wiggling, taunting dance.

I tried to get my hands around his neck, but he grabbed my wrists and fended me off. "Yunie owes me ten dollars!" he shouted as we struggled.

"Quentin, I will kill you!"

"But how can you kill what you looooove!"

I wanted to shut him up, so I did, the best way I knew how. I attacked his lips with mine, smothering the four-letter L-word right out of him. He let go of my arms, freeing me to run my fingers through his hair in what was possibly and without exaggeration my favorite thing to do in the world.

Without breaking our kiss, he gripped me under my knees and hoisted me into the air. I thought he wanted to keep me there, suspended in time and space, until he took a step to the side and pinned me against the tree, hard enough to send a shower of leaves down around us. I gasped in the thrill of his body crushing even deeper into mine.

I kicked off the trunk and toppled forward onto him, folding myself in half to stay in contact with his mouth. My hands dove for the skin under his shirt and ran into his tail wrapped around his waist, a boundary that would have been unfamiliar to anyone but me.

"Wa—" he said, his words muffled by our never-ending kiss. Lying on his back like that, he couldn't draw his head far away enough to speak clearly, so he resorted to grabbing my ponytail and yanking on it sharply. "Wait!" he said again, clearer this time.

I scowled at him as angrily as I ever had. Quentin looked up at me like it wasn't his fault we'd stopped. "Nineteen, remember?" he said. "Your words, not mine."

Ugh. I remembered. Past-Genie could be a real drag. Now-Genie wanted to cut ties to every inhibition she'd ever had, to feast, to howl at the moon with glee. If I could have chosen to be two different people at that moment, I would have.

But he was right. And in the spirit of taking him seriously, I slowed the roaming of my hands to a crawl, and then finally to a rest. Under the fabric of his shirt I drummed my fingers against the rock-hard resistance of his abs, conquered territory that I wasn't ready to give up yet. They would have to redraw the map as far as I was concerned.

"Fiiiiiiiiiine," I grumbled. "We won't break my rule. My stupid, stupid rule."

Quentin nodded sagely. Right before he grabbed my hips, arched his spine, and flipped me over so that he was on top.

"We won't," Quentin said, his expression of prudence replaced with the most wicked smirk I'd ever seen. "But we can skirt it pretty close."

I grinned and pulled him back in for more.

■ ■ ■

I woke up to the sound of my alarm clock vibrating. I reached over to hit the snooze button but ended up slapping Quentin in the face.

"Huh?" he said in a daze from where he was lying beside me. He'd been asleep as well, the first time I'd ever seen it happen.

"Turn the alarm off," I groaned, my eyes shut against the morning light. "You're closer."

His body rustled and twisted over the grass. "Ow," he muttered. "I think you broke me. I haven't been this sore since I was trapped under the mountain."

Maybe I'd only dreamed of last night. The whole thing could have been a mirage to an overwhelmingly thirsty traveler. A manifestation of my pent-up desires.

But the twigs burrowing into my hip and the chill in the air told me yes, I had slept outdoors in a forest. Quentin and I had indeed made up with a vengeance, and now there were a whole new bunch of items to keep secret from Yunie. At least until she dragged them out of me by force.

Wait.

That meant we weren't in my bed. Or my house. Or Earth. Which meant that alarm noise was coming from—

Quentin and I both bolted upright. We were able to catch the last remnants of grayish dawn making their escape, daylight returning even faster than it had left. I stared at Quentin, my eyes wide with dismay.

His earrings were buzzing.

. . .

Quentin and I burst back onto the scene with the others. We were in such a hurry that I hip-checked more than one tree into splinters on the way over.

I missed the chance to see what gods did at night. Maybe they kept operating twenty-four seven. When we arrived they looked at us like we'd only been gone a few minutes. I couldn't tell if they'd moved.

"Ears!" I yelled at everyone. "*Ears!*"

Even though the jewelry he wore was trying to fly away from his head like trapped insects, Quentin was able to stay much more on point. "How good is the signal on these?" he said to Guanyin. "Are they still working?"

She looked horrified that she couldn't refute the charges. Guanyin's good craftsmanship spanned planes. Which meant that somewhere back home in the Bay Area, a human being and a yaoguai were about to run smack dab into each other.

Why? I screamed at myself. Why had I not learned my lesson? Don't stop, don't rest, don't forgive yourself until the problem was solved. The yaoguai who'd managed to get through the portal before Princess Iron Fan attacked. The only thing keeping them away from humans was a flimsy promise made to the Shouhushen, who they'd obviously figured out wasn't around to watch them. Christ, the entire campus could be swarming with demons right now.

"They won't stop!" Quentin shouted, clutching his head.

Guanyin passed her hands over his ears and undid whatever magic she'd used to bind them there. They buzzed and lurched in her hands so violently that she cried out and dropped them on the ground. In one last spasm, they flared with energy and burst into melted drops of pewter. The gold color was fake, after all.

The fact that I'd lost a gift from my father hurt. But losing the earrings themselves didn't hurt as much as seeing Quentin without them on. It felt like every moment we'd shared while he'd worn them had been stripped away.

And in the place of those memories, I now had a disaster of my own making. It wasn't difficult to make the mental connection. The harder the demon alarm buzzed, the more humans in peril. So many that the system had overloaded.

This is your lot, the voice inside my head whispered. It was the same one that spoke to me as a child while I stared at an opened birthday gift, my parents' voices screaming in the background. *Destined to fail. A girl who breaks what she touches.*

I turned to the gods, whom I wanted to collectively throttle. In my frantic state their hesitance last night seemed more like cowardice. "How far away is this energy that's trapping us here? As the crow flies?"

The Great White Planet raised a finger toward a part of the gnarled forest that appeared identical and arbitrary to me. "At your speed? Probably an hour, if the way were clear. But making our way through that growth could take us a day or more."

"We'd want to approach carefully," Erlang Shen said. "Announcing our presence could be the last mistake we make."

Uh-uh. Not good enough. I wasn't going to waste more time having a friggin' woodland adventure.

I snapped my fingers at Guan Yu. "Big man. Can you clear a path? I don't care how messy or loud you are."

The red-faced warrior's eyes lit up with glee. "Ha!" he bellowed. "I like the way you think, Shouhushen!"

Guan Yu unslung his massive polearm and wound up with a two-handed grip like a batter at a home run derby. Above him, the keen edge of the blade caught the light before it suddenly disappeared from the speed of his swing.

Nothing happened.

Erlang Shen was about to make a smartass comment but Guan Yu pre-empted it, holding up his hand. "Wait for it."

The forest in front of us shifted to the right. It was as if someone had raked a scalpel across the backdrop of an old movie set and pulled apart the canvas. The trees slid off their stumps and crashed over on their sides. The crescendo of snapping branches accompanied the big reveal of a deforested path the length of a soccer pitch.

Quentin let out a low appreciative whistle.

"That's pretty good," I said to Guan Yu. "But can you do it on the run?"

. . .

"I'm not asking you to slow down," the Great White Planet said in my ear, his teeth clacking together as he spoke. "But maybe you could give these old bones some consideration."

"Cram it," I said. I didn't care how rough a ride I was, hopping from stump to stump. I never heard Yoda complain about piggybacking on Luke while he was somersaulting through the swamp.

I'd made it clear that dignity was no longer a priority to our group. That was why the Great White Planet was clutching to my back for dear life. I trusted Guanyin could keep up with a fast pace.

Ahead of us, Quentin and Guan Yu were having the time of their lives. The Green Dragon Crescent Blade danced in its wielder's hands as it shredded through the forest, and sometimes not even in Guan Yu's hands. I was pretty sure the warrior god could control the polearm without touching it. On more than one occasion it spun with a mind of its own, zooming in arcs to the left and right before returning to him.

The trees that took too long to fall out of our way were pounced on and obliterated by a squad of Quentin clones. He made up a single-handed offensive line that blocked for the rest of us, only instead of padded dummies, the obstacles were multiton piles of lumber.

Even Erlang Shen got into the act, whipping splinters out of the air with lashes of water. "You know that whatever is generating this qi will hear us coming," he shouted.

"Don't care," I shouted back.

"I'm just saying, powerful beings tend to have good hearing," he went on. "For example, gods can pick up on the sounds of distant, uh, vigorously combative romance, shall we say?"

My cheeks started to burn.

"At first I thought the two of you were locked in mortal struggle," he said. "I almost went to check on you. For your safety."

"Screw you!" I yelled.

"I don't think I would survive the encounter!" he said gleefully. "I mean, I never heard the monkey make such a noise, even when I fought him to the . . . aaagh!"

A weird-looking spiky fruit the size of a pineapple smashed into Erlang Shen's face from above. I looked up to see a Quentin, perhaps the real one, giving me a wink from a tree branch.

I blew a kiss at him. Dunking on people we both hated, together. The truest sign of coupledom there ever was.

■ ■ ■

The Great White Planet's estimation was about right. Without my phone I had no way to time our exact progress. But I guessed roughly an hour had passed, once we ran out of trees.

I let the old god off my back and jumped down from the last stump. With the forest behind me, I gazed into infinity.

The next level of this game was an endless marble floor that housed absolutely nothing. The yawning expanse ahead of us could have been the size of a true continent. Polished flatness every which way you looked.

It was almost oppressive, how smooth and even the white stone plain was. The soothing effect of the campus' flatness back on Earth was magnified here into the nerve-wracking thought that I was about to be pressed down and griddled.

The campus, I thought bitterly. "We have to go."

"Genie," Guanyin said. "I have a bad feeling about this. Something's not right."

I wheeled on her, suddenly furious. She'd been the one to say that we had to finish the Mandate Challenge in order to go home, and the thought of slowing down now caused me to lose it.

"What, do you want to quit again?" I snapped. "I have to get back to Earth, now! We don't have eternity for you to piss away, figuring out what you want to do!"

There was a time I would have severely hurt someone for making Guanyin flinch the way she did now. I couldn't stomach my own handiwork, so I turned my back on her and marched onward to the end.

I watched my feet the first few steps. They crossed over the boundary between forestland and stone plain. So far, so good. No barriers, death traps, or illusions.

We set out in a row, spaced apart from each other. The Magnificent Seven but down one. You could have scored our meaningful walk to a cowboy's harmonica.

But any musical accompaniment would have been tainted quickly. There was a droning in the air that started not too far into the plain. I thought I was hearing things, but the gods frowned along with me each time it increased in volume.

The noise was atmospheric, as if every single molecule of gas around us was contributing to the soundwaves. Perhaps Princess Iron Fan had become the sky itself. I shuddered at the thought.

I knew that taking a peek with true sight would blind me, perhaps permanently. The waves of magical power were so thick that they were nearly tangible, like the arms of a kelp forest parting to let us closer before they swallowed us whole.

The infernal droning became more and more intense. We must have been walking toward its source. It scrambled my neurons to the point where I no longer had any idea how long we'd been traversing this empty floor. The ground seemed to suck at my ankles. Only sheer bullheadedness kept me wading through the quicksand.

Suddenly, a lucid thought flickered through my head. I'd heard a sound like this before. When Quentin had summoned Guanyin to Earth the first time, he'd chanted in a way that made it seem like there were hundreds of him packed into the room, a monkish overtone concert.

This was like that, times a million. This was someone's *voice*, amplified to the nth degree. The amount of power needed to turn a vast outdoor expanse into an echo chamber made me queasy.

And yet we kept going. Understanding that I was listening to a person, to language, let me identify syllables like droplets making up the ocean.

Shui le shui le shui le shuile shuileshuileshuile . . .

Sleep. The imperative form. Someone was casting a sleep spell, the most basic of basics, but with the energy of a thousand birthing suns behind it. I saw a dot on the horizon, the singularity at the source.

We kept going. We kept going until that dot on the plain turned into a shape, and the shape turned into a man.

It was the Jade Emperor.

26

THE KING OF HEAVEN LOOKED MUCH DIFFERENT FROM THE LAST time I'd seen him on Earth. The puffy, sweaty, middle-aged bureaucrat was gone, switched out for a gaunt, starved hermit who hadn't seen the underside of a roof in a long time.

His face was burned and hardened by exposure, like fired clay. Fraying, unadorned robes hung loosely off his shoulders. His eyes were closed in meditation, and he sat cross-legged on the white marble floor.

Erlang Shen began to shake with laughter. Silently at first, and then with growing force. He doubled over. Dropped to his knees.

"I can't believe this!" he shrieked, wiping the tears from his eyes. "This is too much! Really!"

He collapsed and rolled over onto his back, clutching his ribs, kicking into the air, pedaling an imaginary bicycle. He'd lost it completely. Everyone else was like me, straitjacketed with fear.

"Don't you get it?" Erlang Shen cried with joy. "*He's* the threat! He's the cause of all of this! He brought us to this plane and trapped us here! You don't know him like I do! Everything that happened to us was because he willed it so!"

None of that made any sense. Erlang Shen was seeing what he wanted to see, drawing conclusions that aligned with his hatred.

I couldn't tell him so. My throat wouldn't work. Neither would my arms and legs. The sense of wrongness shooting through me was paralyzing. If the Jade Emperor was casting *sleep* like this, a single bullet with enough powder behind it to level a city, then the command should have devastated us. But we were still awake. Which meant something else was the target.

Erlang Shen sat up suddenly, like a revenant. "Come on!" he yelled at us. "None of you see the irony in this? The Jade Emperor's the person whom we had to kill this entire time! After everything we've been through, this is a gift from the Way!"

He singled me out. "Nothing to say? No little quip about how I went to Hell for wanting to kill him and now I get permission, signed and stamped by the Universe? No mockery? Nothing at all?"

I couldn't respond even if I wanted to. None of us could. In his mania, Erlang Shen had missed his uncle opening his eyes, just a crack.

■ ■ ■

The pyroclastic flow of energy that washed forth from the Jade Emperor wasn't magic. Magic altered reality. This *was* our new reality. Oblivion, at his behest. He was less of a god and more of an eldritch horror.

My eyelids were taped open, immobilized. I could feel my atoms being shaken apart. The solid light that represented the King of Heaven's power was visible to my naked eye. It washed over

Quentin, Guan Yu, Guanyin, and the Great White Planet like it did me, rendering us into photo negatives, robbing us of color, freezing us like backdrop paintings.

But not Erlang Shen. The thundering sea parted around him. Deigned to let him through. He didn't even seem to notice what was happening to us in comparison to himself.

In frustration at our silence he screamed incoherently and flung his fist in our direction. Then Erlang Shen turned back to his uncle with murder in his eyes.

With the water he'd held on to he formed a long, slender blade. He stalked toward the Jade Emperor, who still sat unmoving in repose.

"None of you have any idea how long I've waited to do this!" Erlang Shen roared. "A year passes on Earth for every day in Heaven? Well, a *decade* passes in Hell for every day on Earth! *A decade of torment for EACH! DAY!*"

Erlang Shen was far away. Tinny. Ringed by darkness. I was having an out-of-body experience watching him. Despite everything that had transpired between us, I was overcome with only one desire: to scream at him to run away. To save himself.

He stood before the Jade Emperor and gripped his uncle by the shoulder with one hand, raising his weapon high with the other.

"Here's to a better Universe," Erlang Shen said. He plunged the weapon down.

The Jade Emperor caught the tip of the blade with his fingers. The water evaporated.

Erlang Shen lost his balance and stumbled forward. The Jade Emperor reached up with his other hand and gripped his nephew by the throat.

Making a slow, deliberate show of it, the King of Heaven finally, fully opened his eyes, sending a fresh wave of annihilating power over us. He looked at the group in turn, the Great White Planet, Guanyin, me, Quentin, and Guan Yu, pointedly ignoring the strangled cries of Erlang Shen.

He got to his knees, and then to his feet, never taking his hand off his nephew. The motion caused his robes to slip from his shoulders, revealing a body that had been flensed of its former softness. He was covered in thick knots of tendons and ligaments like a braided bullwhip, and each twitch of his muscles caused Erlang Shen to gag in pain.

"*Children*," he spat at us. He made the word sound like the most vile kind of creature imaginable. "You complete and utter *children*."

Erlang Shen hammered at the Jade Emperor's wrist, but his attempts to free himself were no more effective than a schoolyard bully back home trying to escape Quentin's wrath. The difference in strength was that big.

"You ingrates have *no* idea what I do for you! You mock me when you think I'm not looking! You spit on my commands! And the first chance you get, you try to *replace* me, just like I knew you would! I *counted* on your treachery! You're nothing but children! Grasping, overweening children!"

He shook Erlang Shen like a rag doll. "And why are *you* here?" the Jade Emperor screamed in his nephew's face. "How did you manage to worm your way out of Hell and into the Mandate Challenge?"

The missing piece that I'd mentioned to Quentin. It was being unveiled, inch by inch. But I still didn't know where it fit yet. The Jade Emperor had planned for a Mandate Challenge to occur in his absence, but why? Why disappear in the first place?

243

"My flesh and blood," the King of Heaven said, summoning a fresh reserve of contempt. "How pathetic you look. Do you miss your eye? Is that what this is about? *Here!*"

He viciously smashed his own forehead into his nephew's. The blow tore a gash in Erlang Shen's skin like an old scar had been reopened. The blood that flowed down the rain god's face made a pattern, a crying wound where a third eye could have been once.

"Do you know why I never listened to you?" the Jade Emperor said. "Why I kept you in your place?"

Tears streamed down Erlang Shen's face, mixing with his blood. He couldn't get a sound out around his tongue blocking his throat.

"The reason I treated you like garbage is because you *were* garbage," the Jade Emperor said to him. "I bet not once while you were brooding in the shadows, plotting your revenge, did you ever realize that you were useless trash. You assumed I was afraid of your power? No. I was never afraid of you, boy. I rejected you because you were too *weak* to help me rule. You *always* were."

With a final sob, Erlang Shen gave up. Stopped resisting. The most defiant person I had ever met closed his eyes and accepted his fate.

The Jade Emperor crushed his neck.

■ ■ ■

It was the lightness. The utter lack of weight the Jade Emperor gave to any of us. I had known how little he cared about humans, but to see him cast aside his own family was more than I could stand.

I screamed, and to my surprise, the Jade Emperor heard me. He looked at me and tossed the corpse of Erlang Shen to the ground, where it lay still and bent. His nephew already forgotten, not worth wiping his hand over.

The Jade Emperor stuck his tongue out and wagged his head in sarcastic, undignified mockery of my incomprehension. "You look confused," he said. "Since there's nothing more disgusting than a face of an idiot human who doesn't know what's going on, I'll tell you what this is about."

He extended his finger. Not to point at me. But at Guanyin.

"I needed *her*," he said. "The Goddess of Mercy." He gestured at Guan Yu, the Great White Planet, and Quentin, all of whom were still locked up by his raw power. "The rest of you are chaff. I don't know how Princess Iron Fan managed to let so many of you survive, but no matter. The witch sent me what I asked for."

The Jade Emperor left me reeling as he closed in on Guanyin. There was no end to how much I'd ruined everything, no bottom to the pit I'd dragged us into. She wouldn't have been here if not for me. I was a living, walking mistake, and my friend was going to suffer for it.

Guanyin made eye contact with me, her gaze full of desperation. I saw one of her arms twisted behind her back, her fingers working over a spell. She was using her body to hide the motions from the Jade Emperor. I couldn't tell what she was casting until a warm glow appeared to the side of me.

It was a portal.

Creating a rift out of this plane was not going to work. Guanyin said so herself. But she was trying anyway. Putting her life into it. In the last moments before the Jade Emperor did who knew what to her, her only thought was to get me home.

But we got caught. The Jade Emperor noticed the weak,

flickering shine of the portal and laughed. Under the crushing weight of his spiritual power, it was like a candle at the bottom of a deep-sea trench. He came over to me and grabbed me roughly by the back of my neck.

"What do we have here?" he said. "A rift to Earth? Interesting." He thrust my face toward the flickering glow. "Let's see what channels we can get."

Up close to the portal, my eyes swam in a sea of amber. I saw Earth as a planet, a swirling blue and green marble, before plummeting down, zooming in, freefalling into the western half of North America, landing nearby the college campus before I could register the distance that had passed.

Suddenly I was inside a building undergoing construction, an off-campus apartment complex similar to Ji-Hyun's. The top floors were still nothing but I-beam skeletons. Hunched figures perched on the girders and stalked through the shadows. Yaoguai. I could see through their shrouds of concealment, the layers of magic moving along with their bodies.

They weren't using the spell by sitting still and keeping quiet like I thought when I'd negotiated our truce. The demons had mastered a perfect mobile camouflage, the kind that would let a hunter remain invisible to its prey. And every single one of them was fixated on a human walking down the street toward the construction lot.

Yunie.

I recognized her face, her stride, the way she held that stupid shoulder bag that was too big for her. I used to have nightmares and cold sweats about my friend being pursued by yaoguai, and now she was blundering straight into a nest of them, her life on offer without the cost of a chase. Those demons were hungry and wounded. I couldn't have put her in more danger if I'd tried.

I couldn't protect her. I couldn't protect anyone.

Please, I begged, not knowing whom I was speaking to. I gasped for air I didn't deserve. *Make it stop.*

The Jade Emperor yanked me back. I lost sight of Yunie and wailed like a child.

"Oh, you look like you want to go home," he said, *tsk*ing. "You know, I think I might let you. This isn't business for a human girl, no matter how strong she is. Tell me, Shouhushen. Would you like to give up and go home?"

"Yes," I sobbed. I was so broken it came out as two syllables.

"I'll send you home," he whispered. "But just you. You'll have to leave everyone else behind. Oh, what I'll do to them. You can't imagine."

He twisted my head around so I could face Quentin and Guanyin. I could barely make their forms out through my tears. Quentin had managed to move a few paces toward me. His mouth was bleeding from a self-inflicted bite. Guanyin was shaking with effort. She couldn't hold the portal open any longer and was on the verge of losing the spell. There wouldn't be another.

Between two worlds, I made a choice. There was no way to say if it was the right one. But as with all of my choices, I could and would hate myself later.

"So?" the Jade Emperor said. "Are you going back to Earth?"

He let me drop my arms onto his shoulders to steady myself. They felt like jelly. He glanced left and right at the two useless blobs that were my hands and smirked. He released me out of pity, knowing that whatever I did next, it would eat me up inside.

He was kind of right.

My fingers clenched like I'd stuck them into a wall socket. They made an audible bone-crunching noise as they dug into the Jade Emperor's shoulders.

"You first," I said.

His eyes widened. I shoved his head into the portal, and it snapped shut, leaving the rest of his body on this plane.

27

EVERYTHING STOPPED.

The suffocating spiritual pressure emanating from the Jade Emperor ceased. It felt like gravity had cut out on a space station. Even though my feet were still planted on the ground, my newfound freedom gave me the sensation of drifting.

The endless chanting of the sleep spell stopped, too. It must have required the maintained attention of its caster. Who I presumed was the guy lying on the floor without his head.

Footsteps came running up behind me. I turned, expecting Quentin, but found the Great White Planet instead. Man, I kept forgetting about him.

"You—you killed the King of Heaven!" the Great White Planet cried.

"Was I not supposed to?" I slurred.

"No!"

I laughed. Having been blasted with so much spiritual power was only now catching up to me. It made me loopy. Intoxicated. Being out of my mind was better than facing the repercussions of my actions and the damage I'd caused.

249

I pitched forward and dry heaved. Quentin and Guanyin caught me before I hit the ground. They propped me up on either side. Guan Yu started to help, too, but backed off once he saw they had me. Good guy, that Guan Yu.

"He was gonna kill us," I said. "Couldn't let that happen. Not even if—not even if . . ."

Not even if it meant the end of the world. I shut my eyes so I wouldn't cry at what I'd done. The window that had closed. Whatever ruin waited for me back on Earth was on my shoulders. Yunie. Oh god, Yunie. I'd—I'd—

Guanyin gripped my upper arms. "Genie, I swear to you, everything will be okay on Earth." She shook me hard, trying to get through. "Your friends will be okay. I give you my word. Genie, listen to me!"

She was lying, of course. This whole business was a lie. Telling ourselves we could do the right thing. There was no such animal as the right thing. It was less real than dragons.

A high-pitched shriek startled us out of our huddle. It came from Guan Yu.

The warrior god looked like he'd seen a ghost. He pointed his weapon, the tip trembling as his hands shook.

The Jade Emperor was sitting upright on the floor.

As a favor to those of us who'd missed it moving, the body lurched again, staggering to its feet. This time we all shrieked.

The Jade Emperor was still headless, but decidedly less so than a few minutes ago. The sawed-off surface of his neck tilted at us, and I got ready to puke, but instead of being filled with gore, it was a blank void, almost digital in its emptiness. And around the edge of his wound, the surfaces were reconstituting themselves, cell by cell, pixel by pixel. The Jade Emperor's nose, ears, eyes, and the rest of his skull came back from the foundation upward, as if a team of invisible tiny bricklayers was working overtime to restore a giant statue.

I'd come to understand that each god of Heaven had a personal power, a domain of reality that was theirs to command. Erlang Shen's was water. Guanyin's was time. The Jade Emperor's unique ability appeared to be regeneration. Cellular self-dominance. The perfect specialty for a self-concerned god.

His new head was closer to the one I recognized. Jowly and soft, untouched by the sun. The shade of the skin didn't match the rest of his body. He came to his senses and looked around, taking stock. And then his eyes widened.

"No *no* NO!" he screamed. "What did you *bai chi* do? You've ruined everything!"

I ran at him and closed my hands around his throat. He must have still been recovering, because he seemed to lack the spiritual force and physical strength to fend me off. Only three different gods and a Monkey King pulling me away kept me from doing to him what he'd done to Erlang Shen. Heck, his powers meant I could kill him again and again, for eternity. Not the worst way I could spend the rest of my useless life.

"The sleep spell!" the Jade Emperor shrieked. "You broke the sleep spell! Did none of you think about what I was casting it on!?"

The ground underneath us began to shake.

■　■　■

I was a girl from the Bay. I knew my quakes, from s-waves to after-shocks. I could tell you the Richter score of any given tremor down to half a point.

So I immediately knew that this earthquake, even if it was in a different dimension, wasn't normal geology at work. There was an insistent thrashing to it that felt like someone lacing their fingers through the bars of a gate and yanking back and forth out of rage.

I felt the others losing their balance, but I grabbed the Jade Emperor again to make a stable structure. "What are you talking about?" I shouted.

"I left the court of Heaven and came here in the first place because I had to hold it off! Someone always has to hold it off!"

"Hold *what* off?"

"Anarchy. Apocalypse. The Anti-Way."

Saying those words out loud calmed the Jade Emperor. He laughed in resignation. "The secret you learn once you become the ruler of Heaven," he said as if we had all the time in the world, "is that you have one, and only one, duty. To make sure Heaven survives. Nothing else matters. And today, because of you, I've failed."

From a center point off in the distance, the plateau bulged upward. The stone should have broken into fault lines, but instead it warped, elastic, like fake rock painted on a flat canvas.

The bulge grew bigger and bigger, and reality around it got thinner and thinner, until with a birthing, nuclear hiss, it ripped asunder. The film strip of the movie playing in my eyes tore apart and let the white projection show through the gap.

Something crawled out of it.

An arm the size of a blue whale reached out of the void between the rocks. It crashed down onto the plateau, spreading its giant fingers over the terrain, gripping for purchase like a tentacled alien landing on Earth and deciding *Yes, this'll do*. Another arm, the mate to the first, elevated itself from the rift and pushed at the other side. Triceps as big as a subway car flexed and pushed until they pressed their owner upward.

What little logic that remained to me, after the fires of shock and dread had burned my mind to ashes, was expecting a massive, horrible head to poke its way out of the hole. Humanlike, to match the arms. Or perhaps an animal's, like a yaoguai. But no head came. Instead the titanic shoulders that emerged had nothing in between them.

The headless, mountainous torso rose into the air, a tectonic act, a new range forming, until it paused, seemingly stuck by its waist. Its pectorals blinked. They *blinked*. Like *eyes*. Right where its nipples would have been, the skin of its chest folded rapidly in the unmistakable pattern of a pair of eyes adjusting to the light.

"Nüwa have mercy on us," the Great White Planet whispered, his entire body reliving a nightmare. "It's a Primordial!"

"*Xing Tian*," the Jade Emperor said. "The embodiment of resistance. It is *hundun*, chaos, un-creation. The destruction that constantly lurks behind the veil." He gazed upward at the monster with an almost appreciative calmness, in the same way a skier might stop to recognize the beauty of an oncoming avalanche. For the moment, it was far enough away that it was still a landmark.

"Xing Tian cannot be killed," he said. "It cannot be fought to any end. When it rouses, it can only be appeased and suppressed, as it has been for eons by the holder of the mandate. I originally came here to reinforce the wards that keep it from tearing through the boundaries of Heaven and Earth and obliterating the Universe."

The missing piece. I understood everything now. The Jade Emperor had detected Xing Tian stirring and rushed here to contain the threat. But he didn't want to be trapped in this duty forever, when someone else could possibly shoulder the burden.

In a spectacular display of *wu wei*, letting events unfold to his advantage, he waited for a Mandate Challenge to be called in his absence, knowing that strong gods would step up. He'd sent Princess Iron Fan to filter out the most powerful challenger and discard the rest. The plan had been to swap whichever god it was into the job of keeping Xing Tian at bay, like a fresh battery.

It was Atlas tricking Hercules into holding up the firmament in his stead. And the rest of us had fallen for the gambit, right until the point where I'd veered off script.

Finally comprehending the chain of events that led us here did absolutely nothing for our situation. The *thing* blotting out the sky twisted around. The false eyes on its chest lowered their gaze until they spotted our group standing there, dumbfounded.

Xing Tian's reaction was as immediate as ours was slow. I'd never truly appreciated the term *abomination* before I saw it painted on the giant's expression. Its eyes turned to furious slits, and the torso's cavernous navel suddenly expanded to encompass its entire waist, forming a fleshy abyss like a whirlpool out of Greek myth.

It's screaming at us, I thought. *It hates us more than anything in the world. Its very purpose is to hate us.*

Had Xing Tian lungs connected to its navel-mouth, I was one hundred percent sure that the noise from its roar would have liquefied us outright. But the colossus was horrifically silent, making our voices sound like they were cutting through the aftermath of an explosion.

"Run!" the Great White Planet said. Whatever level of familiarity he had with these types of beings gave him his wits back while the rest of us were stunned stupid. "We have to run!"

The Jade Emperor laughed again. "Where? Now that it's fully awake, it'll pull down the walls of the Universe."

"Anywhere but here!" the Great White Planet snapped.

This time there was no need to carry the old man. Terror made us all equally speedy. We sprinted back in the direction we came, even the Jade Emperor with his defeatist attitude. For someone who'd accepted his fate, he was pretty damn fast.

The sky turned darker over our heads.

A ponderous crash behind us nearly sent me flying into the air. I glanced back to see we'd just managed to avoid getting squashed by the monument of Xing Tian's hand, slapping the ground. From its position stuck in the rift, it'd flung itself out as far as it could reach to try and kill us. It was so big it had crossed the distance with one flop.

It wasn't going to stay stuck long. The hand clawed into the ground, fingernails punching deep into the stone. Xing Tian pulled with the force of a million pack animals and heaved forward, a man on the verge of successfully climbing out of the ice he'd fallen through.

The shadow from its other hand loomed overhead, blotting out the light. We were going to get crushed if we stayed our course. Maybe the gods of Heaven had watched as many terrible movies as me where people were flattened by trying to outrace a rolling boulder, because we all cut sharply to the side, right in the nick of time. The gust of wind from Xing Tian's falling-log fingers twisted my knees up and sent me tumbling.

Is this what it's like to fight me? I thought as I hit my head on the stone floor. *How completely unfair.*

Out of the corner of my eye, I saw the Jade Emperor open a portal for himself with great difficulty. Xing Tian's spiritual gravity made it no sure thing. The King of Heaven wriggled through the miniscule window, disappearing down to his thighs before the rift snapped shut, leaving chunks of his legs behind. He'd simply regenerate them later.

I hadn't the notion to be upset about his comical, lizard-like escape. If nowhere was safe from Xing Tian, then the most the Jade Emperor had secured himself was dying in his own bed.

Quentin picked me up off the ground. "We have to make a stand!" I yelled. "Why aren't we fighting?"

"We can't!" Quentin said, echoing the now-gone Jade Emperor. "It's more than a god! It's a concept! It's resistance itself! It can fight back forever until it wears us down and kills us!"

He pulled me away from the giant hand that was beginning to stir again, and I heard the unthinkable spill from his lips.

"We *lose*, Genie!" he said. "There's nothing we can do! We've lost, and it's over!"

I couldn't believe it. Quentin would never say that. Not when the two of us were together and there was something left to struggle against.

Xing Tian pulled back both of its hands this time, opting to push itself upward instead of pull itself along the ground any farther. Its torso raised into the air, a gigantic barn being raised, nearly causing a vacuum in the atmosphere. It shifted ponderously, like it was getting ready to try standing up for the first time. I couldn't imagine how big it would be if it got to its feet. We all backed away from its growing height.

Except for Guanyin.

. . .

At that moment, I would have sworn up and down that somehow, Erlang Shen had planted his future-glimpsing eye in my forehead, as some kind of parting curse. Because I could see the threads of possibilities weaving themselves together into one singular outcome.

"What are you doing?" Quentin shouted at her. "You can't fight it!"

Guanyin smiled, and her face shone with light. "Since when am I a fighter?"

She beckoned Guan Yu closer and whispered in the general's ear. The stoic god's face crumbled. He nodded and muttered something back.

"No!" I cried. I tried to grab her and pull her away from Xing Tian, but Guan Yu tackled me by the waist as hard as he could and ran in the other direction.

"Quentin!" I screamed. I tried to find purchase with my feet so I could push back. "You can't let her! Stop her!"

Quentin shared one last glance with Guanyin, their centuries of friendship unable to buy them a proper farewell. She pointed with her chin at me, and Quentin turned away with tears streaming down his face. He caught up with Guan Yu and grabbed me right when I almost slipped free. Together they managed to keep me from digging my heels in.

I could no longer hear what I was screaming. Guanyin walked up to Xing Tian.

The monster had shoved one knee under itself, readying to get up. But upon spotting the easy prey, it clasped its hands together above its headless shoulders in a double hammer-fist. It wanted more than to kill her. It wanted to erase her existence.

Xing Tian's hands came plummeting down. In response, Guanyin whipped her arm upward, as if she were hurling a submarine fastball. Her motion ended with a snap of her fingers.

The behemoth stopped where it was. But the stay of execution was short-lived. There was too much of Xing Tian, and it was too strong. It broke through Guanyin's fourth-dimensional restraints, the only being I had ever seen do that, and resumed its deathblow.

Guanyin seemed to have expected this. She hurled another invisible fireball of time at the hands coming to crush her, and they stopped again.

This wasn't a solution. Xing Tian kept powering through her magic, reaching her in stuttering steps like a buffering video stream. It truly could not be resisted. Guanyin's barrage of time freezes lasted shorter and shorter, until the monster's massive fists lay right over her. The skin on its chest was folded into a tortured caricature of rage.

In her last moment, she reached up and placed her welcoming hands on Xing Tian's. It was then I saw what had eluded everyone else but her—how much pain and suffering this creature was in.

And that much pain, the Goddess of Mercy would never ignore.

Guanyin released all of her good karma. All of it.

■ ■ ■

To call the wave of energy similar to a bomb blast would have been an act of disrespect. There was nothing dangerous or hurtful about the glow that wrapped snugly around us. It was bliss. A state of grace. This was what the denizens of Hell must have experienced all those years ago when Guanyin's freely given blessings washed away their sins.

And the cruelest thing about it was that when the light receded, her body was still there. In a twisted way, I wanted her to be smashed to bits. Vaporized. If there was nothing left of her, then I could have struggled through the guilt of abandoning her to her fate.

But she and Xing Tian were both present, motionless. The giant had been trying to crush her, but now, in its kneeling posture, with its hands clasped and extended, it looked like it was praying to the goddess for relief.

Mercy had been granted. Xing Tian's mockery of a face was no longer in agony. It was calm and still, as if it were an acolyte in the presence of its master.

Guanyin stood before her supplicant. She was as perfect and beautiful and lifeless as the statue in a shrine. She was gone.

■ ■ ■

I surged forward again, only to be caught by Quentin.

"Genie," he funeral-whispered. His face was wet against my side. "If we wake Xing Tian, her sacrifice will have meant nothing."

I pounded my fist on his back, hard enough to injure him. He made no noise as I hit him over and over again. Quentin only hugged me tighter and tighter as my strength sapped away. My arm fell on him one last time, and I broke down sobbing. My chest collapsed under the weight of despair, and I gasped without end.

A large glow appeared in the air close to us, demonic purple instead of Heavenly amber, and a furry snout poked through.

It was the fox. The one I'd seen saying goodbye to her mate, the werewolf who'd made the doomed last stand against Princess Iron Fan. She forced her way into this plane until her top half was visible. She extended her paws and beckoned us, asking for an embrace. Something about the way she couldn't come any farther out of the newly formed rift made it seem as if she were restricted, tethered to safety by her legs. Other animal limbs—deer hooves and octopus tentacles and the like—peeked through around her. An entire zoo crammed into a phone booth.

A little speck with a big voice perched on the fox's head. "Of course you had to be in the last plane I looked!" Tiny said.

I stared at her without comprehending her form or her words. She might have been offering me something. I wasn't sure I wanted it.

"We wouldn't leave you stranded, not after what you've done for us!" the yaoguai queen said. "Now hurry! This portal spell is really hard to maintain!"

28

A ROUGH, CHOPPER-ESQUE NOISE WHIPPED QUENTIN'S VOICE into froth.

Genie! he might have been shouting.

It was the pounding of blood in my own head. The fluorescent lights hurt my eyes.

We'd been dumped unceremoniously in an empty lecture hall somewhere on campus. My body was draped across two different rows of seats. A great green chalkboard stared at us, judging.

The fox and Tiny and the mass of her surviving yaoguai followers who'd lent the spiritual juice necessary to punch a new hole from Earth to Xing Tian's lair were nowhere to be seen. Maybe they'd been hurled down a different fork in the road.

The bootleg portal had kicked my ass as thoroughly as Princess Iron Fan. But even if the journey had been bump-less, I wouldn't have moved. I wanted to decompose, rot away. I'd given up my bones.

"Genie!" Quentin shook me.

Get up, Guanyin's voice said to me. *You still have work to do.*

I don't. I can't. Please don't make me.

You have to, Genie.

261

"Genie! You have to get up!" Quentin shouted. "There's traces of demons everywhere!"

Yunie. I bolted upright. I had to save my friend. If it was still possible.

■ ■ ■

The solemn, detached, Bodhisattva-like thoughts I'd had about honoring Guanyin's lesson to me vanished the instant we hit the street outside the lecture hall. What replaced them was sheer human panic. A flailing fear of death that lacked any dignity whatsoever. I would beg the Universe not to take Yunie. I would offer it money, the toys from my childhood, my hair.

Without Quentin's earrings, the only lead we had was the glimpse of the street the Jade Emperor had shown me. I turned true sight on and spun around like a lighthouse, the least efficient way to use it but my best option right now.

There. Not too far from Ji-Hyun's apartment. The same unfinished building I'd seen through the portal. The fires of demonic energy blanked out anything behind them. I couldn't spare the time to make out more details or describe the location to Quentin for a jump. Instead I ran.

I ran like an animal. The lower I got, the more forward motion I could get into each step. I was nearly climbing on all fours, my hands dallying with the idea of yanking on the ground for more speed.

Pushing myself over the ground like this made me incredibly fast. People noticed me—oh boy did they notice. The wind I created knocked over cups, startled dogs, set off car alarms. I didn't care.

Coming to a stop in front of the unfinished building required plowing a yard-long furrow into the asphalt. I hurled myself through the wall of insulation sheeting. The hallway was tissue paper as I scraped it into ruin. And then—

There, in the largest room, was Yunie. Surrounded by demons. She was reading them a book.

I'd made so much noise coming in that she and every other pair and trio and quintuple of reptilian, birdlike, and compound eyes stared at me.

"Uh, hey," she said. "Can you hang on for a second longer? We're at a good part."

■ ■ ■

Seeing that I was catatonic, Yunie remained the picture of calm. She finished up what she was doing with the yaoguai, got up, and silently took me by the hand. She led me out of the room.

We passed demons who looked like they should have been slaughtering the B-movie cultists who'd arrogantly summoned them. They were already working on undoing the damage I'd caused to the building. A giant termite chewed at the wall studs I'd snapped, drooling glue-like saliva over the weakened points to hold them together.

I walked arm in arm down the street with Yunie as if she were showing me how beautiful this day was. Quentin came around the corner and she nodded at him. You know, to be neighborly. He fell in beside us without a word, understanding that this was her show.

Somewhere through the fuzz in my head, a bell jangled. We'd entered a nearby coffee shop. It was private in the way that only a really packed place could be. No one noticed the bat demon hanging from the ceiling, also wrapped in concealment. It was licking a croissant.

We sat down at a miraculously empty table without buying anything. It looked like it had been scavenged from one of the school libraries. I recognized the gray Formica from Ji-Hyun's tour.

"You and Quentin probably want to know what's going on," Yunie said.

I didn't nod.

"It'll be easier to show you than explain." She reached into her purse and took out a giant phone the size of a small tablet. It wasn't hers. She thumbed through the image library until she found a video. After plugging in some ear buds, she handed the phone to me. I pressed play.

The recording was of a different building than the one we'd left. A small campus gym made out of aged brick, not one of the big glass-walled ones that was open all hours. The footage must have been shot by a neighbor across the street, maybe for a noise complaint because it was night. And a series of loud crashes came from the double door. The sound of a crowd running into locked pushbars.

"What exactly is happening here?" I said.

She looked glad I was speaking again. "After the demons came through the pool, they panicked and scattered everywhere across campus."

"*Why do you know this?*" I shrieked.

"Shhh," Yunie said. "Keep watching."

Another crash, this time with sparks. The sign of concealment failing. "Holy mother!" the person recording yelled. "Look at this!"

I was. The picture was incredible, the camera phone expensive.

The operator a good shot. I could make out with perfect clarity the doors bursting open and a horde of demons piling into the street.

It was a testament to the videographer's modern priorities that they didn't run away or hide. They screamed and swore but kept recording, even when one of the slavering demons spotted the human holding a funny metal rectangle. It opened its crocodilian jaws and got ready to pounce.

"Jesus, is this person dead?" I said. I looked around the underside of the phone for blood.

"You're going to miss the best part!" Yunie hissed. She turned it back over.

"*Stop right there!*" a very familiar voice said in the recording. The camera panned to the side, catching a blob of light before focusing on a very familiar face. Yunie's.

In the video, my friend rode a majestic white horse. The stallion had antlers and armor encasing its flanks. I recognized the proud, strong shine in its eyes. It was Ao Guang.

I remembered my *Journey to the West*. Dragons could turn into horses. The Guardian of the Eastern Sea had transformed into a mount for my friend.

He reared up on two feet and neighed ferociously. Yunie stayed in perfect control. She looked like a Valkyrie, come to collect the souls of the fallen.

"Wow," she said, examining the yaoguai from her perch atop the dragon horse. "You—you are an eclectic-looking bunch, aren't you?"

She pointed at a feathered, raptor-y one in the front. "Are you like a *dinosaur*? Are demons allowed to come in dinosaur? How does that work, paleontologically speaking?"

The yaoguai went mad, half at her flippancy and half from her spiritual presence. I'd been told repeatedly that my friend was the type of person that yaoguai liked to eat best, but it was startling and horrifying to see the effect Yunie had on them. Drool went flying. Teeth snapped together. They rushed at her and Ao Guang with such hunger that I had to look up at the Yunie next to me to assure myself she'd survived.

Yunie in the recording faced the demon charge with poise. She reached into a bejeweled saddlebag and pulled out a scroll. With only a few feet left to go before they reached her, she unfurled it.

A wash of light burst forth from the scroll's contents. The yaoguai recoiled, spitting and screaming like vampires in the sun.

"All right, listen up, assholes!" she yelled. "My name is Eugenia Park, and I bear the seal of my friend Eugenia Lo Pei-Yi, the Divine Guardian of California! I carry her mandate, which demands and compels your obedience!"

I could make out writing on the scroll. Long, flowing classical strokes that glowed in amber. The characters were steeped in Guanyin's magic. And on the bottom, shining white-hot like cigarette burns, were my chop seals.

Yunie was holding the scroll I'd stamped before I left. Guanyin had done a bit of reverse-forgery and laid out the terms of the truce I'd negotiated with Tiny on the blank paper, sealing the whole deal with powerful magic. She must have given the contract to Yunie during that brief period where she'd disappeared to check the Earth end of Ao Guang's rift.

"You will get back inside, calm down, and stay there until

further notice!" Video Yunie roared. She was really in her element. "The Shouhushen has given her word that you will be cared for so long as you follow her rules! Disobey and you'll be in for a world of hurt!"

My friend sounded so confident and authoritative that I doubted she needed the protection of the scroll. The demons' momentum had been broken. They were confused as hell.

"I know my friend and what she's capable of," Yunie said. "Ask yourselves if you want to make her angry. Ask yourselves if you want to make *me* angry."

If there were two things yaoguai respected, it was fearlessness and the threat of force. Both of which Yunie had provided in spades. They gave up. The yaoguai turned around and shuffled back into the gym. Yunie watched them and nodded in satisfaction, scratching Ao Guang's horse ears as she maintained her vigil.

"Wow," the person recording muttered.

The noise caught Yunie's attention. She wheeled Ao Guang around. "You!" she yelled, pointing straight at the camera. She spurred her mount into a furious charge across the street.

"Oh shi—" was the last sound the person made before they dropped their phone and the video cut out.

■ ■ ■

"So yeah," Yunie said. She sounded a little apologetic.

"What in Heaven's name did I just watch?" Quentin said. He didn't have the benefit of sound. Or being there when the video was taken.

"While you guys were on your voyage to Mordor or whatever, Guanyin came to me and asked if I could act as your last line of defense," Yunie explained. "She told me exactly what to do and when to do it in case you didn't come back right away. Wrote me out a checklist of trouble signs and emergency contacts and everything. I just followed her instructions to the letter."

I said nothing.

Yunie glanced at Quentin and back at me, nervous. "Ao Guang and his crew helped out a lot. They managed to sneak most of the new arrivals into your forest preserve. He was really glad to be lending a hand, too. He kept screaming 'For the Shouhushen!' and 'As the Shouhushen wills it!' Guy's a little intense for someone his age."

It was like she was speaking a third language. A tongue that was unfamiliar, coming from her.

"The rest I checked up on, gave them human food, that sort of thing," she said. "There were a few mishaps, but nothing a ton of forget and conceal spells couldn't fix. And I stole that guy's phone, I guess. I look a lot better in that video because it was the third time that night I gave that speech. The first time I did it I was so scared I nearly crapped myself."

When I still remained silent, she got truly worried.

"Genie, I'm sorry I went behind your back," she said. "Guanyin told me you'd flip if you found out I was helping with magic stuff. She said it was like your biggest fear, so we kept it secret. You're not mad at me, are you? Say something. Please."

"I didn't know you could ride a horse," I murmured.

She squinted at me and then looked away in embarrassment.

"I learned at summer camp. I never told you because I was afraid you'd think I was a snob."

That was what set me over the edge. I burst into fresh, heaving sobs and hugged Yunie to my chest. My tears ran down my face and into her hair.

They would always look out for me to the very end. Guanyin and Yunie. My two sisters. My Heaven and Earth.

Yunie squeezed me back, not caring about the scene I was making. "Apparently the magic wouldn't have worked if you weren't a really good Shouhushen," she said. "And the reason I was able to channel your authority was because I'm the reincarnation of some powerful soul. At least that's what Guanyin told me."

She patted my head. "Where is Guanyin, anyway?"

29

WE TROD UP THE STAIRS TO JI-HYUN'S APARTMENT IN SILENCE, a mourning procession. Yunie had taken the news about Guanyin much worse than I thought she would. I remembered reading a psychology article saying that you tended to like someone more after doing them a favor, and my friend had done the goddess and me the mother of all solids.

Ji-Hyun met us at the door. "Your grandpa from the country is here," she said to me. "He mentioned something about losing a family member. I'm sorry."

The older girl slipped into the hallway. "I'll give you guys some privacy."

"Ji-Hyun, wait." Tossing aside any worries about whether we were close enough yet, I leaned in and wrapped up Yunie's older cousin in a hug. "Thank you," I said. "For everything."

Ji-Hyun grunted in the affirmative. "Any time, Stretch."

After she left, the three of us filed in. An amazing sight waited for us. The apartment was clean. Clean-er. Ish. The booze refuse had been scraped off a dining table. Around it, a perimeter of mopped floor. The space that wasn't completely vile looked like a castle holding out in a siege.

The Great White Planet sat at the table. He held a cup of steaming tea between his hands. A consummate host, Ji-Hyun.

On some level I expected him. My wizard headmaster needed to come and explain to me what on god's green earth had happened. "So you're going around showing yourself to humans now?" I said.

The old man shrugged. "Does it matter? I see you've opened your circle as well." He tilted his head at Yunie.

"She gets the biggest pass in the history of all passes," I said. "You ought to make her an honorary goddess for what she's done."

"I wouldn't say no," Yunie said.

The Great White Planet smiled wanly and patted the empty seat across from him like he owned it. "Come, sit."

There was space enough for three. I felt a sense of balance, flanked by Quentin and Yunie. Maybe the three of us should have teamed up from the beginning. I wished the Universe had picked a different way to tell me so.

"Guan Yu and I managed to find our way back to Heaven," the Great White Planet said. "Once Xing Tian was neutralized, we could travel freely once more."

"The Jade Emperor beat you there, though," I said.

"He did. We arrived to see the King of Heaven sitting firmly on his throne once again. By then he knew Guanyin had succeeded. He'd already circulated the 'official' story of what happened."

He paused, knowing this was a possible blowup moment for me. But I hadn't the energy. "What is the official story?" I asked.

"It's very close to the truth. As soon as the Jade Emperor detected the menace of Xing Tian, he heroically went off on his own to face down the existential threat. Concerned for the rest of our safety, he told no one where he went. After the blunders of lesser gods woke the monster, the kind and noble Goddess of Mercy sacrificed herself to make up for her error. He would have gladly held off Xing Tian himself until the end of existence, but fate had other plans."

The Great White Planet waited to see if I would have my outburst at that last part. When he saw that I was calm, he continued.

"The Jade Emperor, in his benevolence, understands why the Mandate Challenge was called," he said, his monotone betraying his disgust. "But seeing as how the crisis is over and he, the incumbent ruler of Heaven, is still around, the window to consider new rulership has closed. In a further display of generosity, he forgives the court of Heaven for its treasonous actions, as well as the individuals more directly involved."

With that, the saga was over. The Jade Emperor had gotten everything he wanted. It had been his journey the whole time, and the rest of us amounted to only a bump in the road. "Did you tell the rest of the gods what really happened?"

"I tried to. But my word is worth less than dirt now. I bungled the most important task in millennia by trying to replace my boss while he was legitimately combating the end times, remember? Guan Yu raised his voice as well, but no one listened. Or maybe they believed us and didn't care. The Jade Emperor's consolidated his power too well."

The Great White Planet fiddled with his teacup but didn't drink. "Guan Yu left the court of Heaven to go on a personal voyage. He no longer wanted to have anything to do with such corruption. As for me, I was thanked for my service and forcibly retired for making these statements. Lei Gong or Zhenyuan or another one of the Jade Emperor's henchmen will take over my job. I'm lucky that I wasn't sentenced to Hell, honestly."

They were good eggs, the general and the inspector. Guan Yu's honor and the Great White Planet's integrity showed me there was some decency among the people high above us. Just not enough to make any meaningful difference whatsoever.

"Nezha?" I said. "Erlang Shen?"

"Nezha's loss was mourned—a young god struck down before his prime." The Great White Planet's voice quavered. "As for Erlang Shen, what of him? He was a traitor, and his presence in the Mandate Challenge was a foolish experiment with an outcome that should have been expected. He couldn't contain his rage, and the Jade Emperor killed him in self-defense. What else needs to be said?"

The hurt in his eyes told me that he needed to say much, much more about his former prize student. The Great White Planet condensed the volumes into a few pithy lines of advice.

"You remind me very much of Erlang Shen," he said to me. "A youth who saw too far into the future and was blinded by the possible. I'm warning you now. Don't go down his path. Stay focused on what's in front of you."

It was advice that might have kept Guanyin alive. "Was Erlang Shen a good contender to replace the Jade Emperor, before he lost his third eye and started to plot against Heaven?" I asked. "You've been the grade-keeper for so long. You must know."

The old god aged another hundred years in front of me.

"He was flawless," the Great White Planet said, his voice hoarse. "Before the Jade Emperor took away his eye, he would have developed into the perfect ruler of Heaven."

I disagreed with him about who would have made the perfect ruler. But then, everyone was biased toward their favorites.

The Great White Planet stood up. He seemed shorter than I remembered. I hadn't meant to cause him pain. "I should go," he said. "Would you like to know what your final score as the Divine Guardian of California was?"

"That's okay," I said. "I feel like there are other things that matter more than grades."

He nodded as if I'd passed the last category of his test, the part that wasn't scored with a number. "There certainly are, Shouhushen."

The inspector of the gods left like a normal person. Through the door and down the steps, back to Heaven or wherever his retirement led him. I wished him well.

My friends had let me do all the talking but figured now was the time to speak up. "Okay, I understood exactly none of that," Yunie said. "Other than I want to punch this Jade Emperor person in the balls."

"We all do, Yunie," Quentin muttered. "We all do."

She ventured the question cautiously. "Is Guanyin . . . really gone? I know you told me what happened, but I still can't believe it. If she's physically still there, in that place . . ."

We couldn't give her an answer either way. We had none. The Goddess of Mercy was who we usually turned to when we didn't have a clue.

The beginning of a thought flickered through my head, but it was extinguished by the calendar alert of my phone going off. The device lay exactly where I'd left it, plugged into Ji-Hyun's wall socket. I'd set the meeting alarm to remind me of an important deadline.

"I have to go see about a guy," I said, getting up suddenly.

■ ■ ■

Quentin paced uneasily around the perimeter of the fountain. It was a small, modern art-y sculpture made up of black and white squares set at angles, as if a chessboard had been shattered and rearranged. The sun was deceptively high. Really, there were only a few hours left in my long weekend.

"Genie," Quentin said. "I don't think this is the time."

On the contrary. There would never be a more appropriate time to talk to Ax than now.

He arrived late. I guessed that was the power move du jour, instead of being early. I sat down on the concrete lip of the fountain. Ax took a seat next to me so we could talk without facing each other, like spies doing a drop-off. He rudely ignored Quentin again.

"You look like you've been deep in thought," he said.

"I have," I said. "And I'd like to hear your pitch again, before I give you my decision."

Ax leaned back, precariously close to falling into the water. "What pitch is there to give? The future belongs to the risk-takers. Those who are willing to gamble. It's as simple as that."

A stiff breeze would knock him over and completely soak him. "Like you?" I said. "You took a great risk by quitting school and joining the Nexus Partnership?"

"I did indeed," he said, his mouth leaking liquid metal into the air. "I risked it all. I was a Dean's List student at this school, so you could say that me dropping out was like throwing my advantages away and being reborn as a completely new person."

Ax couldn't have known, but my eyes were blazing away with true sight, inches from his face. My lie detection was on in full force, the first time I'd ever used it on an unsuspecting human. Every untruth he spoke would make it appear as if quicksilver spewed out of his mouth. Word bubbles drawn by a cartoonist with metallic paint.

"There's no guarantee things will work out for me," he said as mercury trickled from his lips. "I'm performing a high-wire act without a safety net."

"Ax, what does your mother do for a living?" I asked.

He was surprised, both by the question and the fact that I hadn't asked about his father instead. "She's the CEO of a hospital in Anderton," he said. That was true.

"Anderton, where the venture capital families live," I said. "Do you know what my mother does for a living, Ax? She does the books for a billiards supply company in Redpine."

"Oh," he said politely. "The one the train passes?"

"Yup," I said. "The one by the train tracks, with that big vertical sign that needs painting. She gets paid under the table. In fact, I think her main job is helping the owners cheat on their taxes."

I could tell he suddenly found my musk less palatable. "Okay. You're telling me this because?"

"Because I think you and I might have a very different definition of risk," I said. "Ax, does the work you're doing with the Nexus Partnership mean everything to you?"

"Of course it does. It's my reason for living. You can't be a part of this group unless you're passionate about the mission. Why do you think we ask you to quit school?"

Yes, yes, quitting school, blah blah. "But what would you do, though, if your ideas didn't work?" I asked. "Say your baby company never made it to fruition."

"I'd try another, and another," Ax said. "I'd never quit."

Bubble. Another lie.

"So you're telling me that you would eat failure after failure, without end, until you were old and gray?" I asked. "You wouldn't, say, go back to school? Get your degree and a nice safe job? Take a gap year and travel? I'm sure your parents would support you in any of those options."

"Of course I wouldn't do any of those things," he said, clearly insulted. "I'm on my own in the world. There's no going back to my former life."

This time the metal lie balloon was so big it would have killed a small flock of birds had it been solid. I watched it pulse and throb before returning to the conversation at hand.

"See, that's the difference, Ax," I said. "People like you have the luxury of failing more than once. The world will pick you up, dust you off, and send you on your way, nothing lost and nothing gained. You get to keep going, and going, until you get the result you want. And if you do decide to give up, there's a nice cushion for you to land on. That's why you have mottoes like 'fail fast,' and 'failure is the best teacher.'

"People like me don't get to fail," I continued. "Not ever. When people like me fail, we don't bounce off a soft surface. We hit the ground hard. We lose so very much. We don't survive long enough to learn anything."

I peered as far down my nose I could at my own mouth. It was clear. Maybe the detection didn't work on me to begin with.

Ax got up and dusted his hands off. He didn't have to waste his time listening to this.

"I get it," he said. "The answer is no. Frankly, I'm disappointed you've made this into some kind of bizarre class resentment thing. We don't discriminate by socioeconomic background."

You might not care about your advantages, my dude, I thought to myself. *But the Universe we share sure as hell does.*

In one small irony, a mote on the scales of life, Ax stumbled a bit in his hurry to leave. Not a lot. The more spectacular finale would have been if he'd tumbled back into the fountain and gotten soaking wet. It would have been the finale to the kind of kids' movies I used to watch, where the jerk villain got messy as a comeuppance.

His little pitch forward, however, did take him far enough that he ran into the steadying hand of Quentin, who he'd done his best to pretend wasn't there. Quentin dusted him off and grinned at him like an anglerfish.

"Easy there, chief," he said to Ax. "You almost had a bit of bad luck. Can't have that now, can we?"

Only Quentin could scare someone that bad by being that friendly. My hundred thousand dollars fled the scene. We watched him go.

"Are you sure about this?" Quentin said. "Maybe it was a risk worth taking after all."

"I'm sure it'll keep me up at night," I said, completely serious.

30

I WAS PLANNING TO TAKE THE TRAIN HOME. THAT WAS WHAT we'd agreed upon. Instead I got a call with an unpleasant surprise.

Both my parents had come to pick me up at the college. In the same car no less. Mom must have been dying.

In the parking lot, I saw my dad standing outside his car. I could make out my mom's silhouette in the passenger's seat. I walked over to them. Most of the other people around were students coming in the other direction, returning to school after their weekend trips off-campus. They carried empty picnic coolers and bags of car trash. One guy struggled to take his surfboard off his roof rack.

I got into the back seat of Dad's car. It took me a moment. I hadn't ridden like this in years, Dad driving and Mom in the front. It regressed me to my younger years like a sledgehammer. The hairs on my neck stood on end. We were silent for a minute, until Dad got past the local town traffic and merged with the highway traffic.

"How was your trip?" Mom said.

"How's your heart?" I snapped.

"*Genie!*" Mom shrieked.

"Dears," Dad pleaded.

We hadn't lost our touch. The reunited band was playing its greatest hits right off the bat.

And then Mom did something weird. She calmed herself and de-escalated. "Genie, I want to know how your trip was," she said. "That's all."

Jesus, she really was dying. I was being stupid, provoking her to anger. What was I trying to do, push her blood pressure over the edge?

I fought back against the suffocating grip of childhood this car had me in, and rattled off banalities. "The trip was great," I said. "I learned a lot. Ji-Hyun was a wonderful host. Don't let me forget to send her a thank-you gift."

"I won't," Mom said. "And how was the party? Did you have fun? Did you drink a lot?"

I nearly kicked the car door open so I could jump out while it was still moving. That's why they'd both come. My parents had found out that I'd lied by omission about a party with alcohol and leering college boys. They were going to drive me out to the desert, and burying my body was a two-person job.

"You . . . knew about the party?" I said.

"Of course I did," Mom said, her upset-meter beeping a little at the insult to her intelligence. "I'm not an idiot. You're a teenager at a college."

"And you're our daughter," Dad said. "We know plenty that you don't tell us about."

The one upside of what had happened to my family was that I could no longer receive double-parent dressing downs like these. But now the hydra had regenerated and was going to attack me from both sides. I thought about lying my way out of the situation. Or protesting that I didn't drink or have fun.

But that risked ruining my mother's relative tranquility. She wanted guilt, so I would have to give it to her. I sighed.

"Yes," I said, steeling myself for the inevitable scolding. "I drank too much and partied a little too hard. I got slightly sick."

"Good," she said. "Not good that you got sick, but good that you had a lot of fun and drank and tried something new."

The car kept going, but in my head the brakes had slammed to the floor. My brain came screeching to a halt. I wanted to roll down the windows and scream for help. An alien had kidnapped my mother and replaced her with a malfunctioning duplicate. I was equipped for demons, not aliens. This was a government situation.

"You're glad I went to a drinking party?" I said incredulously.

In the glimpse I caught of her in the windshield reflection, my mother swallowed a lump in her throat. "Genie, I was hoping you would have the time of your life this weekend," she said. "I was hoping you would fall in love with that school. I know you want to go somewhere farther away. But I thought if you truly loved that place, then maybe you would stay in the Bay, closer to us, where we could see you more often."

Subtlety. Recognition of my choices. Hoping instead of screaming. I wanted to grab my mother and shout *Are you even Asian anymore?*

"That place is hella expensive," I said. "There's no good way to pay for it."

"There's no good way, but there's ways," Mom said. "We can always take out more loans, work more jobs. It's worth it if you love it."

She was saying that we should double down on our past mistakes. Lean into the jaws of the shark. "Do you know what would happen to us with more debt?" I said.

"No," she said. "But that's not the point. You worry too much about things being clear and certain. Who knows? Sometimes things work out."

Dad saw that I had extreme difficulty responding. So he changed the subject to a nice, easy, soothing topic of conversation. "Your mother and I are getting back together."

I choked on my own saliva. My heart couldn't take this. It was going to explode long before Mom's did.

"For the health insurance," he explained while I tried to self-Heimlich. "It turns out that the policy I get from the gym is really, really good. It'll cover medication, specialists, regular checkups."

He thought of a joke that he really liked and sent it through the Dad-filter until it came out covered in lint. "It's what they give us instead of money!" he said.

I didn't laugh. This wasn't a fairy-tale ending. This was a slow-rolling disaster in the making. My parents were not good for each other. They were going to make each other miserable. They were going to trap each other in French Existentialist hell.

"Are you sure this is a good idea?" I said, when I should have been painting warnings on the windshield in my own blood.

"No," Mom said. "What did I tell you about being certain? We don't know. But we're doing it, and that's that. I don't want to hear any lip from you about it."

Knowing what they'd done to each other in the past, this was a sacrifice. And they were making it for me. To free up some resources for my education, my continuing improvement as a human being. They were willing to get back on the Wheel of Suffering right where they'd left, in order to give me the push I needed to break free.

I didn't like it one bit. I owed it to them to mention the alternative I'd passed up. If they thought quitting school for the money was a better idea, maybe I could go crawling back to Ax and beg him for a second chance. I told them about his offer.

"That sounds like a terrible idea," Mom said. "College kid nonsense. They think they know everything at that age."

"I'm glad you told him no," Dad said. "It feels like it would have turned you into a different kind of person than you are."

"You're too smart to work for a dumb boy like that," Mom said. "Go into business for yourself if you want. You'd be good at it."

Oh the ever-loving irony, hearing them of all people extoll the virtues of entrepreneurship. I was thankful they weren't yelling at me for rejecting the easy money. But my father's words stung a little.

Becoming a different kind of person than I was was the point. Growth meant change. Adapting to the circumstances of the Universe.

That certainly had been the point of Guanyin's lesson to me. I needed to become the kind of strong person who could hold a loss, like her. She wanted me to be a leader who stayed firmly in the present, maximizing the amount of good I could do, rather than dwell on past wrongs or dream about the future. She wanted me to be a leader who could sacrifice.

I'd learned. After everything that had happened this weekend, I'd absorbed the message.

Hadn't I?

No.

I bolted upright in my seat and scraped my head against the car roof.

"Ha! Haven't seen you do that in a while," Dad said.

I pulled out my phone, fingers scrabbling for the onscreen keyboard. I almost locked myself out with wrongly entered passcodes, I was so manic right now.

Guanyin may have been the ultimate embodiment of all that was good in the cosmos. But that didn't mean she was right about everything. She could be flat-out wrong sometimes.

Like about me, for instance. I wasn't a saint. I wasn't a worthy follower of her enlightened way of thinking.

To borrow Kelsey's term, I was a beast. A rage monster. I was no better than a yaoguai, an iron demon in the shape of a girl. I had to embrace that reality.

I managed to fit five typos into "are you there?" before sending the message on my phone.

"Who're you texting?" Dad asked teasingly.

The other animal I knew and loved.

"what's up? high five cheeseburger guy on bicycle" Quentin texted back.

Yunie had given him her spoils of war, the phone she'd jacked from that unfortunate bystander. It replaced his old Swedish bricklike model, the one he must have reached a decade into the past to buy. Now Quentin could finally message me like a normal human being.

I steadied my thumbs and wrote out my plan. The block of words was so long it went past my entire vertical screen. Quentin must have been looking at the "message being composed" ellipses for a good five minutes.

Once I was finished, I hit send. My thesis statement.

"r u serious?!?!?! fingernail polish briefcase cat" was his response.

Okay, so he needed a bit of time to get the hang of emojis. I dove into a furious back-and-forth with him that was intelligible once you stripped out our excesses.

Your plan, he said. *It's not a plan. It's speculation. Madness.*

Life belongs to the risk-takers. I asked you if it was possible. Not if you liked it.

I don't know. You've done that trick exactly once in your entire past life as the Ruyi Jingu Bang. I don't know if you can anymore. Not only that, there's the damage it might do to your mind. There's no precedent for what you're describing.

I'll train so that I can pull it off. With you.

I don't know how long it will take to relearn. We may never succeed.

That's the gamble, isn't it? I don't care how long it takes. We'll be together while we try. Even if it's a lifetime.

Quentin took his time replying to my insinuation that he and I would be together our whole lives. The modern declaration of love, folks. A sideways comment over a text message.

"we'll start tomrw," he wrote back. "peach peach peach kissy face kissy face kissy face."

I don't think he understood what the peach emoji implied. I'd have to explain it to him. Or show it to him. My face flushed at the memory of the night he and I had spent together under a sky beyond Earth.

"So," Dad said. "Do you think you might put that school on your list of top choices?" There was a strong note of hope in his voice.

I relaxed into my seat and stared out the window. The highway carried us into the falling night.

"I think it's likely I'll go back there someday," I said. "I mean, I left something very important behind."

31

IT HAD BEEN A WHILE SINCE I'D LAST BEEN IN THIS PLACE. THE ground was as white and marbley as I'd remembered. The same electric blue ceiling of sky.

I took a single long, deep inhalation. My updated pre-serve ritual, which Coach Jameson had taught me. Over the course of my volleyball career, the relaxation technique had gotten me to somewhere in the middle of the pack in aces, instead of dead last like I normally was.

I needed that same luck right now. If I screwed this next part up, it would mean the end of the world.

I ran. My steps caused mini-gales as they pushed the air. The rock vibrated with my impact.

I hit top speed and left my feet. I went soaring over the ground and delivered a flying knee to the ribs of Xing Tian.

The titan went skidding across the stone floor, its flesh squeaking with friction against the smooth surface. Its pectoral eyes blinked awake in astonishment. Xing Tian got to a standing position. And looked up at me. I would have been slightly taller than it, even if it had a head on its shoulders.

It screamed its lungless oath of rage, silently overacting with its torso-face. It reared back to give me a right hook that could kill a god.

I caught its arm from behind.

Xing Tian turned to look. It instinctively recoiled in the way an animal without a nervous system might respond to a predator. The monster may not have been capable of true fear, but on some level it knew it had to play defense now.

"That's right, buddy," the second giant me said, my words forming a hurricane. "Behold my final form."

. . .

I smacked Guanyin on the face repeatedly.

"Genie, she's not a passed-out drunk!" Quentin said. "Be careful with her!"

"Did you give her enough karma?" Yunie said. "Maybe you have to do it a couple of times for it to take." She mimed rubbing her hands together. "You know, like a defibrillator. *Clear.*"

This was the other big risk of the plan. I didn't need to restore her back to full power; I only needed to wake her up. If I couldn't do that, then this whole venture was pointless.

Wait. A defibrillator. I reached into my pocket and rummaged for my chop seals.

Guanyin choked and arched her back against the marble floor. She started to breathe again.

Okay. Phew. I was glad she stirred before I ripped her shirt off and slammed my stamps of authority into her heart to jolt her with magic energy. That was a dumb idea.

The Goddess of Mercy's eyes fluttered open. "Wha—" she said.

She bolted upright and nearly smacked me in the nose with her forehead. "No!" She understood that if she was awake, so was Xing Tian.

"It's okay," I said, cradling the back of her skull in case she flopped back down. "We got you covered. Everything is going to be all right."

"But Xing Tian!" She pushed me away and staggered to her knees, forcing her way through the gap in our huddle. She gazed up at the events happening in the distance.

"JESUS CHRIST, GENIE!" she shouted, needing to borrow profanity from me in order to express her shock. "IS THAT TWO OF YOU?"

Against the backdrop of the sky, a giant version of me traded blows with Xing Tian, aided by a second giant version of me. It was like a mountain range had come to life and started fighting with itself. Lincoln and Washington ganging up on Jefferson while Roosevelt shrunk down to normal size and rescued the Goddess of Mercy.

Okay, maybe not the best analogy, but in my defense, it was hard to concentrate when I could see three viewpoints in my mind at once.

"Two of me plus one more right here," I said. "The ultimate form of the Ruyi Jingu Bang."

Nezha, rest his soul, had keyed me onto the concept. Me and my fellow triplets were more than mere hair-clones. We were split bodies, each one alone stronger than I was by myself.

"Quentin's not a three-headed mountain monster though," I

said. "We were planning on holding that in reserve, in case things got super ugly."

Guanyin couldn't process this. "Genie, what—this is—I don't—"

"I'll explain on the way out," I said.

"*Halabeoji*," Yunie called.

Ao Guang came trotting over, his hooves clip-clopping elegantly against the stone. Yunie had groomed him to the nines for the honor of transporting the Lady of Mercy to safety. His mane shone like a shampoo model's, and his armor glittered like magic.

Quentin helped Guanyin into her mount and took Ao Guang's reins. We shared a grin. We looked like the pictures of ourselves in my children's book. The Monkey King and the Ruyi Jingu Bang, leading a holy figure atop a dragon horse.

"Xing Tian can't be defeated," I said as we walked away, cool guys not looking at the titanic donnybrook happening in the background. "But Guan Yu and the Great White Planet helped me do some research, and it can be stalemated. You proved that. All I did was swap myself in for you, and substitute blissful peace for . . . you know. Anger-fightin'. My usual."

Guanyin twisted frantically in her saddle, still trying to comprehend the scale of what was happening behind her.

"Believe it or not, the hard part was learning how to transfer part of my good karma to you to wake you up," I said.

"I was surprised she had any to begin with," Quentin said. I clubbed my life partner in the back of the head.

"Genie, this is *monstrous*!" Guanyin cried. "You're going to leave two-thirds of yourself behind on this plane, holding off Xing Tian!? You'd be struggling for eternity, your mind split into parts, never able to truly focus on a single priority! You'll never be free of this duty!"

"Gee, sacrificing myself in a never-ending battle for good? That sort of sounds like someone I know."

"This isn't funny!"

"Sure, it's a little awkward," I said. "I was wondering if the version of me that's talking to you would have to come back here to swap places with a me over there on a regular basis. You know, take shifts to make things fair. But I think that's unnecessary. It feels like we're like the same person at the same time."

To prove my point, a big-I gave normal-myself a thumbs-up the size of a grain silo, and then went back to wrenching the ankle lock I had on Xing Tian.

"So yeah, constant struggle," I said. "Such is life. If you feel that bad about it, there's a chance we may come up with a better solution before the end of time. We have a pretty big brain trust now."

One of Ao Guang's crab generals waited for us by the glowing purple portal, its claws extended to serve as a platform that Tiny could stand on. She bowed at Guanyin as we approached, though without zoomed-in vision, the gesture was barely perceptible.

"Genie, wait," Guanyin said. She slid off her dragon mount and took me by the shoulders, staring me in the eyes. "Are you . . . taller?"

"Ugh, yeah," I admitted. "I kept growing through high school."

"Through high school?" Guanyin suddenly looked stricken. "Learning to do this, it had to have taken at least—*Genie, how long have you been trying to rescue me?*"

I bit my lip. Guanyin grabbed Yunie and lined us up in front of her. She examined our faces.

"You're not girls anymore," she murmured. "You've gotten older. You're young women now."

She hiccupped. And trembled. And began to weep.

I pulled her close and hugged her hard. "Genie really wanted you to be there for our college graduation, but we weren't quite ready at the time to pull this off," Yunie said softly. "We're sorry we couldn't come sooner."

Guanyin bawled into my shoulder. The Goddess of Mercy, who had seen countless lives come and go over the centuries, weeping over a few lost human years. She had a little bias for individuals in her after all.

I let her finish crying it out. Tiny had gotten much better at holding rifts open, so there was no rush to jump through.

"Oh man, we have so much to catch up about," I said to Guanyin. "The last few years have been absolutely bonkers."

"You should see how Genie's managed the yaoguai on Earth," Quentin said. "It'll blow your mind. The situation's incredibly bizarre right now, but you can't argue with the results."

"We also went on all these spiritual adventures," Yunie said. "Both across Earth and the other planes of reality." She turned to Quentin. "We had to have legitimately saved the world like what? Two or three times?"

Quentin shrugged like he'd lost count.

I stroked the Goddess of Mercy's hair. "My parents are doing fine," I said. "Despite the stress I put them through, they've weirdly never been better. Life after college was crazy eventful. I don't know if the story's as interesting as the spirit stuff, but it felt about as difficult. It turned out okay, though."

"I want to hear about it," Guanyin said, her voice muffled against my collarbone. "I want to hear about every little detail."

I sighed. "If that's the case, then I've also got to tell you about our plans for the mandate."

Guanyin jerked away. I'd ruined the moment. "How could you bring that up?" she said, still holding on to me. "That doesn't matter anymore!"

"I think it matters," I said. "Let's do some math here."

I glanced around at my surroundings. "I'm the Shouhushen of the Blessed and Erroneously Named Kingdom of California on Earth, and I'm stronger than I've ever been before," I said. "I have Sun Wukong the Monkey King—who's also leveled up quite a bit, mind you—at my beck and call."

I reached over and slapped Quentin's ass. He raised an eyebrow, silently promising to pay me back later when we were alone and in private.

"I've earned the respect and trust of *two* fanatically loyal armies of the supernatural, one demonic and one draconic," I said. I gestured at Tiny and Ao Guang. The powerful ant yaoguai saluted, and the Guardian of the Eastern Sea did the horse-whinny equivalent of promising me his liver.

"And I'm *literally* the only force holding back the end of the world," I said, pointing at the shifting, tumbling, Genie-shaped horizon. Even though I was sixty-six percent occupied with preventing the apocalypse, I'd never felt so full of energy before. It was a total rush.

"Also you have me," Yunie said.

"I also have Yunie." An addition of no small consequence. "Taking all of those things together means that if *I* want to talk about the fact that the goddess who truly won the Mandate Challenge has returned to the living and needs to be fitted for her crown post-haste, and *Heaven* refuses to listen . . ."

I cracked the knuckles of one hand by itself, another trick I'd learned. "Well, maybe then we have a little problem that needs addressing."

Guanyin was startled by what and whom I was threatening. "Genie," she begged. "Please don't overthrow the entire order of the gods just to put me on the Throne of Heaven."

I would make no such promise. I simply grinned and let her fret.

Besides, it wasn't like I was ready for an undertaking of that size immediately. Or any sort of adventure at all right now.

After everything we'd been through, we needed a break. We needed to rest, train, prepare, grow. Figure out what parts of ourselves needed to change, and which parts needed to stay the same.

We had time. Tomorrow was a new day.

"Let's go home," I said to my friends.

ACKNOWLEDGMENTS

Thank you to all my friends and family. Even Karen.

I'd also like to thank my wonderful editor, Anne Heltzel, and magnificent agent, Stephen Barr.

And finally, to the fans of *The Epic Crush of Genie Lo*, the first book I ever published—thank you for sticking with me.